Ascension of the Chosen

Tournament of the Gods Book #4

By Timothy L. Cerepaka

An Annulus Publishing Book

Annulus Publishing, Cherokee, Texas, 2016

Published by Annulus Publishing

Copyright © Timothy L. Cerepaka 2016. All rights reserved.

Formatting by Timothy L. Cerepaka

Contact: timothy@timothylcerepaka.com

Cover design by Elaina Lee of For the Muse Design

ISBN-13: 978-0692681367

ISBN-10: 0692681361

Acknowledgements

I would like to thank my uncle, James Wilhite, for helping me get this manuscript into publishable shape. I'd also like to thank the rest of my family for supporting me while I wrote this novel. You guys rock.

Acknowledgements

Chapter One

WHEN BRAIM AWOKE this morning, he realized that he was gripping the handle of the sword that was leaning against the dresser next to his bed. He let go of the sword handle, trying to figure out why and how he had grabbed it during his sleep.

Must have had a bad dream or something, Braim thought. He rubbed his eyes. *Doesn't look like anyone is in the room with me, though.*

Braim sat up and looked around his room again. It was indeed empty, aside from himself. The shutters on the windows were closed, with tiny rays of light sneaking through the cracks. It was also rather cold this morning due to a cold snap that had swept over World's End last night, causing Braim to shiver as he pulled his blankets more tightly around his body. He wasn't sure how early it was due to the fact that the shutters were closed and he had no clock in his room, but he guessed that he had awoken at his usual time at sunrise.

It was so quiet that Braim considered just sitting there for a while or maybe going back to sleep. After all, despite having gotten a full eight hours of sleep, he was still quite drowsy. He was hungry and thirsty, but not enough to convince him to get up and get dressed.

Just as Braim was about to go back to bed and sleep for a little while longer, he suddenly remembered something important he had to get to this morning. Tashir had asked Braim to come down to Last Beach to do some more sword training at the crack of dawn, and if the weak rays of the sun peeking through the cracks in the shutters meant anything, then dawn was practically here.

Shaking his head, Braim jumped out of bed, threw on his red tunic, combed his hair in the mirror above the sink in his bathroom, splashed some ice cold water on his face to wake himself up, and then was out of his room in a second. He dashed down the hallway to the inn's exit and heard the innkeeper, Mishak, shouting from what sounded like the kitchen area, "Mr. Braim! Would you like some breakfast? Delicious coffee, just the way you like it!"

"No thanks, Mr. Mishak!" Braim shouted back as he grabbed the door and pulled it open. "Got an urgent appointment to keep. No time to eat."

"Very well," came Mishak's voice, which sounded disappointed. "Will leave you some food in room for when you return, in case you hungry."

"Thanks, Mr. Mishak!" Braim shouted, and then he ran out the door, closing it behind himself on the way out.

The air outside was cold and crisp, unusual for World's End, which was usually a warm island due to the fact that it was located so far south. But Braim didn't focus on the cold. He just ran as quickly as he could through the wide-open, largely empty streets of World's End. He found it odd how few katabans were out this morning, but with the sun not high in the sky yet, that was probably because they were still asleep.

In any case, Braim enjoyed the empty streets because that meant there was no one to get in his way or slow him down. Still, he found the empty streets to be little worrisome, as he was used to them being full of katabans going about their daily business. Perhaps that would change as the day progressed ... or maybe it wouldn't, considering how depressed many katabans seemed nowadays.

It's all of the bad news, Braim thought as he rounded a corner, hoping that Tashir would not be too angry at him for being late. *Kind of hard to remain upbeat and normal with at least three major threats to Martir currently active.*

But Braim pushed those thoughts out of his mind for now in order to focus on the present. He just needed to get to the beach as quickly as he could, because he wasn't sure he'd have time to train for the rest of the day if he was late.

Because Braim ran fast, he reached Last Beach in about ten minutes. By the time he did, he was hot and tired and even sweating, even though Last Beach was even colder than the rest of the city due to the cold wind blowing in from the south. As he expected, Tashir stood on the beach, already swinging his sword around in practice, but curiously enough, Tashir was not alone. Yoji, the young bald mage who was in the same bracket as Raya, was sitting underneath a grove of trees nearby, reading a large, thick book without a title on its cover or spine. The young mage seemed engrossed by the book, but Braim didn't know what was so interesting about it, though he didn't care enough to ask.

As soon as Braim stepped onto the beach, Tashir noticed him

and immediately stopped practicing with his sword. Lowering his blade, Tashir walked over to Braim. The aquarian makhimancer didn't look angry at Braim's lateness, but maybe he was just hiding it.

"Braim," said Tashir, his gurgly accent slightly distorting Braim's name. "I was wondering where you were. Did you forget about our appointment?"

Panting, Braim nodded. "Almost. When I woke up this morning, I'd almost forgotten about it. I had to skip breakfast to get here on time."

"Skip breakfast?" Tashir repeated. He frowned. "It is never wise to skip meals, Braim. Especially when you are learning to wield a sword, which takes a lot of energy out of you. It is better to train with a full stomach than with an empty one, in other words."

Braim's stomach growled, like it agreed with Tashir, but Braim ignored it and said, "Nah, it's fine. I can get lunch later or something. I'm ready to train now. I even brought my sword. See?"

Braim lifted up his sword to show it to Tashir. Tashir didn't look like he agreed with Braim skipping breakfast, but then he shrugged and said, "Fine. But don't complain when you find it hard to perform the very basic sword techniques I'm going to teach you."

"Don't worry, I won't," said Braim. Then he glanced at Yoji, who was still reading his book. "What's Yoji doing here? Is he trying to learn makhimancy, too?"

"No," said Tashir, shaking his head. "The Hollech Bracket Challenge is for later in the morning, so Yoji came here to have a quiet place to study in preparation for it."

Braim looked at Tashir in confusion. "But how does he know what the Hollech Bracket Challenge will be about? Has Alira said anything about it?"

"As usual, no," said Tashir. "But Yoji explained to me that it will probably have something to do with thievery, deception, and horses, so he has been reading up on all three areas extensively since winning the last sub-bracket challenge three or four weeks ago now."

"Oh," said Braim. "What about Raya? She's supposed to be in this challenge, too, right?"

"Yes," said Tashir, "but I don't know whether she is studying for it or not—I doubt it for obvious reasons—but I have not interacted with Raya much since she and Alira returned, so I am not sure what she is doing."

"Knowing her, Raya probably expects to win without any effort," said Braim. He rolled his eyes. "And then she gets insulted when I call her silver spoon. Do all members of royalty lack self-awareness like her or is she special?"

"Not all royalty is as spoiled as Raya," Tashir said. "Regent Kaserous, the Regent of East Yudra, is well known for her humility. Raya, as far as I can tell, is simply young and foolish, though she seems much more thoughtful ever since her kidnapping."

"Maybe getting kidnapped by a psychotic prison escapee did her some good," Braim said, stroking his chin. "Anyway, what about Alira? What's she doing? Has she recovered her magic yet?"

"I don't know," said Tashir with a shrug. "Last I heard, Alira was trying to get her powers back and has been making a little progress, but whatever the golems did to her must have been severe, as every time I have seen her, she always seems depressed. I believe she will be presiding over the Tournament, however, regardless."

"Right," said Braim. "Speaking of the golems, I haven't heard anything about them recently, either. Have the gods taken them out yet?"

"I'm just as in the dark about the golems as you," Tashir said. "And that is what troubles me. I don't know much about these golems, but it seems to me that the gods should have no trouble destroying creatures that are clearly not their equals. Yet the gods have not announced that the golems have been destroyed."

"Which means they're still out there," said Braim. "Yeah, you're right. That *is* suspicious. The golems can't be *that* powerful, can they?"

"I doubt it, but there may be other complications that the gods have run into," said Tashir. "Tamra and the Void, after all, are still active threats."

The mention of the Void made Braim look to the south. Across the last stretch of sea after World's End was a massive, black wall that seemed to be eating at the sky. It was as solid as a wall, but Braim knew that the Void was an intelligence not to be underestimated. He wondered if she was looking at them now, listening to their every word. He wondered why the Void hadn't simply tried to consume World's End whole now, considering how powerful she was, but maybe the Void feared the gods or had some other reason for not doing it yet.

In any case, Braim didn't want to focus on the Void, so he

looked at Tashir again and said, "Right, right, almost forgot about those two. Any news on Tamra? I haven't seen her since she attacked those four gods."

"None whatsoever," said Tashir. "It seems like Tamra has vanished into thin air. I have spoken with some of the Soldiers and they said that none of the gods know where she is, though they suspect she is somewhere in the Northern Isles."

"Well, I hope they stop her soon," said Braim. He looked up at the sky, which was clear this morning. "The last thing we need is a crazy mortal like her running around stealing the souls of the gods."

"I'm not sure how she can possibly be a threat to anyone, though," said Tashir. "You said that she lost her arm when she tried to use the Soul Collector on you, correct?"

Braim winced at the memory, even though it had been about a week ago when that happened. Still, the scene of Tashir lying on the floor screaming in pain as the stump where her arm had been bled profusely had left an impression on Braim's memory that was unlikely to go away anytime soon.

So Braim nodded and said, "Yes, but remember she has the souls of four gods in her body. She might be able to harness their power to heal herself, maybe even make a new arm entirely. No telling what she can do now."

"I suppose that is possible," said Tashir. "Anyway, the sun is rising ever higher in the sky. If we're going to practice sword-fighting, then we should get started right away."

"All right," said Braim. "That's what I'm here for. Let's get started."

But then Tashir paused and looked at Braim. He had a

questioning look in his eyes, which made Braim a little nervous because Tashir had the head of a shark and so sometimes he looked more intimidating than he intended to.

"What is it?" said Braim. "Did you forget something?"

"No," said Tashir, shaking his head. "I just wanted to know if you had regained your magical powers yet."

Braim frowned. He scratched the back of his head. "No. They're still gone. Can't use any spells or anything like that."

"Oh," said Tashir. "All right. Just wanted to make sure. Because if you could use magic, then I could have taught you makhimancy. Without magic, however, you can't learn it."

"Yeah, I know," said Braim. He folded his arms and looked back toward the city. "I've thought about going to the Ghostly God and demanding that he come up with something he could use to restore my magical power to me, but he's never around because he's technically not allowed to be here. Still, it's frustrating to lack magical powers after you've had them for a while."

"I cannot imagine how hard that must be," Tashir said. "No one is born with magical talent and skill, but when you learn it, it becomes such an important—and sometimes even necessary—part of your life. Are you sure you can't relearn it on your own?"

"I've tried," said Braim. "I've tried several times to cast even the most basic of spells. But whatever that bracelet did to me, it completely took away my ability to do any magic."

"You mean you can't do any magic at all?" said Yoji.

Braim looked to the right and saw Yoji walking toward them, his large book tucked under his arm. Even though it was early in the morning, Yoji looked wide awake and ready to take on the day, which Braim decided had to do with the fact that Yoji was still quite young and so didn't take as long to wake up as Braim or the other godlings did. He didn't know the mage's exact age, but Yoji seemed to be even younger than Raya.

"Yeah," said Braim, nodding. "It sucks."

Yoji stopped a few feet away from them and tapped his chin thoughtfully. "And you've tried to get your magical powers back?"

"Well, not really," Braim said. He shrugged. "I don't even know *how* I'm supposed to get them back. I had a friend of mine who lost his magical powers once, but he got them back in a way I can't really replicate."

Braim expected Yoji to simply nod and say some words of sympathy, but to his surprise, Yoji snapped his fingers and said, "I think I know how to help you get your powers back."

"You?" said Tashir. He sounded quite skeptical. "What do you mean?"

"I mean exactly what I said," said Yoji. "I know how to restore a mage's magical power."

Braim and Tashir exchanged skeptical looks, prompting Yoji to say, "I'm not just saying this. I really do know a way. I read about it in a book once."

"Well, that certainly is reassuring," said Braim, looking at Yoji. "I mean, reading something in a book definitely makes it sound more truthful."

"I will have you know, Braim Kotogs, that I am a prodigy," said Yoji. He stood up straight, although due to his skinniness that did little to make him look more mature. "When I was ten, I was already performing complex magical spells such as the Elemental Titan Spell and also doing interdisciplinary study in fields as far apart as divination and geomancy. I've debated adults three times my age and beaten them in debates. So I know what I'm talking about, even though I am younger than both of you."

Braim held up his hands in a pacifying way. "All right, all right, I believe you. But what's this method that will restore my magical power, anyway?"

"It's easier if I show it to you than to tell you about it," said Yoji. "We can go to my apartment in the city and do it there. Should be safe."

"But what about Braim's sword training?" said Tashir, gesturing at the sand with his sword. "Isn't that the whole reason he got up this morning?"

"Who cares about learning how to swing a sharp piece of metal around?" said Yoji, waving off Tashir's concerns rather dismissively. "After all, you can learn sword-fighting any old time, but you can't always regain your lost magical abilities."

"He's got a point there, Tash," said Braim. "As much as I like learning how to use a sword, if there is any way at all that I can regain my magical powers again—especially in light of recent events—I think I'd rather do that instead. Maybe we can do this sword training later?"

Tashir scowled and looked away. He just shook his head and walked down to the beach away from them without another word. Drawing his sword, he started practicing again, swinging his sword even more ferociously than before.

"Guess that's a no, then," said Yoji. "Anyway, we don't need him to get your power back. The two of us can do it together. I can assure you of that."

Braim nodded and followed Yoji back up the beach toward the

city. He still looked over his shoulder, however, at Tashir, who he felt bad about abandoning like this after agreeing to train with him. He hoped that Tashir wasn't too angry at him, because the last thing he needed, on top of all of his other problems, was to have one of his only friends too angry at him to even speak with him again.

Chapter Two

PRINCESS RAYA MANA, Princess of Carnag and daughter of King Malock and Queen Hanarova, stood outside the door to the room of Judge Alira. She had been standing there for a few minutes already, but those few minutes had seemed like forever to her, probably because she was still groggy from having gotten up so early this morning.

And I look so horrible, too, Raya thought, wincing when she remembered how her hair and face had looked in the mirror this morning. There were no mirrors in the room she stood in to look at, but she was glad for that because she didn't want to look at her own face at the moment. *Even after I cleaned up as best as I could, I still look awful, simply awful.*

But Raya had had to get up anyway, because the night before she had received a gray ghost from Alira summoning her to Alira's chambers in the morning. Alira had not said exactly what she wished to speak with Raya about, but Raya assumed it had something to do with the Tournament. A part of her hoped that Alira would tell her what the upcoming Hollech Bracket Challenge was going to be about, but knowing how fair Alira was, Raya didn't get her hopes up too much. She looked around the room in which she stood, feeling a little bit bored. She was not normally one to study her surroundings, but she had nothing better to do at the moment.

She stood in a small room, pretty bare and obviously meant only as a place to pass the time before going into Alira's room. A staircase had taken her up here, one that started at the lobby of the Temple of the Gods. It had been a fairly tall staircase, as Alira's room was located well above the streets of World's End, and Raya would have preferred not to walk up it, but it was the only way to get up to Alira's room, so she took it anyway.

Raya leaned against the wall. The only illumination in the room came from a glowing stone embedded in the trim above the door. But the stone's illuminating life did not extend to the staircase, which was still quite shadowy. Now Raya knew that there was nothing in the staircase that could harm her, but seeing the shadows of the staircase reminded her too much of the Void's shadows.

Don't think about the Void, Raya told herself. She looked away from the staircase. *Do that and you'll just get anxious.*

Of course, it was hard for Raya not to think about the Void, because the Void had killed Keeper. Perhaps *killed* wasn't the right word, seeing as Keeper had been an automaton, which meant that he technically did not really 'live' in the same way that human beings did. Still, the fact was that Keeper was gone and there wasn't any way to repair him because the pieces of his body had been left behind in the ethereal. Raya had considered going back to the ethereal to gather his parts, but knowing that the Void had taken over the ethereal had made her decide that it would be better for her health not to do that.

13

Even so, Raya wished that she could. Keeper had been her protector, even if Raya had only been aware of that for a while. Ever since Keeper's death, she had felt far less safe than ever. Perhaps that was because of the Void, the golems, and Tamra, but it was also because she knew that Keeper had been designed by her parents to protect her. Raya had not seen or spoken with her parents at all since Keeper's death, so she didn't know if they knew about his demise. She wished that she could be with her parents anyway, though, because with everything that had happened recently, she wasn't sure if she would ever see her parents again.

I should chin up, Raya told herself. *After all, today is the day of the Hollech Bracket Challenge. And if I win—no,* when *I win, because it is obviously my destiny to win—then I won't have to worry about my personal safety ever again.*

Of course, Raya tried not to dwell on the fact that the gods were worrying about *their* personal safety at the moment. So she instead thought about Carmaz, who she hadn't heard from at all since she and Alira had left Ruwa. She didn't know if he was still alive or not. For that matter, she didn't know if Herune and the Hermit were still alive, either, but she didn't really care about them as much as she cared about Carmaz. She could live with their deaths, but she wasn't sure if she could live with Carmaz's.

I wish the gods would at least tell us if Carmaz is all right, Raya thought. *They have been so silent. I guess they just want us to focus on the Tournament, instead of worrying about what's going on in the wider world, but I hate not knowing whether Carmaz is alive or what the golem army is doing or anything like that.*

Raya was snapped out of her thoughts when the door to Alira's room opened and Alira stepped out. The Judge looked much the same as she always had, with her glasses showing severe-looking eyes behind them. She wore silver robes, her bald head reflecting the light shining from the top of the doorway. Despite that, she didn't seem quite as powerful as she used to, no doubt due to the fact that the golems had blocked her magic.

"Hi, Alira," said Raya, waving at her. "How are you?"

Alira looked at Raya with some uncertainty. Then she looked at the staircase and asked, "Did anyone follow you?"

"No," said Raya, shaking her head. "I'm all alone. Why?"

"I don't want anyone eavesdropping on our conversation," said Alira. She then stepped back into her room and said, "Please come inside."

Curious, Raya stepped through the open doorway into Alira's room. As Alira closed the door behind her, Raya looked around at the Judge's room, because this was the first time she had ever been inside it before and so didn't quite know what to expect.

It was a medium-sized room, with a large wooden wardrobe standing against the opposite wall, its doors cracked open slightly, allowing Raya to see other silver robes like the one Alira was currently wearing hanging within. A bed lay on the right side of the room and on the left was a door that seemed to lead into a bathroom, because Raya caught a glimpse of a tub through the partially-opened door, as well as the scent of some kind of orange soap.

The massive Rulebook lay open on a tall wooden podium. The words written on it were in a language Raya couldn't read, but it looked like Alira might have been flipping through the pages at some point. There was a quill and ink pot next to the Rulebook, though Raya didn't see any paper or parchment for Alira to write upon.

Alira walked past Raya to the window. She then pulled the curtains apart, peered out briefly, and then closed them. She turned to face Raya, an odd look on her face that Raya had rarely seen before on Alira's face: Fear.

"What is the problem, Judge?" said Raya. "You still haven't told me why you summoned me. After all, you *never* summon any godlings to your personal chambers, so I believe it must be something important."

"You're right," said Alira, nodding. She took her glasses off her face and wiped them off with her robes. "I don't. I prefer my privacy and have no reason to socialize with you godlings. My whole and only purpose is to judge the participants of the Tournament and determine who will ascend to godhood and who will not. Nothing more, nothing less."

Raya smiled, though it was a somewhat nervous smile because she didn't quite like Alira's monotonic voice, which contrasted with her fearful expression. "Oh, of course. I mean, that sounds rather boring, in my opinion, but—"

"But today something has been on my mind and I wasn't sure who to talk to," said Alira. She replaced her glasses over her face and looked at Raya with a frown. "You are the closest thing I have to a friend—more like an acquaintance, really—which is why I summoned you here."

Now that puzzled Raya. Raya hadn't thought that Alira might think of her that way. Sure, the two of them had escaped Ruwa together, and Raya had even saved Alira's life once, but to Raya

16

that had not meant anything. Of course, since Alira didn't have any friends whatsoever, maybe that explained why she considered Raya her 'acquaintance.'

In any case, Raya said, "Is it something related to the security of World's End? Because if it is, you might want to tell the gods about it."

"No, nothing quite so serious as that," said Alira. Then she shrugged. "Well, I mean, it is serious—*very* serious—to me, but not so serious to anyone else. Except maybe to you, assuming you even care."

Raya's impression was that Alira was clearly bad at putting her feelings into words. The Judge seemed so hopelessly lost and confused that Raya actually felt sorry for her, even though Alira was probably still a great deal more powerful than Raya was or ever would be (unless Raya won the Tournament, anyway).

So Raya said, in a much gentler tone than she normally used when addressing Alira, "Alira, you sound awfully confused. Why don't you start at the beginning?"

Alira nodded. She rubbed her forehead, looking disturbed. "All right. Do you recall how the Void stabbed me after you and I escaped from the ethereal a week ago?"

"How could I not?" said Raya. "I thought you were going to die. The only reason you survived was because Atikos healed you. And even then, I heard she struggled with that."

"She did," said Alira. She touched her chest, where the Void had stabbed her. "Wounds created by the Void are different from wounds created by Martirians. The Void's tendrils cut into your very essence. It is possible to recover and heal, but it still badly wounds no matter what."

17

"Of course," said Raya. "But what does this have to do with your problem? Did Atikos not heal you correctly?"

"Atikos did a fine job, seeing as she is the Goddess of Healing," said Alira, shaking her head. "The problem, Raya, is … well, I'm not sure how to say this, but I am dying."

Raya's hands flew to her mouth in shock. "Dying? Why?"

"I'm not sure," said Alira. She winced when she touched the spot on her chest where the Void had stabbed her. "But I think the Void must have left part of herself in me when she penetrated me. Atikos healed most of the damage, but she told me that she couldn't remove all of the Void's darkness. I asked her not to tell anyone about that."

"Why?" said Raya. She stepped forward. "Shouldn't we know if the Judge of the Tournament of the Gods is dying? What if you die in the middle of one of the upcoming Challenges?"

"That would indeed be quite inconvenient," Alira said. "But I don't want to alarm everyone or create even more stress for the others by telling them that I am dying. Besides, why else do you think I am pushing forward with all of the last Challenges in one day? I don't want to die before the Tournament ends, so I am going to get them all done as quickly as possible."

"What will happen if you die?" said Raya. "And why are you telling me about this if you didn't want to tell anyone else?"

"Because …" Alira bit her lower lip. "Because, despite my cool outward appearance, this does weigh heavily on me. Raya, you don't understand. I have *no* idea what awaits me on the other side. When I die, where will my spirit go? Do I even have one?"

"Why wouldn't you?" said Raya. "I mean, certainly, you can be rather uptight and boring, but you seem as alive as anyone else

I've ever known."

Alira shook her head. She walked over to her bed and sat down in it, sinking her face into her hands at the same time. "But I am not like everyone else you've ever known, Raya. That is the point. I am truly one of a kind. The Powers created me for one task, and one task only. I am not even sure I am supposed to live past that task."

There was more emotion in Alira's voice than Raya had ever heard in it before. While Raya was no stranger to random emotional outbursts, she didn't quite know how to handle it coming from Alira like this. It wasn't like she knew anything about the Powers or the afterlife, after all, so there wasn't much she could say to assuage Alira's fears of death.

Then an idea occurred to Raya and she said, "Then why don't you talk to Braim? He was dead and came back to life. He could tell you what lies beyond."

Alira looked up at Raya, annoyance on her features now. "How many times must I say this? I'm not like the rest of you. When you die, you know that you will go to the Spirit Lands or wherever it is that Braim came from, but me? I can't be sure. The Powers did not create me with the intent of letting me live a long life. I may end up like your automaton bodyguard, Keeper, who had no soul and who is likely gone forever now."

"Don't say that," said Raya. "You don't know that. Sure, you might be different from the rest of us, but that doesn't mean you won't go to the places that we'll go when we die. I bet you will."

"You don't know that, either," said Alira. "I would like to believe that, but the Powers never confirmed that when they created me. They gave me one mission to complete. And, even if the Void was not killing me on the inside, I fear that I would die once I complete that mission, because after that I would have no further purpose in life."

"Then why are you still judging the Tournament?" said Raya, throwing her hands into the air. "If I were you, I'd say no. Grinf can judge the Tournament, can't he? He did that with the final two sub-bracket challenges, didn't he? Why not have him take your place so you can live?"

"Because I am not selfish," said Alira. She wiped some tears out of her eyes, which startled Raya, as she had not known that Alira even could shed tears. "And because I am impartial, unlike Grinf or the other gods. They cannot judge the godlings as well or as accurately as I, nor do they know the Rulebook as well as I do. The Tournament could not finish with one of them acting as the Judge in my place."

"It still seems dumb if you ask me," said Raya. "I know that the Powers are supposed to be even wiser than the gods, but it seems to me like this is cruel and unnecessary. What good would your death do for the world?"

"The real question, Raya, is what good would my *life* do for the world after the Tournament ends," said Alira. She sniffled. "I never told you this, but back on Ruwa, after Carmaz rescued me from the golems, he asked me what I planned to do after the Tournament was over."

"He did?" said Raya. Jealousy shot through her at the idea of Alira and Carmaz being so close like that, but she tried to hide it so that Alira wouldn't notice. "Well, that's ... that's just like Carmaz. He's a thoughtful guy, which is why I intend to make him my husband after I win the Tournament."

Alira looked at Raya with a puzzled expression on her face, then shook her head and said, "Anyway, I didn't have a very good answer for Carmaz at the time. And for most of my life—as short as it has been—I've only focused on the present, on what I am supposed to do, without ever asking what comes next."

"What comes next is what you want to come next," said Raya. "Isn't it obvious?"

"No, it isn't," said Alira, shaking her head. "Outside of judging the Tournament, what good could I possibly do for the world, or even for myself? Especially with my magical abilities almost entirely gone. They are returning slowly, but even if they do, it isn't like I know how to use them for anything other than punishing cheaters and rule-breakers. I don't even know what I want for myself."

Alira sounded like she was completely at the edge of despair. Raya, feeling concerned for Alira despite her normally less-than-positive feelings toward the Judge, walked over and sat down on Alira's bed next to her. She then put one hand on Alira's back, causing Alira to look at her in surprise.

"Alira, it's going to be all right," said Raya. "I know how bad everything seems at the moment, how awful it all is, but that doesn't mean it *has* to end badly for you or anyone else."

"How can you possibly know that?" said Alira. "I am going to *die*, Raya. It might be because of the Void or it might be because the Powers designed me to expire after I complete my mission, but I am going to die nonetheless. And what is worse is that I know that I have no reason to live, no reason to keep going after the Tournament is finished."

"Well, I—"

21

"And I'm not just talking about all of the other problems in the world," said Alira. She waved her hands in a random direction. "Even if the golems, the Void, and Tamra are defeated, my life will still be meaningless and without direction, assuming it continues past the Tournament. There is no hope for me, at least none that I can see."

Raya rubbed Alira's back, even though she wasn't at all sure if it would help. "Maybe all that's true, but maybe not. Listen, Alira, I know you and I haven't exactly gotten along that well, what with you assigning me to the bracket that I wanted nothing to do with and me arguing with you about it, but I think that deep down you are a good person and I want to help you."

"Help me?" said Alira. "How?"

Raya smiled. "Well, assuming you do live past the Tournament and we can remove the Void's darkness in you, then you could come live in Carnag Hall back home."

"What would I do in a palace like that?" said Alira. She wiped some more tears away from her face. "Waste away the rest of my days, however long that may be?"

Raya shook her head. "No, silly. We can help you figure out what to do with your life. My parents won't object. They're both good people who always strive to help those in need. They wouldn't ever say no to you or anyone else I might bring in."

Alira's expression was still quite depressed, but she sniffled and said, "Thank you for the kind offer, Raya. It isn't what I expected from you."

"Why not?" said Raya, not hiding the offense in her voice. "I'm a *very* generous and kind person. You shouldn't be surprised at this kind offer from me at all."

"Of course," said Alira, though Raya thought that the Judge was just humoring her now. "Sorry."

Then Alira hesitated. There was something in her eyes now that Raya had only seen once before, that same desire from when she and Alira were cornered and almost killed by the Empty followers. It made Raya feel uncomfortable, but she didn't look away because she didn't want to offend Alira.

"Raya …" Alira seemed to be struggling to find the right words. "There's something … I need to tell you."

Raya cocked an eyebrow. "What? More bad news?"

"It's hard to categorize it as 'good' or 'bad,'" said Alira. "It all depends … depends on your definition of those words, I suppose."

"Well, just spit it out already," said Raya. "I'm all—"

Raya didn't get to finish her sentence because Alira interrupted her with a kiss. The Judge's lips locked onto her own, soft and moist. Raya smelled the Judge's odor, which was that same orange soap smell from before. Raya didn't even quite realize what was happening until she realized that Alira was too close for her comfort.

Abruptly, Raya pushed Alira away, breaking her off her kiss. In fact, Raya pushed Alira away so hard that Alira almost fell off the bed, while Raya jumped off and walked away as fast as she could.

"Raya!" Alira called. "Wait, where are you—"

"I'm getting ready for the Tournament," said Raya. She could still taste Alira's lips on her own, but she didn't look back over her shoulder at the Judge. "Gotta prepare for the Hollech Bracket Challenge, after all. See you there."

Raya opened the door to Alira's room and was out in an instant, slamming the door shut behind her. Then she dashed down the staircase, feeling confused and disturbed by what just happened and, most importantly, wishing that it had never happened at all.

Chapter Three

CARMAZ KORVA WALKED through the ruins of what, not more than a few days ago, used to be his hometown of Conewood. It was still early morning, though the sun was rising rapidly and would no doubt be bright enough to see by in just a few hours. Even so, the morning was humid and hot, making him somewhat sweaty, despite wearing a much cooler shirt than he normally did.

Carmaz stopped in front of one ruined hut. Aside from the hole in the roof that appeared to have been created by a golem smashing it in, the hut still stood on its foundation. The door was closed and locked, but because it was made out of weak wood, Carmaz kicked it in with a single blow from his boot and stepped inside to see if there were any survivors.

The hut was dark, though with the first rays of the sun streaming in from the outside, Carmaz could see that it was indeed empty. A table in the center of the one-room hut was buried underneath the remains of the bashed-in roof, but it seemed like whoever had lived here had escaped some time ago.

Carmaz sighed in relief. No corpses. That was probably the best news he'd received in the last week, because it seemed like every destroyed village he went to was full of corpses. Nor were there any golems lying in wait. Not that there ever were, because the golems were a constantly moving army that never stayed in any one place for longer than a day or two, but Carmaz always worried that Stalac or Lady Dia might order some of the golems to stay behind and ambush anyone tracking them down. That hadn't happened yet, but that didn't mean it wouldn't.

Stepping back out of the hut, Carmaz looked around at the village he had spent much of his life in. The town water well in the center was completely destroyed, crushed to pieces, making it impossible to gather water from it anymore. The fishing shack, where the local fishermen kept their fishing supplies, appeared to have been uprooted and thrown into another hut. There was no way to tell if anyone had been inside that hut when the shack had been thrown on it, mostly because the heavy shack had crushed the hut underneath it. Considering Carmaz couldn't see any blood or body parts, he assumed no one had been in it at the time, but he was in no mood to investigate for obvious reasons.

A part of Carmaz just wanted to leave entirely. Herune had warned him that tracking down the golems like this was foolish. He had said that Carmaz should stay with the Hermit and him until the gods came and dealt with the golems, but as far as Carmaz could tell, the gods weren't coming, and in the mean time people were suffering and Carmaz was the only person who could help them.

Or the only person who wants *to help them, anyway,* Carmaz thought. He shook his head. *Focus on the mission. Try to find as many survivors as you can. If possible, give proper burials to the deceased.*

That was when Carmaz heard a small girl crying somewhere nearby. He looked in every direction until he located the crying, which was coming from another ruined hut on the other side of the destroyed well. The young girl's cry sounded rather hoarse, like she had been crying for hours, but it was still quite audible. Carmaz wondered why he hadn't heard it when he first entered the village, but quickly forgot about that question, deciding to instead focus on rescuing the little girl, whoever she was, and finding out if she knew about the locations of any other survivors from the attack.

The door on this hut had been knocked in and the left wall had fallen, but the girl's cry continued unabated, which told Carmaz that this girl was probably not badly injured, just scared.

"Hello?" Carmaz called out when he reached the bashed-in door. "Can you hear me? I'm a friend. Not one of the golems."

The girl's crying stopped immediately. Then a small and scared, but familiar, voice said, "Carmy?"

Carmaz recognized the pet name and voice immediately. A sense of dread filled him, however, because of what that meant. Nonetheless, he said, in a strong voice, "Yes, Frissa, it's me. Stay where you are. I'm going to get you out of there, all right? Just hang on and you'll be safe."

"O-Okay," came Frissa's small voice. "I'm scared … Big rocks attacked …"

"I know," said Carmaz. "Just hang in there for just a little while longer, all right?"

Carmaz grabbed the door and pulled as hard as he could. Because it had been punched in, the door was hard to remove, but Carmaz kept putting all of his strength into pulling open the door.

27

Eventually, he succeeded, pulling the broken door out of the doorway and leaning it against the hut's outer walls. He then stepped into the hut and blinked.

Like the other hut, this one was small and smelled like mud. It was partially exposed to the elements due to the collapsed wall, but that didn't matter to Carmaz, because he soon spotted Frissa—a young girl with dark, innocent eyes and curly black hair—hiding underneath a table. She started when she saw him, but even though Frissa knew him, she did not come out from under the table to greet him.

"Hey, Frissa," said Carmaz. He smiled, hoping that that would be enough to calm her down. "It's me, Carmy. Are you hurt?"

Frissa still didn't move an inch from her hiding place. Carmaz noticed she was gripping a knife in her tiny hands. "Are the rocks gone?"

"The rocks?" Carmaz repeated.

"Walking rocks," Frissa said. She stumbled over the words, likely due to the fear in her mind. "The ones that smashed everything and killed everyone."

"Oh," said Carmaz. "You mean the golems. Yes, they're gone. They are long gone. I don't know where they went, but I know that they are nowhere near this place and probably won't return anytime soon."

Frissa sniffled, but then ran out from under the table and slammed into Carmaz's legs. She wrapped her small arms around his legs and immediately started crying. She even dropped her knife, though Carmaz didn't pay attention to that.

He just scooped her up into his arms and let her rest her head on his shoulder, patting her on the back and saying, in a soothing voice, "There, there, Frissa, it's going to be all right. I'm here to protect you from the walking rocks."

Thankfully, Frissa stopped crying, but she continued to sniffle and hiccup. Her small hands gripped his body hard, much harder than he had expected from a little girl her size, but he didn't mind because that meant she trusted him, something he worried had been shattered ever since his exile from Conewood after he was kicked out of the Tournament.

"Everyone's ... gone," said Frissa. Her voice was small and hard to understand due to her hiccups and sniffles, but Carmaz understood it anyway. "Hazur ... Barc ... all of them are ..."

Frissa broke down into sobbing again, causing Carmaz to pat her on the back and say, "It's all right, it's all right. I'm going to get you to somewhere safe, okay? I have some friends who will protect and take care of you. But first, I want to see if we can find any other survivors."

"There aren't any survivors," Frissa said. She sniffled. "The walking rocks killed everyone."

Carmaz had a feeling that Frissa was telling the truth, but he said, "Well, maybe you don't know that. We'll just do a quick search of the ruins, and if we can't find anyone, we'll leave, okay?"

Frissa sniffled. "Okay."

So Carmaz turned around and stepped out of the hut back into the humid early morning air, Frissa in his arms. As soon as Carmaz did that, however, he heard movement behind him and looked up over his shoulder just in time to see a massive stone hammer falling down on the hut.

Alarmed, Carmaz jumped forward, causing Frissa to scream,

as the hammer crashed down on the ruined hut. Hitting the ground, Carmaz rolled back to his feet, protecting Frissa with his body, and then looked back in the direction of the hut to see what had caused that.

Standing behind the now-completely destroyed hut was one of the golems. This one, however, was different from the golems Carmaz had seen before. It was far more humanoid, with a somewhat human face and five-fingered hands that probably weighed more than he did. The golem carried a gigantic stone hammer—the head of which was twice as tall as Carmaz—in its hands, a hammer which was currently resting on the ruins of what had once been the hut they had been standing in moments before.

The golem lifted its hammer off the ruins of the hut and stared at Carmaz and Frissa. Its eyes were stony and dead, much like the eyes of the rest of the golems, but Carmaz figured that it was probably angry at him for dodging its attack. Carmaz, of course, had only dodged it because he was pretty sure that he had Dranyx's luck, but that didn't matter to him at the moment because the golem took one step toward them. Its massive foot crushed the ruins of the hut as the golem lumbered toward them slowly but menacingly.

But Carmaz was not going to stand around and wait for the golem to kill him. He stood up, turned around, and ran as fast as he was able, never looking back even once, with Frissa now crying openly and freely again.

Carmaz heard the pounding footsteps of the golem behind him as it ran after them. That made Carmaz run even faster, his eyes on the Swamp surrounding the village. He figured that if he could make it into the mess of trees, bushes, vines, and mud outside the village, then Frissa and he would be safe.

But as Carmaz headed for the Swamp, something rose from the Swamp's water. Carmaz skidded to a stop, looking at the thing that rose from the Swamp like a demon from the depths of the underworld. Water and mud rolled off its form, until the monster now stood to its full height, revealing that it was another golem, one of the golems that Carmaz had seen before. Like the others, it had a sword hand and a saw hand, which it raised above its head as Carmaz and the crying Frissa drew closer.

Skidding to a stop, Carmaz ran to the right, away from both golems, in the direction that seemed free of golems. But then two hands burst out from the earth in front of Carmaz's path, again forcing him to stop as something pulled itself out of the earth.

This creature was nowhere near as bulky or huge as the golems, but its stone skin pegged it as one of them. But it was incredibly thin, much thinner than any golem Carmaz had seen before, and small, maybe about a head shorter than Carmaz was. Its joints cracked as it rose from the ground, pulling itself out inch by inch. Its face was monstrous, with short blunt teeth and blank eyes. It looked more like a corpse rising from the grave than a golem.

Carmaz backed up as quickly as he could, while also glancing to the left and to the right. The golem wielding the hammer was coming from the right, while the one that had risen from the Swamp was coming from the left. That left only one direction open, the one directly behind Carmaz, so he turned around, with Frissa still crying, and dashed in that direction, again moving as fast as he could.

But he only made it a couple dozen yards before a stone drill burst through the ground before him. Once more coming to a stop, Carmaz looked as yet another golem—this one closer in size to the skinny one, although much bulkier—emerged from the earth. It was vaguely humanoid, though it had no real head to speak of and its right hand was a stone drill that looked quite capable of tearing through Carmaz's chest and ending his life.

And once again, Carmaz had to back up, only this time he realized that he was trapped between the four golems. They had cut off all possible avenues of escape. Carmaz looked around again just to make sure he wasn't overlooking any possible escape routes, but when he saw that he was indeed stuck, he almost despaired, because he knew that he couldn't defeat all four of these golems on his own, especially while protecting Frissa at the same time.

"C-Carmy?" said Frissa. She had stopped crying now, though she sniffled every now and then. "Are the rocks going to squish us?"

"No, no, Frissa, they won't," said Carmaz, although every word that came from his mouth sounded like a lie even to him. "Of course they won't. We'll get out of this situation alive and well, so don't worry, okay? I'll figure it out. Just take it easy right now."

"O-Okay," said Frissa. She squeaked when the golem wielding the hammer made the earth tremble slightly with a particularly loud stomp of its foot, gripping Carmaz so tightly that her tiny finger nails bit into his skin.

But Carmaz ignored that. He looked around, forcing himself to think fast, desperately trying to figure out how to get out of this situation alive. He wished that Herune and the Hermit were with him, but the two mages had stayed behind in the Sanctuary and didn't know about Carmaz's current predicament. Nor did he have any way of contacting them, either, which seemed like a really dumb thing now that Carmaz thought about it.

Carmaz's mind raced as the four golems slowly moved in on Frissa and him. Frissa whimpered, but she must have trusted him more than he thought, because she didn't utter a word. That reassured Carmaz greatly, but it still didn't help him figure out how to save both of their lives.

Think, Carmaz, think, Carmaz thought, glancing at the skinny golem, which walked with strange and unnatural movements like a puppet. *There has got to be some way out of this. You can't die, not yet, not when Ruwa needs you.*

But no matter how hard Carmaz thought about it, he saw no way to get out of this situation alive. The biggest problem was Frissa. If he didn't have Frissa in his arms, clinging to him like he was her actual father, then he would have risked making a break between the legs of one of the larger golems. As it was, however, he wasn't sure he wanted to risk Frissa's life like that.

Not like you have much choice, Carmaz thought. *If you don't risk escape, then you and Frissa* will *be killed.*

That thought was enough to make Carmaz say, "Frissa, I want you to hold on tightly, because I'm going to get us out of here and I don't want to drop you accidentally, okay?"

Frissa didn't answer. She just tightened her tiny grip on him even more, which was surprising because Carmaz hadn't thought she could hold him any harder than she already was. Nonetheless, he was glad she had listened.

So Carmaz dashed toward the golem with the hammer, as the

gap between its legs was wide enough for Frissa and him to pass underneath. And it seemed to be working, because the golem stopped its advancement and watched Frissa and him approach as if surprised.

But then the golem slammed its legs together, immediately cutting off the one chance that Carmaz and Frissa had at escape. The golem raised its hammer high above its head, ready to crush Carmaz and Frissa with it.

Carmaz stepped back, but there was no way he could escape in time. The golem brought its hammer down on them both without another word.

Before the golem's hammer fell onto Carmaz, however, someone behind Carmaz shouted, "Dumb mortals! Get out of the way!"

Someone behind Carmaz shoved Frissa and him to the side. Carmaz staggered and fell, but fell in such a way as to keep Frissa from taking the brunt of the impact. Frissa yelped in surprise, but otherwise seemed unharmed.

But the golem's hammer was still falling toward them fast. And it would have slammed straight down on top of them if it hadn't been caught by someone Carmaz had never seen before. The figure appeared to be mortal, because his skin was organic like Carmaz's, without a hint of stone anywhere on his body.

Yet there was no human in the world who could have effortlessly caught and held back the hammer of that golem like that. The being had skin as green as the leaves of a tree and, while shorter than Carmaz, was far more muscular than himself. The being had grass-like braids, but he was also almost completely naked save for a very thin loincloth around his waist.

The golem, however, didn't seem to realize what it was dealing with. It was trying to crush the fat, green-skinned being under the weight of its hammer, but the being didn't even struggle to hold it back. The green being almost seemed bored, as if he wasn't really trying.

"Stupid golem," said the being in a harsh voice. "Think you can crush me with an oversized hammer? I'd be laughing if it wasn't so pathetic. Of course, you golems don't seem to have brains at all, so maybe you're just that stupid."

With a grunt, the being shoved the hammer off his head. That action caused the golem to stagger backwards, but before it could regain its balance, the being jumped up at him and kicked it in the side of the head. The blow smashed straight through the golem's stone head, shattering it into a million pieces. Its hammer fell to the ground with a *boom*, followed by the golem's corpse itself, the impact shaking the earth and making Frissa yelp again.

The green-skinned being fell to the ground, picked up the deceased golem's hammer with no trouble at all, and then swung it at the skinny golem. The blow shattered the skinny golem into pieces, but that still left two golems: the one that had risen from the Swamp and the one that had drilled from under the earth.

Not that either of them posed much of a challenge to the newcomer. The green-skinned being dashed over to the driller. The driller tried to stab him, but he caught its spinning drill with one hand and snapped it off. Then he stabbed the drill into the driller's chest, forcing it in hard enough to cause the driller's entire form to break apart. Its head and limbs and what was left of its body fell into a heap on the ground, but before the last of its pieces could touch the earth, the green-skinned being leaped toward the last golem.

This golem must have been paying careful attention to the fates of its brothers, however, because it didn't even wait for the green-skinned being to attack it before it swung its sword in his direction. In fact, it actually smacked the green-skinned being in midair, sending him flying uncontrollably into the Swamp waters, which he fell into with a *splash*.

Carmaz—who was sitting up now—stared at the spot where the green-skinned being had fallen. Frissa, too, was watching, though she looked like she was about to cry again. Carmaz almost felt like crying himself, because he was now certain that Frissa and he were going to die.

The golem, on the other hand, seemed to consider it a mission accomplished, because it turned away from the spot where it had knocked out its opponent and resumed marching toward Carmaz and Frissa. Carmaz, seeing an opportunity to escape, got to his feet as quickly as he could while still holding Frissa, but before he could run away, Frissa cried out, "What's that?"

Carmaz looked in the direction Frissa was pointing. He gasped when he saw what she was pointing at.

The trees and vines of the Swamp were coalescing into one. It looked like some kind of mysterious force was bringing them together, forming a giant hand. But it wasn't like the large mud fists that the Hermit created. No, this hand was massive, half the size of Conewood, and constantly growing larger. Trees, vine, mud, and other things flew together, creating a strange sound of wood and mud slapping together, until soon a gigantic hand made of everything noted before dwarfed even the golem.

The golem must have heard this, because it turned around and looked up at the hand. Then the hand's index finger rose, rose higher and higher, and pointed down toward the golem, which raised its sword like it was ready to fight the hand.

But the golem never stood a chance, because the hand's index finger hurtled down toward it at an amazing speed. The finger completely covered the golem in its thick muck and trees, obscuring the golem from Carmaz's view. Mud and leaves and branches flew everywhere as the finger slammed down into the golem. It was like watching the entire Swamp attack the golem, a sight which made Carmaz want to run, but he stood and watched instead.

The assault lasted only a few seconds, at which point the hand stopped slamming into the golem and pulled back its finger. As the hand retreated, it revealed what happened to the golem that it had been attacking … or what was left of it, anyway.

Lying on the earth, prone as a sunk ship, were chunks of the golem. That was the best way for Carmaz to describe it. Covered in mud and other types of gunk, the golem appeared to have been almost completely pulverized. Carmaz recognized its chest—the only part that seemed to be in one piece—as well as its sword, but aside from that, the golem's body parts more closely resembled the old ruins of Castle Ruwa than the mighty stone warrior that had stood there only a couple of seconds before. If Carmaz had not known that the golem had been standing there mere moments before, he would have assumed that it was some rocks left over from an abandoned construction project.

Still, Carmaz didn't go anywhere near it. He just held Frissa closer than ever, watching the massive hand as it dissipated. Trees flew back to their original positions, vines wrapped around their trees again, and mud returned underneath the surface of the waters, until soon the massive, titanic hand was gone, and the area was silent once more, save for the chirps of some bird somewhere in the distance.

"Carmy?" said Frissa. She sounded as awestruck as him. "Did you do that?"

Carmaz shook his head. "No. And I don't know who did."

A harsh, terrible laugh suddenly penetrated the air. It was so sudden and so loud that Carmaz jumped and looked around. At first, he didn't see anyone, until he spotted the green-skinned being from before emerge from the Swamp waters and jump out. He landed on the muddy ground on both feet, laughing hard. He then walked over to the remains of the golem, which he kicked so hard that he snapped them in two.

"Take that, you dumb golem," the green being said. He picked up what appeared to be its head and stared it straight in the eye. "Do you think you can just hit me like that and not expect the full power of my divine wrath to come down upon you? Do you? Huh? Huh?"

Obviously, the golem's decapitated head did not respond. The being snorted and threw the head over his shoulder. It landed in the Swamp waters with a splash, where it rapidly sank out of sight.

"Stupid rock," the green-skinned being muttered. "Always hated them. So boring."

Carmaz—who wasn't sure that he wanted anything to do with this newcomer, even if he did just save their lives—took a step backwards, hoping he could escape before the green-skinned being took notice of them.

But then Frissa waved at the green-skinned being and shouted, "Hey, Mr. Loincloth! Thanks for saving us!"

Carmaz wanted to yell at Frissa not to attract the attention of this obvious being of power, but he was too late. The green-skinned being looked in their direction, as if he had forgotten all about them. Then he walked over to them, moving rather quickly for a man of his weight.

"Who are you?" said Carmaz, holding Frissa close to him as the green-skinned being approached. "Are you a katabans?"

The green-skinned being stopped and put a hand on his chest. "Me? A katabans? Of course not. I'm a god, one of the greatest there is, thank you very much."

"A god?" said Carmaz. "Which one? I don't recognize you."

"Of course you wouldn't," said the god. "I've never had much of a following among you humans, mostly because I was on the other side of the Godly War. Not that I want human worship, mind you, because I think it's the dumbest thing in the world, but there is a very good reason you don't know who I am."

"You're a southern god, then," said Carmaz. He gulped. "Are you going to eat Frissa and me?"

The god smiled, revealing crooked wooden teeth that looked solid enough to bite through bone. "Well, I would certainly like to, but I can't, since this is the northern side of the Dividing Line. If we were on *my* island, then I sure would eat you both up, but I can't even touch you two. Anyway, I came here to take down those dumb golems, not eat humans, even though I haven't had a good human in the Powers know how long."

The god rubbed his large stomach. He then pulled out a bone from nowhere and started chewing on it.

39

"Wait, you're here to help us defeat the golems?" said Carmaz. He sighed in relief. "Oh, thank heavens. I guess Raya and Alira must have gotten to World's End after all."

"Yeah, they did," said the god. He sucked on his bone for a moment before pulling it out of his mouth. "But don't expect any of the other gods to show up anytime soon."

"What?" said Carmaz. "Why? Don't the gods care about saving Martir from the golems?"

The god chuckled. "Human, I guess you don't really know everything that's happened outside of this little spit of mud you call an island. I'll have to fill you in on it, but first, let me introduce myself."

The god gestured at himself with his bone. "My name in your human language is unpronounceable, but it translates to the Loner God. I am the God of Solitude, the Jungle, and Animals … and, as strange as it may seem, I am going to save your island even if I have to destroy it."

Chapter Four

BRAIM HAD NEVER visited Yoji's apartment before. Although he liked Yoji well enough, he never really thought of the young mage as a close friend. An acquaintance, sure, but never closer than that, mostly because Yoji's know-it-all attitude turned him off.

As it turned out, Yoji's apartment was much more spacious than Braim's little room. It was located on the third floor of one of the massive buildings that dominated World's End, but it still offered a nice view of the city. There was a large double-bed in one corner, with the door to what appeared to be a nice, white-tiled bathroom only a few feet away from it. The floor was partly wood, partly carpeted, and the carpeting itself was red and shaggy and quite soft. Long, flowing black curtains covered the windows, while a large wardrobe stood on the end of the room opposite the bed.

But what really caught Braim's attention was the immense amount of books everywhere. Books were stacked on the sofa, on the end table, on the coffee table, on the dining table, at the foot of the bed, and he even caught a glimpse of some in the bathroom. Some were huge and thick, at least a thousand pages in length if not longer, while others were so thin that they were practically pamphlets. A handful had their titles written in Divina, allowing Braim to see one of the books was *Prophecies* by Hanyu, but the vast majority were in a language that Braim could not read or understand. Many of the books appeared quite old, but there were a few that looked brand new. In fact, there were so many books that their collective scent filled the room, overriding any other smell in the place.

"Wow," said Braim, stopping as Yoji closed the door shut behind them with a wave of his wand. "You really like to read."

Yoji walked past Braim over to the nearest stack of books, which was actually taller than him. He then waved his wand at the stack, causing the books to separate and start floating around him like the stars around the world. He glanced at each book as it flashed past his face. "Well, of course I do. Knowledge is power, after all, and books are full of knowledge."

"But where did you get them all?" said Braim, scratching the back of his head.

"A few of them I took with me from Itrija when Tinkar showed up and told me that I'm supposed to be in the Tournament," said Yoji, still without looking at Braim. One of the books stopped in front of his face, but then he shook his head and it went floating around again with the rest. "Just a couple dozen of my favorites."

"A couple *dozen* isn't exactly what I'd call a 'few,'" said Braim.

Yoji didn't seem to hear him, though, because he continued, saying, "But the vast majority of these I got from this bookshop near here. The owner is a katabans book collector who has collected books from katabans writers and even some books written by the gods themselves. He's a very knowledgeable katabans, told me some very interesting things about the gods."

"Such as?" said Braim.

"Well, for one, Kano and Tinkar have apparently had some sort of long-running feud because of some mortal woman Tinkar loved or something," said Yoji. He shook his head. "I didn't really understand it. Anyway, that's not important. What's important is that the book collector agreed to give me these books in exchange for some books from home, as he finds it hard to get books from the Northern Isles and tells me that they are *very* valuable on World's End due to their rarity."

"Okay, but how can you read these books?" said Braim. He picked up a thin volume from a nearby pile and turned it over, frowning at its unintelligible title. "I don't even know what language this thing is written in."

"It's Godly Divina, also known as the language of the gods," said Yoji. Another book stopped in front of his face, but then he scowled and smacked it away. "From what I've gathered, the universal language of the Northern Isles, Divina, is derived from Godly Divina, but the two languages have diverged so drastically over the centuries that mastery in one language does not mean mastery in another."

"Still doesn't explain why you want these books," said Braim. He placed the book back on top of the stack he had taken it from. "Sure, they might have useful or rare knowledge in them, but there's no point in owning a book you can't read, in my opinion."

Yoji glanced at Braim in surprise. "Oh, I forgot to tell you. I learned Godly Divina just so I could read those books. It's supposed to be impossible for mortals to learn—at least according to the book collector—but it only took me a couple of weeks of trial and error to decipher the basic pronunciation and grammatical structure, and then another couple of weeks before I learned how to read and write in it."

"Really?" said Braim. He pointed at the book he had just replaced. "What is that book called?"

"*A History of the Godly War*, by the Historic God," said Yoji without missing a beat. "An interesting book, but the god is one of the southern gods, so he tends to portray the northern gods as idiots. I still learned a lot from it, however."

"Amazing," said Braim. "Is that what you've spent so much time learning? The language of the gods?"

Yoji shrugged. "I'm still not fluent in it, even though I've read sixty percent or so of the books here. Anyway, I don't consider the language to be all that impressive, because the grammatical structure is almost completely at odds with human grammar and their spelling tends to be very unusual. For example, nouns and adjectives are always hyphenated, but then sometimes they aren't and it depends on the context or sometimes the mood of the writer. Also, double negatives don't exist except when you are swearing an oath to a god or goddess."

"Uh huh," said Braim, who found his attention wandering because he didn't care much for the intricacies of divine grammar, even though Yoji clearly found it fascinating. "Let's get onto the reason we're here. You said you had a book that tells how to restore my magical power, right?"

Yoji nodded and returned his attention to the books orbiting him. "Yes, I'm trying to find it. I read it a while ago and probably would have forgotten about it entirely if you had not—Ah ha!"

Yoji pointed his wand and the books ceased orbiting him. One of the books floated toward him. It was an old and thick tome, with a faded black leather cover. It was so old that when Yoji cracked it open, it made a cracking sound that made Braim think it was going to fall apart. Yoji carefully turned the pages with his telekinesis, while the rest of the books floating around him neatly organized themselves into a stack, and in the same order that they had been in before from what Braim could tell.

Braim walked over to Yoji and looked at the book. Like most of the books, it was written in Godly Divina, which was completely unreadable to Braim. There were drawings and strange diagrams that Braim didn't understand, but which seemed important.

"Is that the book you were looking for?" asked Braim.

Yoji nodded, a smile on his face as he flipped through the pages, although he only carefully flipped through them, probably because of their age. "Yep. This is exactly what I was looking for."

"What's it called?" said Braim.

"Roughly translated from Godly Divina, its title is *The Limits of Magic*," said Yoji. "It was written by someone who called himself the Scribbler. Doesn't say what his real name was, but it doesn't matter who he was because this book is very interesting. I've read it twice already and still haven't understood even half of everything in it."

"It looks old," said Braim.

Yoji rolled his eyes. "Of course it's old. The bookseller told me that the book is about five hundred years old. He didn't see much value in it, though, because it doesn't have a famous author

45

and its contents are fairly esoteric."

"Esoteric?" Braim repeated. "What is the book about, exactly?"

"Well, as the title implies, this book describes the limitations and reach of magic," said Yoji. He stopped flipping the pages for a moment, but then frowned, shook his head, and continued searching for what he was looking for. "It's surprisingly modern, despite being five centuries out of date, in its description and conception of magic. Then again, the katabans of World's End have always seemed magically advanced to me, seeing as they can all use magic without wands or magic stones."

Braim nodded, though he didn't really care too much about that. "Is that all he talks about? Doesn't sound too esoteric to me."

"No, there's a lot more, and that was the simplest way I could think of to describe it," said Yoji. "The Scribbler also goes into a lot of detail about various theoretical spells and rituals. At least, I think they're theoretical, since they go against practically every known law of magic that we modern mages have discovered, but he describes them like they were commonplace things in his time. But again, it's hard to tell because I'm not as good at reading Godly Divina as I am at reading mortal Divina."

"What kind of spells and rituals does he talk about?" said Braim.

"He talks about negating another mage's magical abilities, for one," said Yoji, "which isn't possible, or isn't supposed to be anyway. You can't really negate another mage's powers. Only the gods are said to be capable of doing that and even then only rarely."

"But this book also tells about how to restore magical powers to mages who lost them, right?" said Braim.

Yoji nodded. "Yes. There's a spell and a ritual in here that you're supposed to do if you or someone else loses their magical power."

"From the magic-negating spell from earlier?"

"Or from something else," said Yoji. "And I mean 'something else,' because the Scribbler described some creatures that once lived on Martir in his time that could negate magical powers. He didn't dwell on them too much, though. Just said that the gods banished them beyond the Void when they became too much of a threat."

"That's reassuring," said Braim. Then he glanced at a clock hanging on the wall. "Say, how long will this ritual take, anyway? The Hollech Bracket Challenge is supposed to start soon and you're supposed to be in it, right?"

"Yeah, but I'm sure we'll get it done before the Challenge starts," said Yoji, waving off Braim's concern like it meant nothing. "The ritual the Scribbler described isn't time-consuming to set up. Assuming, of course, it even works."

"Why wouldn't it work?" said Braim.

"Because I have never even heard of such a ritual or spell before," said Yoji, glancing at Braim in annoyance. "I didn't even know it was possible for mages to lose their power. I know that magic, like every other skill, can grow less effective over time, but that's only if you don't continually practice and study. Actually losing your innate ability to use magic, though … man, that's another beast entirely, that's for sure."

"I know," said Braim, nodding. "But is there any reason you didn't bring up this ritual before?"

"I forgot," said Yoji with a shrug. "There's just been so much stuff going on recently that I forgot all about this spell. Don't worry, though, because I have a feeling it will work."

"Even though you haven't tested it before."

"Well, sure," said Yoji, "if you want to put it *that* way, it sounds risky, but since you're here, you obviously think it's worth the risk."

"Does the book say what might happen if the ritual doesn't work?" asked Braim.

"No," said Yoji. "Actually, it's written in such a way as to suggest that there aren't any negative consequences at all or if there are any, then they aren't that important."

"What the author considers 'unimportant' might not be so 'unimportant' to me, you know," said Braim. "He doesn't mention how *anything* could possibly go wrong?"

"Well ..." Yoji hesitated. "He *does* say that if you don't do it right, it can sometimes give you things you didn't expect."

"Things?" Braim repeated. "Good or bad things? Magical things? What?"

Yoji shrugged. "It doesn't say. Just that sometimes it may not work out exactly the way you hoped it would."

"If that means my head is going to explode—" Braim began, but Yoji cut him off.

"Here it is," said Yoji. He pointed one finger at a particularly long paragraph that made Braim's brain hurt just looking at it. "The Magical Restoration Ritual." He leaned in closer to read it better. "Yes, this is it. Do you have your wand?"

Braim reached for his wand holster on his belt. His wand was there, but he only carried it out of habit rather than out of the belief that it could actually help him. Still, he drew his wand out of the holster and held it up for Yoji to see.

"Good," said Yoji. "That's the first step. Now let's create a circle over here in the center of the room."

Yoji walked over to the center of the apartment and quickly used his magic to move all of the books and furniture off to the room's perimeter. Then he bent over and traced his wand along the floor, a black, inky substance trailing wherever his wand touched. Braim stood there, watching, until Yoji finished the circle, which was large enough for at least two people of Braim's size to stand inside.

"Okay," said Yoji. He stepped aside and gestured for Braim to enter. "Now step into the circle."

"What do I do after that?" asked Braim.

"You'll see," said Yoji. "Just step into the circle and I will let you know what to do next. Don't disturb the circle, however, because the circle is a crucial part of the ritual and if it's disturbed then you probably won't get your powers back."

As much as Braim trusted Yoji, he still didn't like the warning from the Scribbler about getting 'things' that he might not want. But the alternative was never getting his magical powers back at all, so Braim nodded and walked over to the circle. He was careful to step over the circle's line, making sure not to disturb it, and then he walked into the center of the circle itself. He turned to face Yoji, who had *The Limits of Magic* floating before him, his eyes glued to it.

"All right," said Braim. "What do we do next?"

"According to the book, we must next touch wands," said Yoji.

"Touch wands?"

"Yes," said Yoji. He raised his wand. "The tips of our wands must be touching. I'm not supposed to be in the circle with you, however. Instead, I am supposed to be standing right outside it."

"Okay," said Braim. He raised his own wand and held it out toward Yoji. "Then let's do it."

Yoji walked up to the circle and touched the tip of his wand against Braim's. At this point, the wands started to glow and spark, almost making Braim pull back, but he refrained from doing so because he didn't want to mess up the ritual.

Yoji, on the other hand, was sweating now, though only a little. He looked back at the open book and said, "All right. Now that our wands are touching, I must cast the spell written down here."

Braim raised an eyebrow. "What kind of spell is it?"

"Not sure," said Yoji. "Doesn't seem to belong to any magical field that I know of. But don't worry. I know exactly what I'm doing. You just sit back and relax."

Braim wasn't so sure that he could sit back and relax when he was essentially Yoji's experiment. Nonetheless, he nodded and said, "Then go for it. No time like the present."

Yoji nodded and looked at the book. Squinting his eyes, he said, "Okay. This spell has an incantation, which is pretty unusual, but no worries, because I can chant any incantation easily."

Before Braim could tell him to just get on with it, Yoji began chanting the incantation. But Braim didn't understand it because Yoji was speaking in Godly Divina. It sounded superficially similar to normal Divina, but at the same time, the words seemed impermanent and unreal. Whenever Braim tried to understand them, they passed straight through his head and out his ear. Yet there was a certain authority and even beauty to the words that he couldn't deny, the kind of authority and beauty you would expect from a language called the language of the gods.

As Yoji chanted the incantation in a steady rhythm, Braim felt something go up his wand and his arm. He couldn't see anything out of the ordinary, save for the wands, which glowed and sparked more than ever. Yet Braim couldn't tear his wand away from Yoji's, as their wands seemed to be stuck together by some unknown force.

Again, Braim felt something pumping through his wand and into his arm into his chest. It felt like water, but it obviously was not, though Braim didn't understand what it was until he realized that he was feeling magical energy pump back into him. Right now, it wasn't much, but he remembered how magical energy felt inside his body and the stuff pumping into him felt just like that.

By the gods, Braim thought, a smile appearing on his lips. *I can't believe it. It's actually working. I can actually feel the magical energy flowing into my body. It's amazing. It's wonderful. It's a miracle.*

Braim looked at Yoji. The young mage was continuing to chant the incantation, his voice steady, despite the sweat rolling down his temples and the heat radiating from the touching wands. Braim wasn't sure what the problem was, but hoped it wouldn't hurt him. He almost called off the ritual, but he couldn't open his mouth for some reason.

Then Braim felt something touch the small of his back. He looked over his shoulder and saw a tendril rising from the circle,

51

which had also reached toward him. It had touched the small of his back and was now slowly wrapping around his waist like a snake.

The tendril did not hurt when it touched him, but it alarmed him anyway. He looked up at Yoji, who seemed to notice the tendril as well, because he was also looking at it now. Based on the shock on Yoji's face, the young mage had clearly not expected this to happen. Yet he still chanted the incantation, as if he was unable to stop at all.

Braim tried to jerk his wand apart from Yoji's, but he found that his wand, his hand, and his whole arm were frozen. No matter how much effort he put into pulling away, nothing worked. It was like the ritual was intent on keeping Braim and Yoji standing exactly where they were, but Braim didn't understand why, nor did he want to. He just wanted to escape.

The tendril crawled up Braim's waist to his chest now. Again, it wasn't painful, but it was uncomfortable. It made Braim feel like he was being violated, a feeling he didn't like at all. It reminded him partially of the Void, even though the Void had been far worse than this.

Then it constricted around his body and Braim couldn't breathe. He wanted to gasp for air, but he couldn't even do that. He felt more and more magical energy pouring into his body now, magical energy that he couldn't reject no matter how much he wanted to. Sweat rolled down his face, but it was nothing compared to Yoji's, who was sweating as profusely as if he was standing in the middle of a blazing furnace. And still he chanted, but the fear in Yoji's eyes told Braim that the mage wanted nothing more to do with this terrifying ritual anymore than he did.

It felt like the life was being squeezed out of Braim. His vision shifted in and out of focus. His body started to feel like it was on fire. No matter how much Braim told his arm to pull away from Yoji's, it didn't listen. His eyelids felt heavy and hot. He was certain that he was dying and would be dead soon enough.

But then there was an explosion between the two mages, right in the spot where their wands had touched. The explosion sent both of them flying in opposite directions. Braim spun head over heels in midair until he slammed into a pile of books that fell on him, losing consciousness as soon as he hit the floor.

Chapter Five

RAYA STOOD IN the lobby of the Stadium of the Gods along with the remaining godlings in the Tournament. The other godlings were talking among themselves, speculating about what these last challenges would contain, and just who would win each bracket. Samvan was bragging that he was a shoo-in for the position of Human God, while Tashir was arguing with another Spider Goddess Bracket challenger about whether or not it was useful for a God of Spiders to know how to wield a sword.

But Raya didn't join in the discussions, not because she was uninterested, but because she was keeping an eye out for Alira. The Judge was still nowhere to be seen, even though Raya was pretty sure that all of the godlings were here (except for Braim and Yoji, though she believed they'd be here fast enough). She had been tempted to simply stay in her apartment and refuse to participate in the Tournament outright, but Raya didn't like the idea of forfeiting, not when she was so close to achieving the godhood that she desired.

Still, Raya hoped that maybe Alira would get kidnapped again and Grinf would have to take over as Judge for a little while.

There was no way that Raya could look Alira in the eyes again after their little encounter earlier. She could even still taste Alira's lips on her own, even though she had drunk several cups of water and ate a large meal after fleeing her.

Raya had no idea how to handle Alira's feelings toward her. She wasn't interested in women at all herself and never had been. She preferred men, especially manly men like Carmaz who played hard to get. She only thought of women as either friends or rivals, depending on how she was feeling that day and whether or not they were competing with her for the same man.

There was no way at all that Raya could ever accept Alira's feelings. She would never return them. Never, ever, ever. That wasn't how Raya rolled. She actually found the idea of a relationship with another woman to be rather disgusting and she could never understand any woman who thought that way about other women. It made no sense to her whatsoever, but she didn't want to go and reject Alira outright like that. She could, but she remembered how much pain and angst Alira was going through at the moment and it made her hesitate.

I wish she hadn't done that, Raya thought with a scowl. *Does she even comprehend what she's done? Doesn't she know there's no way the two of us can ever be together? She's not an idiot. She has to know that.*

But Raya wasn't so sure about that. After all, Alira, despite having the appearance of an older woman, was actually not very old. Raya didn't know Alira's exact age, of course, but she figured that it wasn't very high. So even if Raya hypothetically *did* like women, their age differences—even if they weren't obvious at first glance—would preclude any relationship with each other or at least make it very uncomfortable and strange.

Raya was snapped out of her thoughts, however, when a familiar motherly voice said, "Raya?"

Raya looked to her left and saw Malya approaching. The short, middle-aged woman looked as kindly as ever, but she also had worry on her face, like she was aware of Raya's own inner conflict.

"Hi, Malya," said Raya, waving at the swordswoman as she approached her. "You look ready for the day."

Malya brushed back her hair, looking a little bit embarrassed. "Oh, I just decided to make myself a little nicer for the day. After all, this is the final leg of the Tournament. Alira has said she wants to make this the final day of the Tournament, so why not look nice for the memories?"

Raya nodded. She looked down at her own clothes, but they were the same as ever. She had not thought to dress up any differently than she normally did, but now that Malya mentioned it, Raya certainly wished she had and privately wondered if it was too late for her to go back to her apartment and throw on something nice before the Tournament officially started.

"By the way, where is Alira?" said Malya, looking around, a frown on her face. "I haven't seen her at all today. Have you?"

Raya tasted Alira's lips on her own again, but she shook her head and said, "No, of course not. I don't know where she could be."

"This is so unlike her," Malya said, standing on her tiptoes to try to see over the heads of the other godlings, though her short stature meant that even on her tiptoes she probably could not see much. "Alira is always so prompt about appearing. She hasn't been kidnapped again, has she?"

"I doubt it," said Raya. "Maybe she slept in or something."

Malya looked at Raya skeptically. "I have never known Alira to sleep in ever. Granted, that poor woman has certainly faced her share of hardship recently, but I didn't think that that would make her not show up like this."

Raya scratched the back of her neck. "Well, I'm sure she'll show up soon enough. Have you seen Braim or Yoji anywhere?"

Malya shook her head. "I haven't seen either of them today. I thought they were already here at the Stadium. Are you sure they aren't here?"

"Yes," said Raya, nodding. "At least no one else has seen them. Tashir told me that they had gone off together because Yoji had said he knew of a way to give Braim his magic back, but they haven't been heard from since."

"How strange," said Malya. "Yoji always struck me as being excited about the possibility of winning the Tournament. Why would he ever be late?"

"No idea," said Raya with a shrug. "Nor do I really care. After all, if Yoji is out of the Tournament, then that means less competition for me."

"Oh, right," said Malya. "I almost forgot that you are in the Hollech Bracket. Have you been preparing for the challenge?"

Raya folded her hands behind her back. "Well ... it's hard to prepare for a challenge that you don't know anything about, you know. I thought I'd just take it as it comes."

"That's reasonable," said Malya. "Still, the only reason you won the last challenge was because the Void attacked and killed half of your competition."

Raya glared at Malya. "Are you implying that I *don't* deserve to be here?"

Malya held up her hands in a pacifying way. "No, no, no, Raya, I'm sorry if you thought that. I just wanted to make sure you remembered that so you wouldn't get too complacent about whatever this next challenge is."

"Thanks for the warning, Malya, but I think I will do *quite* fine in the Tournament," said Raya, folding her arms across her chest. "I'm not a scared little girl, you know. I am a woman with a lot more experience under my belt than when I first participated in the Tournament weeks ago. So if you will excuse me, I—"

Raya was interrupted by the sounds of the doors to the Stadium lobby swinging open behind her. Raya turned around to see a couple of Soldiers of the Gods march in, but they were not alone. They dragged behind them Braim and Yoji, whose uniforms were slightly burnt and whose bodies smelled like smoke for some reason.

The rest of the godlings also turned to watch the two Soldiers enter the lobby. There were a few whispers and murmurs among the godlings, but no one said a word until the two Soldiers stopped just beyond the doors.

Then the two Soldiers unceremoniously tossed Braim and Yoji onto the floor, turned, and marched out without another word. Raya wanted to ask them what happened, but the two Soldiers were gone before she could utter even one word, slamming the doors behind them as they did so.

"Braim? Yoji?" said Malya. She walked over to the two godlings and looked at them both with concern. "Are you two all right?"

Raya walked up to them as well and looked down at Braim and Yoji. The two were still alive, thankfully, but they looked like they had been caught in the middle of an explosion. Braim's red hair was somewhat darkened around the edges, while tiny bits of wood could be seen in the folds of his uniform. Yoji's bald head was also slightly blackened, though it didn't look like anything worse than a flesh wound to Raya.

"Hey, you two," said Raya. She nudged Braim's head and then Yoji's head as well. "Get up already. The next challenge is about to start, for the gods' sake. Or are you just going to lie there and look like idiots?"

Raya's words seemed to have gotten through, because both Braim and Yoji blinked and shook their heads. Then, as one, they sat up. Braim started dusting soot out of his hair, while Yoji rubbed his head like he was suffering from a terrible headache.

"Ohhhh," said Yoji. He sounded less like his usual know-it-all self and more like a whiny teenager now. "That hurt."

"That hurt?" said Braim, looking at Yoji in annoyance. "Kid, have your soul nearly ripped from your body and then we can talk about things that 'hurt.'"

"What in the world happened to you two?" said Malya. Her hands were on the sides of her face, her mouth hanging open in worry. "You look like you were caught in the middle of an explosion."

Braim immediately stopped dusting smoke out of his hair and looked down at his hands in surprise. "Wait a minute ..."

Without another word of explanation, Braim jammed his hand into his pocket, grabbed his wand, and drew it out of his pocket. He then pointed it directly in front of himself, a hopeful

59

expression on his face.

But nothing came out of Braim's wand. He shook it up and down, as if he believed that that would help, but nothing happened. He then scowled at his wand, like it had insulted him.

"It didn't work," said Braim, looking at Yoji in annoyance. "I *still* can't use any magic."

"Why are you looking at *me* like that?" said Yoji, who was still rubbing his head. "I never said that it had a one hundred percent chance of working. You should be grateful that the explosion didn't kill us both."

"What are you two even talking about?" said Raya, causing the two godlings to look up at her, as if they had forgotten that Malya and she were standing there listening to their every word. "You sound like a bunch of street babblers."

"We were *trying* to get my magic back," said Braim. He pointed at Yoji with his useless wand. "But the ritual Yoji showed me didn't work."

"It's still not my fault," said Yoji. He grabbed his own wand and waved it across his head, causing the blackened spots on his head to go away. "It was an ancient ritual from an ancient book by an anonymous author. Maybe it was just one great big practical joke. Maybe that's why it failed."

"Then maybe you shouldn't have even suggested it in the first place," said Braim. "Or at least proceeded with a little bit more caution than you did."

"You were pressuring me to do it right away," Yoji said, pointing an accusing finger at Braim. "Remember? If you hadn't pressured me, then maybe I could have taken my time figuring out how to do it right rather than rushing to do it."

"I didn't pressure you," said Braim. "You were the one who was trying to do it fast. I had nothing to do with your own sloppiness."

"At least we're not dead," said Yoji. "Did you know that that was one of the possible fates we could have suffered, Braim?"

"It was?" said Braim, looking at Yoji in shock. "Why didn't you tell me that before?"

"Because I didn't want to scare you off before I got a chance to test out the ritual," said Yoji. "Obviously."

Braim's face now looked dangerously pale. His breathing became more ragged, like he had just missed death by an inch. Raya didn't understand it, but then, she never understood Braim very well anyway. Nor was she interested in understanding him, mostly because she still didn't see him as being very special, despite his having returned from the dead.

"You … you should have *told* me that before," said Braim. He gulped. "Okay?"

"Fine, maybe I should have," said Yoji, "but I'm not sure why. Sure, maybe it's nice to know if you are going to risk your own life, but—"

"It's not just *nice*, but *necessary*," said Braim. He shook his head and stood up. "Never mind. I'm getting sick of arguing with you now."

"As am I," said Yoji as he, too, rose to his feet, dusting off his uniform. "Besides, the next Tournament challenge is about to start and I am going to be in it, so I should take advantage of this time to prepare for the challenge."

"Oh, right," said Braim, rubbing his chin. He looked at Raya. "I almost forgot. Raya, you're supposed to be in this challenge, too, right?"

"Of course," said Raya. She tossed her hair back. "And I am going to win it, just as I am destined to."

Yoji looked at her in skepticism. "You really think you're going to win?"

"Why wouldn't I?" said Raya. She glanced to the end of the lobby, but Alira was still nowhere to be seen. "As Princess of Carnag, I am by virtue of my royal birth destined for greater things."

"Being royalty doesn't automatically make you good enough to win a Tournament," Yoji pointed out. "While I don't know what Alira has in store for our challenge, I do know that my extensive knowledge of magic will aid me greatly in winning the challenge."

Raya folded her arms across her chest. She looked Yoji up and down a little bit more critically than before. "You don't look like you'd make a very good god to me. You look more like a scrawny teenage boy, which is of course what you are."

"Raya," said Malya in warning. "Don't be so mean to Yoji. He's your friend, remember?"

"Friend, and also competitor," said Yoji. He waved off Malya's concern. "Don't worry, Malya. While I appreciate your desire to help, I am perfectly capable of taking care of myself. I've faced bullies who have said far worse things about me than anything Raya has."

Raya bit her lower lip. "You mean you aren't offended by my calling you scrawny?"

"It's technically true," said Yoji, gesturing at his skinny form. "No. What offends me more is your obvious sense of entitlement."

"It's not entitlement," Raya insisted. "It's simply a recognition of my destiny. I'm sorry you can't see it. So much for that 'extensive' knowledge of magic."

Yoji raised his hand, like he was about to snap back at her, but then Braim said, "Hey, guys, look! Alira is here."

Raya froze as soon as she heard Alira's name. She looked toward the closed double doors, wondering if she could leave without anyone noticing, but with Yoji, Braim, Malya, and the rest all turning to look in the direction where Alira stood, Raya had no choice but to go along with the crowd.

As Braim said, Alira was indeed there. She stood on the same stone platform as ever, carrying the thick Rulebook in her arms, only this time she seemed to be struggling with carrying the Rulebook, like it had become heavier. Raya tried not to focus on Alira, however, because the sight of the Judge filled her with a lot of strange feelings, so she instead focused on the figure standing by Alira's side.

Raya had never seen this particular figure before. He was tall and bulky, wearing sleek armor that perfectly fit his figure. His skin color was snow white, almost, but he didn't look sick. It was simply his natural skin color, which made Raya think that he was either a god or a katabans. He had no weapons from what Raya could see, but he gave off the impression that he was not someone you would want to mess with.

"Who is that?" Raya whispered to Malya.

Malya shook her head, but Yoji answered, "Fojak, obviously."

"Who?"

Yoji looked at Raya in annoyance. "Fojak, God of

Teleportation. Don't you recognize him? He looks like he does in all of the drawings I've seen of him."

Raya shook her head. "No, I don't think I was ever taught about him."

"Well, he's the god who controls teleportation in Martir," said Yoji, his tone still haughty. "He's not very well-known despite all that, but he does have a small yet devoted cult on Itrija. One of my professors back at my school, in fact, is a member of that cult, but he's good, so I have no qualms with it myself."

Raya stopped listening to Yoji as he rambled on and on about various obscure facts about this Fojak and his followers. She wondered why this god in particular was even here. Was he supposed to help in the Tournament somehow? It looked like he was protecting Alira, maybe acting as her bodyguard. To be frank, that was not an entirely irrational thing, considering how Alira had been kidnapped once before. Still, Raya found it amazing that any god would be Alira's bodyguard, because she thought that the gods in general were too prideful to protect anyone else.

"Godlings!" Alira shouted, her loud and authoritative voice booming across the crowd of godlings, silencing them all instantly. "Welcome, one and all, to the final set of challenges in the Tournament of the Gods. There are now five challenges before you and fifty of you left total."

Raya looked around the crowd suddenly. She hadn't noticed until just now, but this crowd of godlings *was* awfully small in comparison to the crowd of godlings Raya had stood among on the first day of the Tournament, which seemed like a lifetime ago now that she thought about it.

"Since the first day of the Tournament, many forces and

individuals have sought to disrupt the Tournament for their own reasons," Alira continued. "Some of these forces and individuals have even killed some of you godlings, yet none have succeeded in stopping the Tournament yet. And none ever shall, because Martir needs new gods, which is what our enemies do not want us to have."

Raya tried to make herself small and unnoticeable. Right now, Alira didn't seem to notice her, but she still didn't want Alira to even be able to see her. A small part of her still wondered if she could leave without being seen, but she dismissed the thought once more, because it was too late to leave now, no matter how much she may have wanted to.

"Ordinarily, I would spread these final challenges out in much the same way I spread out the sub-bracket challenges," Alira said. "But with the new and dangerous threats that have appeared recently, I am going to try to do them all today, one after another, as quickly as possible. In order for the gods to defend Martir, they need their deceased siblings replaced and a new leader to lead them quickly. And those jobs are supposed to fall on the shoulders of the five godlings here."

Raya looked around at the others. There was not a single godling in the lobby who looked bored. They were all clearly listening closely to Alira's every word, which made sense, because this was perhaps the most important speech she had ever given them. Raya, too, listened while also trying not to be seen, though Alira could probably see her no matter where she hid. Raya wished she had learned how to turn herself invisible.

"We will therefore start today's set of challenges with the Hollech Bracket Challenge," said Alira. She gestured to the left side of the lobby, to the entrance that Raya was very familiar with by now. "All Hollech Bracket challengers must line up in front of that door. Everyone else must go up into the box to view the challengers as they attempt to win the Bracket. And yes, whoever wins this challenge will go on to become the God or Goddess of Deception, Thieves, and Horses."

Raya and Yoji, along with eight other challengers, separated from the rest of the godlings immediately. But Raya took up a spot near the back of the line, not because she liked being last, but because it kept her farther away from Alira than the rest of the godlings. Despite that, Raya noticed Alira glance at her. It was a very brief glance, one that none of the other godlings likely noticed, but it was no trick of Raya's eyes, either.

Meanwhile, the rest of the godlings were walking into the door that led to the staircase that would take them up to the box. Malya, Tashir, and Braim waved good bye to Yoji and her as they entered the staircase and vanished from view, with Tashir making a strange two finger gesture that seemed to be an aquarian good luck symbol of sorts.

It occurred to Raya that she didn't know who any of her friends were going to support. After all, as Alira had just said, there was only supposed to be one winner and he or she would then ascend to godhood. That meant that in order for Raya to win, Yoji would have to lose, or vice versa.

Raya looked down the line toward Yoji. He had made his way to the very front of the line, likely so he could be the first in once Alira let them inside. Raya didn't understand why he did, seeing as that would probably not increase his chances of winning the challenge. Still, Raya felt annoyed at him anyway, though considering she always felt annoyed at Yoji for one reason or another, that wasn't saying much.

Then the door opened and Yoji walked inside, followed by the godling directly behind him. The ten Hollech Bracket contenders all stepped inside in only a few minutes, at which point the door closed behind them by itself and Raya once again found herself standing inside that winding hallway with two doors directly ahead of the group.

But there was something different about this place since Raya had last seen it. The walls, floor, and ceiling looked like they had been completely blown apart by a bomb of some sorts, only to be hastily repaired by someone who wasn't very good at repairing walls, floors, or ceilings. The floor was somewhat uneven and rough beneath her feet; not enough to cause her or any of the others to fall over, but enough to be noticeable.

Didn't Tamra come through here and cause a lot of carnage? Raya thought, looking around. *It must have been her. And then the gods or the katabans or someone fixed it, though they didn't do a very good job of it if you ask me.*

Just then, Alira and Fojak appeared before the godlings. It was much harder for Raya to hide now, as there just wasn't a lot of places to hide with so few godlings. Thankfully, however, Alira didn't seem to focus on Raya so much as she focused on the godlings as a whole.

"Welcome again," said Alira. She gestured to the hallways to the left and to the right that wound out of sight. "Today, one of you will win the Hollech Bracket and ascend to godhood. I do not know which of you will win, but I know that each and every one of you godlings are driven and ready to win. You godlings are the best of the best and I am certain that each of you will do your absolute best even if you don't win."

Fojak said nothing, Raya noticed. He looked rather bored, like he wished he could be anywhere else at the moment. But Raya actually felt safer with him here, because as a god he was much more powerful than all of them put together and so could defend them from any outside threats.

"As for this final challenge, it is both simple yet challenging," said Alira. "You must steal an important object from a god. Whoever succeeds in stealing the object first will be declared the winner of the Hollech Bracket and thus will be ascended to godhood."

Raya gulped. She looked at Yoji, wondering if he felt just as surprised and worried by this challenge as she did, because she didn't think stealing from a god would be that easy. To her dismay, however, Yoji looked like he had been expecting it, although Raya liked to think he was hiding his own shock and fear.

"One god has agreed to let you all attempt to steal an important object from him," Alira continued. She gestured at Fojak, who didn't even react to her pointing at him. "That would be Fojak, the God of Teleportation, for those of you who don't know who he is. Fojak has agreed to allow you godlings to steal his Teleportation Staff, which he has donated to the Tournament for this express purpose."

Fojak merely nodded in affirmation, which made Raya wonder if he could even talk at all or if he was actually mute. In any case, Raya had no idea what the Teleportation Staff even was, although Yoji, as always, looked like he knew exactly what Alira was talking about.

"Fojak has spent the last week designing a course that each of you must complete in order to get the Staff," Alira said. "The course will include many obstacles that will do their best to protect the Staff from potential thieves, including armed guards, among other things. You must find a way around each obstacle in order to advance and reach the end, where the Staff is located. But do not worry. While some of the obstacles hurt, none of them are lethal, though I suggest that you do not let your guard down around them anyway."

Fojak was actually smiling now, like the thought of the godlings getting caught in his traps was amusing. That certainly didn't make Raya feel confident about the challenge, to put it lightly.

But then Yoji raised a hand. "Judge Alira?"

"Yes?" said Alira.

"What happens if two or more godlings reach the Staff at the same time?" said Yoji. "Will there be a tie-breaker?"

Alira flipped open the Rulebook and flipped through its pages until she found what she was looking for. Then she looked at Yoji and nodded. "Yes, but I consider that very unlikely to happen due to the structure of the obstacle course. Still, the Rulebook does cover what will happen in that unlikely situation, so do not worry about it, because I have it all figured out."

Yoji lowered his hand, looking satisfied with that answer, but Raya wanted to know a little bit more. Of course, Raya didn't ask, because that would mean drawing attention to herself and the last thing she wanted at the moment was to get Alira's attention.

"Now, does anyone else have any questions about the

challenge?" said Alira, looking among the godlings carefully.

None of the godlings uttered so much as a word or moved in any way as to suggest they had any questions to ask.

"All right, then," said Alira. "As always, all of the regular rules of the Tournament apply and anyone caught breaking them will be instantly disqualified from the challenge and kicked out of the Tournament. With that out of the way, everyone should pick a door to stand in front of and then enter as soon as I give the word."

With that, Alira and Fojak vanished. As soon as the two of them disappeared, the godlings separated, going down the hallways to find doors they could use to enter the course. Raya, of course, immediately went for the doors at the front of the group. She stood in front of the left door, while Yoji stood in front of the right.

"Are you ready, Raya?" said Yoji, looking at her. He drew his wand out of his robe pockets, like he was ready to start casting spells right away.

Raya, not wanting to show Yoji even the slightest sign of weakness, nodded confidently. "Of course I am. Are you ready to lose?"

Yoji rolled his eyes, but said nothing in response, because at that moment Alira's voice echoed through the hallways, though it sounded like it was right in Raya's ears:

"Hollech Bracket Challengers, you may now enter the obstacle course. May destiny's chosen win!"

With that, the doors in front of Raya and Yoji opened. Raya glanced at Yoji one last time before she marched through the open doorway, certain that she was going to be able to handle whatever lay beyond it.

At least, she thought that until she found herself facing a very large, very mean-looking wolf with teeth as sharp as knives. And its breath smelled like blood.

Chapter Six

CARMAZ, FRISSA, AND the Loner God walked through the thick undergrowth of the Swamp, heading back to the Sanctuary, which was essentially the base of operations for the tiny resistance against the golem army on Ruwa. Frissa walked on Carmaz's left, while the Loner God was on his right. This was entirely intentional, because Carmaz didn't trust the Loner God at all and he wanted to keep as much distance between the deity and Frissa as he could, even though Frissa didn't seem to quite grasp how dangerous the Loner God was. She was just amazed at how he had managed to destroy the golems so effortlessly that she kept trying to look at him as they walked, though the Loner God himself seemed to barely acknowledge Frissa's existence.

Nonetheless, Carmaz listened to the Loner God as he explained what had been happening on World's End since Carmaz was kicked out of the Tournament. Carmaz was especially disturbed by the mention of the woman known as Tamra, who, if the Loner God was telling the truth, was possibly an even larger threat to the world than the Void was.

But Carmaz was glad to hear that Raya and Alira managed to

make it back to World's End alive, at least. He had worried that they might not have, but when the Loner God mentioned that that was how the gods became aware of the golems, Carmaz sighed in relief, which the Loner God—caught up in telling his own story—didn't seem to notice.

"And then I told the others what they could do to themselves and I ran away," the Loner God finished. "Last I saw, the other gods were still discussing what to do about all of this mess. I haven't been in any other divine meetings since then, so not sure if they have actually come up with a plan of action or not."

The Loner God sounded incredibly dismissive of his siblings, which was something Carmaz found he liked, if only because he, too, didn't have much respect for the gods in general.

"Doesn't really matter either way to me," said the Loner God, shaking his head. "I don't need their approval to put an end to this madness."

"Then why haven't you already?" said Carmaz. He glanced over his shoulder, but did not see any golems following them. "Look at what you did back there. That was—"

"Amazing!" Frissa finished. She looked around Carmaz's legs at the Loner God, awe on her face. "You're the best god ever."

The Loner God looked at Frissa like she had grown two heads. "Mortal girl, do you even know what I am?"

Before Frissa could respond, Carmaz—wanting to keep the interaction between the two to a minimum—said, "You still didn't say what took you so long to get here or why you haven't used your amazing power to simply crush the golems outright."

The Loner God scratched his chin as he kicked aside a log in his path as though it were a twig. "Well, that's part of the problem.

While I am of course far more powerful than any of those pathetic golems, the golems aren't quite as weak as they seem."

"What do you mean by that?" said Carmaz.

"It's hard to describe," said the Loner God, "but one thing I noticed about the golems was that they have this strange, dark aura covering them. It feels like the Void is protecting them and making them stronger than they normally are."

"Stronger?" Carmaz repeated. "What do you mean by that?"

"I don't know," said the Loner God, shaking his head. He then pulled out a bone from nowhere and started to chew on it. "Obviously, this protection doesn't extend to every golem, as I just proved, but it's making even me a little hesitant to attack them head on. I've thought about sinking the island instead, but that would be too difficult and would probably be more trouble than it's worth, to be honest."

Carmaz's face paled. "Did you just say you were planning to *sink* Ruwa?"

"Sure," said the Loner God, nodding as if he talked about sinking whole islands every day. "We gods have done it before. There used to be a lot more islands in the world than there are today, but we gods were a bit immature in our younger years and so island sinking was a fairly regular occurrence, especially during the Godly War. But again, while I'd like to do that, I think the golems would survive that somehow, so I must come up with a different plan of action."

While Carmaz was relieved to hear that, he still found it depressing that the only god who was willing to actually step in and help the Ruwans just happened to be one of the gods who hated mortals and thought that sinking an island full of them was a reasonable way of dealing with an enemy invasion. Granted, it was better than no divine aid at all, but Carmaz still wondered if he was going to regret this.

But Carmaz was curious enough to ask the Loner God, "Why are you even helping us? I thought you southern gods hated mortals."

"We do," said the Loner God, still chewing on his bone like it was a great piece of candy. "*I* do. I think you mortals are dumb, self-centered, short-sighted, and incredibly tasty. For the vast majority of my existence, I've had nothing to do with your kind except whenever some of the dumber members of your species have wandered onto my island near the Dividing Line, at which point they become my next meal."

"So you aren't helping as a matter of compassion, then?" said Carmaz.

"'Course not," said the Loner God. He laughed. "I'm helping because even I know that the Void, Tamra, and the golems are a threat to everyone on Martir, including myself. Trust me, if Ruwa was not where all of the fun was, I'd be back on my island alone, enjoying the peace and solitude and snacking on the bones of the mortals who've ended up on my island accidentally."

Carmaz nodded, although secretly he was considering setting the Loner God on a wild goose chase, grabbing Frissa, and running away as fast as he could. This despite knowing that Frissa and he were technically safe, because the southern gods could not eat him or her on this side of the Dividing Line even if they wanted to.

"Basically, I'm here because I know that these golems are at some point going to come after me, and I decided I'd rather

75

destroy them first than let them get a shot off at me," said the Loner God. "And I decided to do it quickly, too, because one thing I learned during the Godly War was that whoever strikes first usually wins."

"So you're the only god we can expect to help, then?" said Carmaz.

"For now," said the Loner God. "Though if you ask me, I don't expect any of my dumb siblings to come to an agreement anytime soon. We barely functioned as a cohesive unit even when Skimif was alive, and ever since his death relations among us have become even more strained."

"Surely all of that will be fixed when the Tournament is over, though?" said Carmaz. "Because then you will have a new God of Martir to lead you all."

The Loner God laughed, a harsh, loud bark of a laugh that almost made Carmaz and Frissa jump. "Oh, that's rich. I mean, sure, if we had someone to tell us what to do and didn't take any crap from us, we might get some stuff done, but frankly I don't find any of the mortals competing for the position of God of Martir to be very inspiring. Even Braim isn't worth talking about, in my opinion."

"You seem very cynical about this," said Carmaz.

"Of course I am," said the Loner God. "Skimif used to be a mortal before he became the God of Martir, in case you didn't know. Granted, he did put some effort into leading us, but I was never really all that inspired by him. I'm just too independent, I guess."

The Loner God didn't sound disappointed by that at all, despite his words. If anything, he seemed to take great amusement in the idea that none of the godlings were qualified for the job. It made Carmaz wonder whether the Loner God actually cared about helping defend Martir or if he just saw everything as one big game meant to amuse him and nothing more. It was a troubling thought.

Nonetheless, Carmaz had to ask, "So what happened to this Tamra lady you just told me about? Where is she?"

"No idea," said the Loner God, shaking his head as his feet slashed through the muddy ground. "We lost track of her after she escaped World's End. She could be anywhere for all we know. I thought about going after her, but decided I'd rather deal with these golems first and search for her later."

"And she can steal the souls of gods?" said Carmaz in disbelief. "I didn't even know it was possible."

"It isn't normally, but my brother, the Ghostly God, decided to make it possible because he's too stupid to know which areas he needs to leave alone," said the Loner God. "Now we have a mortal running around Martir with four divine souls in her body, though she thankfully doesn't have that power anymore because Grinf destroyed the device she used to do that. Doesn't make her any less dangerous, however."

"Right," said Carmaz, nodding. "Anyway, we should be reaching the Sanctuary soon."

"The Sanctuary?" said the Loner God. "Is that what you are calling your little hidey-hole?"

"It's the only place on Ruwa that is actually safe from those golems," said Carmaz, glaring at the Loner God in annoyance. "If you don't like it, why don't you just go and kill the golems yourself? It's not like you need to come with us."

"Because I want to meet with the one you call the Hermit," said the Loner God. "That's his name, right?"

"Yes," said Carmaz. "Technically, his actual name is Herune, but he has a son with the same name, so we just call him the Hermit to avoid confusion." He then looked at the Loner God with slightly more curiosity. "Why do you want to talk to him? Do you know him?"

"Yep," said the Loner God. He then tossed the rest of his bone into his mouth and swallowed it in one gulp, which didn't seem to bother him at all. He then glared at Carmaz. "But my reasons for wanting to meet him are none of your business. You just need to take me to him."

Carmaz's personal alarms went off. While the Loner God may not have been able to actually eat the Hermit or any other mortal here, that didn't mean that the deity had kind intentions for them. For all he knew, the Loner God might want to hurt the Hermit.

Even so, however, Carmaz knew that there was nothing he could do to get the Loner God to tell him his real motivations for wanting to meet with the Hermit, nor could he try to trick the Loner God by leading him in the wrong direction. He'd just have to hope that the Loner God was not as malicious as he seemed.

Their journey through the Swamp didn't take them very long. After a short while, they arrived at the entrance to the Sanctuary, which was two large, old trees bending toward each other to form an arch of some sort. The Sanctuary was covered by the thick red vines known as soldier's blood, which Carmaz pushed aside to allow Frissa and himself to enter. The Loner God tried to follow, but Carmaz turned and held out a hand, causing the deity to stop.

"What?" said the Loner God. He sounded annoyed. "Do I

need to wipe my feet off on the mud before I'm allowed inside?"

Carmaz shook his head. "No. I just don't want you in here at the moment. I want to give the others a heads up so they will know who you are, especially the Hermit."

"You dare tell me, a god, where I can and cannot go?" said the Loner God. His red eyes glowed dangerously. "Mortal, you have no right telling me where I may go."

Carmaz wanted to argue, but then he felt someone tugging at his pants and looked down to see Frissa looking up at him. Her eyes were big and wide, which made it hard to ignore her.

"Carmy, why can't you let the fat green man come in with us?" said Frissa. "He saved us. Doesn't that make him a friend?"

"See?" said the Loner God, nodding at Frissa. "Even the little mortal girl thinks I should be allowed in. Are you going to break her little heart by saying no?"

Carmaz bit his lip. He was tempted to tell the Loner God to shove it, because he frankly didn't want the Loner God anywhere near Frissa or him, but it was hard to say no to Frissa's face.

So he sighed and said, "All right, Loner God, you can come in, but please don't threaten anyone, all right?"

The Loner God shrugged. "I have always believed in not making promises that you can't keep. So I can't really promise that I won't threaten any mouthy mortal like yourself who doesn't show me the proper respect that I, as a god, deserve."

Carmaz scowled. "I thought you southern gods believed that mortal worship was dumb."

"Hey, just because I don't want a bunch of stupid mortals groveling at my feet like a bunch of slaves doesn't mean I don't deserve to be treated like the superior being that I obviously am," said the Loner God. "After all, I am still a god through and through, and being a god, whether northern or southern, means you are entitled to certain things that mortals are not."

Carmaz just shook his head in disapproval, turned, and entered the Sanctuary, with Frissa by his side and the Loner God following. The Loner God was muttering under his breath in a language that Carmaz didn't understand, but he understood the annoyed tone well enough.

The Sanctuary was not a very large place. There was perhaps only enough room for six or seven people in here, but there was usually just three: Carmaz, Herune, and the Hermit. There wasn't anyone else because Carmaz, Herune, and the Hermit had agreed to keep the Sanctuary's location to themselves so it would not be found out by Aorja Kitano, even though none of them had heard a peep from Aorja since Herune had knocked her into the mud around the golem spire a week ago; that, and they had not been able to locate any survivors to join them.

The light from the Swamp outside shone through the soldier's blood vines, making everything look a dark, bloody red. Herune sat in one corner on the opposite side of the room, boiling what appeared to be swamp soup based on its scent, while the Hermit lay on an old mattress that Herune had taken from the Hermit's old miniature fortress, behind a green sheet that acted as a curtain dividing the Hermit's 'room' from the rest of the Sanctuary. Herune looked up when Carmaz entered, a surprised look appearing on his bushy features when he saw the Loner God.

"Carmaz?" said Herune. He stood up, drawing his wand from his cloak and pointing it at the Loner God over Carmaz's shoulder. "What the heck is that … that *thing* following you?"

"That thing?" the Loner God repeated. "Well, that's certainly the tamest insult anyone has ever lodged at me before. Can't say I'm too offended, to be honest, even though it is highly disrespectful."

"He's the Loner God, the God of the Jungle, Solitude, and Animals," said Carmaz, gesturing at the Loner God over his shoulder. Then he patted Frissa on the head. "And this is Frissa. She's the only survivor from Conewood. Frissa, this is Herune, and that old man lying down over there is the Hermit."

Frissa waved shyly at Herune. Herune smiled at her—much to Carmaz's surprise, as he had not thought that Herune liked kids—but then his expression returned to seriousness when he looked at the Loner God again. "Did you say that this creature is a god?"

"Oh, so I'm a 'creature' now?" said the Loner God, his voice dripping with sarcasm. "I can tell that biting, creative insults ain't your strong suit, bearded mortal."

"Yes, I did," said Carmaz. "He's one of the southern gods. He rescued Frissa and me from a bunch of golems that ambushed us in Conewood."

"Ambush?" said Herune. "That makes it sound like they expected you to come there. Are you sure they weren't just stragglers?"

"Positive," said Carmaz, nodding. "Their attack was too coordinated and planned to be the actions of a couple of stragglers looking to get a quick and easy kill. I think the golems must have known I was going to be coming back to Conewood and so left a handful of their men there to kill me."

"But why?" said Herune. "You aren't that big of a threat to their operations, are you?"

"Of course he isn't," said the Loner God, walking past Carmaz until he stood between him and Herune. He folded his short arms across his chest. "But my guess is that the golems don't want to take any chances, so they left some guys to take you out so they wouldn't have to worry about you."

"But it still doesn't make any sense," said Carmaz. He put one hand on his chest. "I'm not special or powerful. I'm just an ordinary human being. There's no reason why they should target me in particular."

"You were the first human to learn about them and their plans, though, weren't you?" said Herune. "They must think that you know something about them that we could use against them. Perhaps they think that you know their weakness."

Carmaz shook his head. "I don't know any of their weaknesses except that they tend to be slow. Even then, that's not much of a weakness when they have strength and defense to make up for it."

"It is very strange," the Loner God said, stroking his chin. "Either the golems know something we don't or they are very bad at threat assessment. Considering how easily I beat those four back there, I vote for the latter."

Carmaz thought that the Loner God's theory seemed reasonable. But it still bothered him anyway, because Stalac and Lady Dia had seemed like rational and intelligent beings to him, and he saw nothing rational or intelligent about leaving behind even just a tiny handful of golems to kill one human being who didn't pose much of a threat to them on his own.

There's something about me that scares them, Carmaz thought. *Something they recognize but we don't. The question is, what?*

Carmaz's thoughts were interrupted by the sound of the Hermit yawning behind the curtain in front of his bed. Then the Hermit pushed aside the curtain, revealing the old man's long, white beard that flowed down to his knees. He looked tired, like he had not gotten much sleep, even though the elderly mage had been sleeping for a few hours now at least.

"Carmaz?" said the Hermit with another yawn. "I thought I heard your voice. How did the mission go?"

"Not very well," Carmaz admitted. He patted Frissa on the head. "I only managed to save this young girl, whose name is Frissa. There were no other survivors in my hometown that Frissa or I knew of, and we didn't have time to search for more because we were so busy trying to survive."

The Hermit nodded, but then his eyes fell on the Loner God and his mouth fell open in horror. He became as still as a statue now. In fact, the Hermit looked so still that Carmaz almost believed that his spirit had left his body right there and then and his body had not yet gotten the message.

The Loner God, on the other hand, looked quite at ease. He waved at the Hermit casually and said, "Hi there, Hermit. Long time, no see."

Herune looked between the Hermit and the Loner God in surprise. "Wait. You *know* this god, Father?"

The Hermit snapped out of his shock. He immediately pulled the curtain back in front of himself, but then the Loner God waved his hand and some of the soldier's blood vines grabbed the curtain and ripped it off its pole and tossed it onto the ground, thus exposing the Hermit to the others again. The Hermit pulled his legs up onto the bed, a look of fear on his face as he held his

83

staff before him like a sword.

"Now, now, now," said the Loner God, shaking his head. He put his hands on his hips. "Is that any way to treat an old friend?"

"Old friend?" said Carmaz. He and Herune exchanged puzzled looks and then looked at the Hermit again. "Since when have you and the Loner God been 'old friends'?"

"Never," said the Hermit. He sounded quite serious. "We have never been friends. We met once, a long time ago, but we never liked each other."

"He's right about that," said the Loner God with a chuckle. "I don't even have any friends anyway. Still, it was worth saying that just to get that expression on his face. You mortals are so easy to mess with that sometimes I don't even have to try."

"But you two *do* know each other," said Carmaz. "How? When?"

"Should I tell them or should you?" said the Loner God, addressing the Hermit. "Doesn't matter either way, but I thought I'd give you an opportunity to tell your side of the story."

The Hermit looked like he was going to keep his mouth shut, but then he relaxed slightly and said, "In my younger years, as you know, I was a member of the Dark Tigers. As an assassin, my leader sent me all over the Northern Isles to complete missions given to us. On one of these missions, I went to the island of Destan, located at the edge of the Northern Isles, to kill a prominent Kikasan politician who had gone there to negotiate a trade deal with the locals."

"And then what happened?" said Carmaz.

"Then I ran into a terrible storm in the area," said the Hermit. He shuddered. "Absolutely awful. Waves taller than mountains, endless rain pouring from the sky like some unknown sea beyond the clouds was running over, and it was so cold, too cold for a native Ruwan like me. My ship sank and everyone on it died, except for me. I survived by clinging to a piece of driftwood and I drifted across the Crystal Sea for days afterward."

"And then he washed up on my island," the Loner God said. "Remember that, Hermit? I do, because you were the first human I'd had on my island in a while."

The Hermit, however, didn't seem nearly as pleased by his memory of that day as the Loner God. "I recall it quite well, Loner God. I also recall how you tried to eat me."

"It's what we southern gods do," said the Loner God. "We were born with a taste for human flesh. Trust me, despite you mortals having the collective intelligence of a bunch of frightened ducks, you taste great."

"We do?" said Frissa. She lifted her finger up to her mouth and immediately bit it, but then just as quickly said, "Ow! I don't taste good and that hurt."

"Frissa, please don't bite yourself like that again," said Carmaz, patting her on the head. "That's not a good habit to get into."

"Okay," said Frissa, who sounded more than willing to oblige with Carmaz's request. She looked at the Loner God with betrayal in her eyes. "But you lied and said humans taste good."

"Dumb girl," said the Loner God, shaking his head. "But whatever. Where were we again?"

"At the point where Father washed up on your island," said Herune. "What happened after that? How did Father even survive, if you wanted to eat him?"

"I outsmarted him," said the Hermit simply. He sounded quite proud of himself. "I told the Loner God that I suffered from a terrible disease that could only infect gods if the god in question ate me. The disease—I forgot what I called it—could kill a god. It was a good lie."

"No, it wasn't," said the Loner God quickly. He scowled. "It was a dumb lie. And you didn't even really fool me. I saw right through your trickery from the start, but I played along with it because I didn't think you looked very appetizing."

Despite the Loner God's protests, Carmaz could tell that the Hermit's version of events was a lot closer to reality than the Loner God would ever admit. Of course, Carmaz kept such observations to himself, because he didn't want to anger the Loner God any more than he already had, especially in this tense situation.

"You keep telling yourself that, Loner God," said the Hermit. "But I suppose that is why you allowed me to gain enough strength that I was able to build my own raft and use my magic to return to the Northern Isles?"

"Again, you didn't look appetizing to me," said the Loner God. "Unlike some of my siblings, I have very high standards for my mortal meals, and you simply failed to meet them. What did I care if you built a raft and left? Didn't hurt me one bit."

"Regardless, the fact is that I don't know why you are here," said the Hermit. "Or why we should trust you."

The Loner God quickly explained to the Hermit what he had told Carmaz and Frissa on their way here. Both the Hermit and Herune listened to the Loner God's story, the Hermit stroking his beard, while Herune's expression became more and more distraught with every word that came from the Loner God's mouth. The Loner God didn't do much more than state the facts, but by the end of his story, Herune was tugging at his beard and passing back and forth across the same part of the Sanctuary's floor, clearly agonizing over the Loner God's news.

"So for now, it looks like the only divine help you're getting is me," said the Loner God, jerking his thumb at his chest. "We can't count on the other gods to show up anytime soon, at least not until they get their shit together and come up with a halfway decent plan anyway, and I think it far more likely that Uron will return before that happens."

"And then there are the Void and this woman named Tamra," said the Hermit. He made a humming noise, but it was not a happy one. "I didn't think it was even possible for a mortal to steal the soul of a god. That is indeed disturbing, especially because no one knows where she is."

"Yep," said the Loner God. "But one problem at a time, I always say. I came here to destroy the golems. Where are they?"

"Their army was last seen heading north," said the Hermit.

"Why?" said the Loner God.

"Because there are more settlements up that way," said the Hermit. "And their current mission appears to be 'destroy all life on Ruwa.'"

"Well duh," said the Loner God, rolling his eyes. "Though now that I think about it, I wonder how they intend to travel to other islands, seeing as Ruwa is pretty far away from anywhere, isn't it?"

"We don't know that, either," said the Hermit with a sigh. "We think they might try to build some ships, but I am doubtful they could find the necessary supplies on Ruwa to build vessels large enough to carry their numbers and weight across the sea for even a brief period."

"I guess their long-term thinking must be retarded by the fact that they are rocks, which aren't exactly known for any sort of thinking at all," said the Loner God. "But never mind. Having them all in one place like this makes it that much easier to destroy them all in one go. How has your luck been in stopping them?"

"Poor," said Carmaz, shaking his head. "Very poor. They move a lot faster than you'd think, so by the time we track them down, we're usually too late to stop them."

"It doesn't help that our magic is not always effective against them," Herune added, stopping his pacing long enough to look at the Loner God. "Their leader, Lady Dia, is actually immune to Martirian magic."

"Or just immune to *mortal* magic," said the Loner God. "She hasn't faced a god like me before, has she? I'll just find her and crush her like a pebble. Then I'll smash the rest of her rock collection and Martir will be safe once again."

Carmaz wanted to say that the Loner God was bragging, but after seeing the kind of power that the Loner God wielded earlier, he was in no mood to question the Loner God. Besides, despite distrusting the Loner God severely, he had to admit that he was happy that they had such a powerful being on their side anyway. It made him believe that they might just be able to beat the golems after all.

"You make it sound very easy," said the Hermit.

"Of course I do," said the Loner God. "I'm a god. Everything is easier for us than it is for you mortals. Really, you mortals probably don't need to actually do anything at this point. You can just sit back and let me handle everything from here on out."

"Let *you* handle everything?" Carmaz repeated. He looked at the Loner God in suspicion. "But this is our home. We have to defend it."

"Not anymore," said the Loner God. "And, just to be clear, I am not saying this out of some misguided sense of compassion for you mortals. I just don't want you to get in the way of me slaughtering the golems by the bushels."

"Excuse me, Loner God, but this is our home, one we have had to live on and defend for as long as I can remember," said Carmaz. He gestured at himself and the others. "My ancestors have lived and died on this island, trying to survive every day, while you gods ignored our cries for help no matter how earnestly we begged. We have every right to defend our home, regardless of what you say."

The Loner God—who was picking his nose—said, "You sound like you expect a southern god like me to actually give a damn about any of that."

"I don't," said Carmaz, shaking his head. "I don't expect any of you gods to give a damn about what we Ruwans have been through; how we've had to fight and struggle for survival all on our own, with no promise or guarantee of the protection of any god. And now, you just waltz on in, proclaim you will save us all, and then tell us to sit back and let you solve all of our problems?"

"Not *all* of them," said the Loner God. He finished picking his nose and flung what he found away. "I really only want to destroy the golems. I don't care much for whatever else you mortals are dealing with here. Nor do I expect praise or thanks from any of you fools."

Then the Loner God looked Carmaz straight in the eyes. The Loner God's blood red eyes were so powerful and commanding that Carmaz found it hard to meet his stare. Still, Carmaz looked at him defiantly, not backing down despite the fact that the Loner God was infinitely more powerful than him in just about every way possible.

"But I *do* expect you to stand aside and let me do what I need to do," said the Loner God. "Otherwise … well, let's just say that it will be a lot more painful for you than it is for me, and leave it at that."

"At least let us help," said Carmaz. He didn't show any fear in the face of the Loner God at all, didn't even tremble or trip over his words. "Me, Herune, and the Hermit … maybe even Frissa here … could all help."

"I think you must have forgotten that my name is the *Loner* God," the Loner God said. "Which, you know, means I typically work alone. And I'm a southern god on top of that and most of us southern gods don't use human servants, so there's nothing you can offer me that I'd want or need."

"We will save Ruwa with or without your permission," said Carmaz. He looked at Herune and the Hermit. "Right, guys?"

Herune nodded, while the Hermit was still stroking his beard and appeared lost in thought. But Carmaz figured that the Hermit probably agreed, seeing as he knew that the Hermit wasn't much of a fan of the gods either.

The Loner God chuckled. "Right. Because you were doing *so well* before I came along. But whatever. Do what you want. I could not care less."

Then he nodded at the Hermit. "Hey, Hermit. I have something I need to discuss with you. In private."

The Hermit looked up suddenly, like he had not been paying attention. "In private?"

"Yes, Hermit, in private," said the Loner God. He gestured at Carmaz, Herune, and Frissa. "Away from the ears of these three. It's about something important that I don't want any of these dimwits knowing."

"What do you—" The Hermit stopped. A look of realization dawned on his face. "Oh. Now I know."

"Good," said the Loner God. "Now, let's step outside this pathetic little hideout that you guys call your 'Sanctuary.' After that, I'm going to go golem hunting, my favorite sport."

The Loner God turned and walked out of the Sanctuary. The Hermit, though, was a little slower than the Loner God, getting off of his bed and shuffling across the muddy ground to the exit. He was clearly very reluctant about speaking with the Loner God, but Carmaz didn't know why and he didn't ask, because the Hermit gave off the impression that he was not going to answer any questions they asked him no matter how reasonable they were.

Then both the Loner God and the Hermit were outside. Carmaz stepped toward the exit, but Herune said, "Don't. Father has probably muted their conversation with magic, so we won't be able to eavesdrop on them if that's what you were thinking about doing."

Carmaz's shoulders slumped. "Then how do we know if we can trust the Loner God not to harm your father?"

"He won't," said Frissa. She smiled. "He's rough, but he's a good guy. He saved us from the rocks."

"She's not exactly wrong," Herune said. "Anyway, I think Father can take care of himself, regardless of the Loner God's intentions. He's a powerful and wise mage capable of performing feats of magic even I can only dream of. I'm not going to worry about him."

"If you say so," said Carmaz. His stomach suddenly growled and he looked back over his shoulder at the large pot full of swamp soup that Herune had been working at. "I'm starving. Is the soup ready yet?"

"Should be just a couple more minutes," said Herune. He turned back to face the bubbling swamp soup. "Should be enough for all of us once it's done, though I don't know if gods even eat swamp—"

The *crack* of a tree being knocked down shot through the air like a bullet. Carmaz immediately bent over Frissa, ready to protect her in case of attack, but none of the trees in the Sanctuary fell over. Still, the *crack* sounded like it had come from just outside the Sanctuary, and it was followed by loud cursing in a language that Carmaz didn't understand. Then there was the sound of something sharp flying through the air and Carmaz thought he saw movement just outside the Sanctuary's entrance.

Frissa whimpered and clung to Carmaz's leg even tighter than before. "Carmy, what was that?"

"I don't know," said Carmaz. He looked at Herune. "Any ideas?"

"No," said Herune. "But it sounded like the Loner God and Father are in danger."

"I'll go check on them," said Carmaz. He pried Frissa's hands off his legs and said, "Herune, you keep an eye on Frissa. If I don't return, take her and run. Get her as far from here as you can."

"What?" said Herune. "But I don't know how to take care of kids."

"You don't need to. You just need to keep her safe," said Carmaz. He then looked down at Frissa. "Frissa, Herune is going to take care of you while I go check on what's going on outside. I won't be gone long, but it is still dangerous and I might get hurt."

"No, Carmy, don't go," said Frissa, hugging Carmaz's legs again. "I don't want you to get hurt. Or die."

"I won't," said Carmaz. "I promise. Now just let go and go stand with Herune. I'll be back in a flash."

Frissa, surprisingly enough, let go on her own this time. She then walked over to Herune, but it was very reluctantly and she kept looking back at Carmaz with every step she took.

Carmaz understood her reluctance, because he didn't want to let her out of his sight again. Nonetheless, he knew she'd be much safer in here with Herune than out there with whatever was attacking the Loner God and the Hermit.

With a final look at Frissa, Carmaz turned and ran out of the Sanctuary, ready to take on whatever had attacked, no matter how powerful it was.

Chapter Seven

BRAIM SAT IN the box with the rest of the godlings who were watching the final Hollech Bracket Challenge unfold on the vision bubbles before them. The box seemed a lot smaller than it had in the past, but that was probably because it had fewer seats than it did before, most likely due to the fact that half of the godlings who had started in the Tournament were gone and therefore there was no more need for extra seating.

In any event, Braim didn't care about that. Nor did he focus too much on the challenge playing out on the vision bubbles, even though Tashir, Malya, and every other godling in the room was watching the Hollech Bracket challengers attempt to steal an object of importance to a god.

It wasn't that the challenge was uninteresting, per se. Nor did Braim not care about Raya or Yoji, because he did, although he wasn't sure who he wanted to win, seeing as he had a hard time imagining either of them as immortal deities who had complete control over a particular domain.

No, Braim was focusing on something that he had noticed about himself after the failed ritual to restore his magical powers, something … different.

Braim tried to remember exactly what had happened after he and Yoji were knocked out by the explosion generated by their wands. He recalled being thrown backwards and crashing into a pile of thick, heavy books, but his next memory was more recent, when those two Soldiers dragged him and Yoji halfway across the city to the Stadium. There was that large gap in his memory, likely due to the fact that he had been unconscious, but that explanation didn't satisfy Braim for some reason.

He looked at his hands. They looked pretty normal: large, slightly dirty, and rough. But Braim was certain that there was something different about his hands now. He couldn't quite place it. It didn't really feel like he had regained his magical powers again, but it also didn't feel like anything else he had experienced before, either.

Then Braim saw the veins in his hands—which he had never seen before—glow. He almost started, but then his veins returned to their original colors so quickly that he almost thought his eyes had been playing tricks on him. But then he felt something flow through his hands that told him that he wasn't imagining anything, that it was all real.

But what is *it?* Braim thought, turning his hands over, hoping to see his veins glow again, although they looked perfectly normal now. *It's not magic … right? I mean, I couldn't cast any spells earlier with my wand. Still doesn't explain what it is, though.*

Braim looked around at the other godlings. No one seemed to notice the veins in his hands glow. They were all too busy watching as Raya, Yoji, and the other Hollech Bracket challengers made their way through the obstacle course to the Staff of Teleportation. Braim was quite thankful for that, because he didn't want them to start asking him questions he didn't know the answers to.

Then Braim's hands started to ache and even burn. He gritted his teeth to hold back a cry of pain. It was like there was a fire in his veins, burning through his whole body. He had to take a deep breath, which helped somewhat, but even then, he could tell that he would have to do far more than that if he was going to get better.

I should leave, Braim thought. *Just step out for a minute and get myself together.*

Braim looked down to the front of the box, where Alira and Fojak stood watching the vision bubbles. Alira held the Rulebook tightly against her chest, her eyes fixated on the images of the Hollech Bracket participants doing their best to beat the challenge, while Fojak seemed wholly uninterested in it. He was yawning and occasionally looking around, like he was bored by all of this.

Just get up and go, Braim thought.

He stood up and made his way out of the seats to the stairs that led to the exit. Braim had to pass by Malya and Tashir, causing Tashir to say, "Braim, where are you going?"

"Bathroom," said Braim without looking at Tashir, even though he didn't have to go. "Will be back in a minute."

Braim didn't stay long enough for anyone else to ask him any questions. He made his way down to the exit, causing Alira to look at him, but before she could ask him where he was going, he just said, "Bathroom, and will be back soon," before opening the door, stepping into the stairwell, and shutting it behind him. He then walked down the stairwell, feeling his body temperature going up higher and higher the lower down he went, to the point where he was wiping sweat off his forehead before he was even halfway down.

Braim wasn't sure where he wanted to go or what he needed to do now. He just knew that he needed to get into some place quiet and alone. Then he might be able to figure out how to handle the strange power in his body that felt like it was tearing him apart from the inside out.

Soon, Braim reached the bottom of the stairs, where he pushed open the door and staggered out into the lobby. He leaned against the nearest marble column, panting hard as he did so. He looked at the veins on his hands and saw them flash again.

What in the world does this mean? Braim thought, although his own thoughts were hardly rational even to him. *Can't ... must ...*

Shaking his head, Braim tried to calm himself down as best as he could. He needed to be calmer in order to think, but he was starting to doubt even that a calm mind would be enough to help him think through the sheer pain he was experiencing. A part of him wondered briefly if Yoji was also suffering from this or not, but from what he could remember of what he saw on the vision bubbles, Yoji hadn't been experiencing any sort of pain whatsoever.

In any case, Yoji was in the middle of that challenge and thus unable to help Braim. That meant that Braim would need to figure out how to deal with the burning in his hands and body that was almost overwhelming him on his own. He put his hands on his

97

head, trying as hard as he could to focus on his desire to become the God of Martir and not the pain that was distracting him.

Unfortunately, Braim had little experience with meditation and thus failed to focus on anything except the overwhelming pain that threatened to knock him into unconsciousness. He pushed himself off the column and staggered toward the exit, thinking that maybe all he needed to do was go to his room at the inn, crawl into bed, and sleep. Then, when he woke up, maybe he would feel better.

But Braim only managed a few steps forward before he fell on his hands and knees. It felt like the power within him was eating him alive. He took another deep breath, but that did nothing except perhaps make it harder for him to breathe somehow. He forced himself to remain conscious for as long as he could, but it was a losing battle and he knew it.

Just then, however, Braim heard someone walking toward him. He looked up to see Fojak walking toward him. He hadn't heard the god appear, but he was glad to see him anyway.

"Braim Kotogs?" said Fojak as he approached. "What is the matter with you? You look terrible. Alira sent me to check on you and make sure you were okay."

Fojak's voice was a lot quieter than Braim expected it to be. Nonetheless, Braim was happy to have someone asking for his health. He tried to speak, but the words just did not come out of his mouth for some reason. It was like the energy burning within his body had melted away his words and maybe even his vocal chords.

So Braim raised one hand to let Fojak know that he desperately needed help, but just as he did that, the veins on his hand glowed again.

Fojak's eyes widened. "Did your veins just … glow?"

Braim nodded, but he still couldn't speak. He reached out toward Fojak, but the god stepped back like he was afraid of him.

"I don't like the looks of that," said Fojak. "I have seen that phenomenon in mortals before, but it was so long ago … how can it be happening again?"

Braim had no idea what Fojak was even talking about. All he knew was that he needed help and he needed it right away. He tried to crawl toward Fojak, but even that tiny amount of effort took almost more energy than he had.

Fojak, meanwhile, was rubbing the back of his head and looking around worriedly. "On top of everything else … never mind. Maybe I am mistaken and that isn't what I think it is, but it is better to be safe than sorry."

Fojak raised his hand, energy sparking from the tips of his fingers. Now Braim wasn't sure what Fojak was about to do, but whatever it was, he didn't think it would be very good, although he was incapable of voicing that thought aloud.

"I don't want to have to do this to the potential next God of Martir, but—" said Fojak, before he was interrupted by a loud *boom* from outside.

Both Fojak and Braim looked in the direction of the exit. The large double doors that formed the entrance to the Stadium lobby appeared to have been punched in, if the fist-shaped dents were any indication. Then another *boom* as whatever was on the other side of the doors punched them again, and, without another word, the two doors fell in with a clattering *clang* that made Braim wince.

Then something huge stepped through the doors, bending over in order to fit in. Then, once it was inside, it rose to its full height, towering over both Braim and Fojak in the Stadium's lobby.

Braim had never seen anything like this creature before. It was vaguely humanoid, but it appeared to be made completely out of stone and rock. It had two fists as large and thick as boulders, while its face—if you could even call it that—was nothing more than a slit for eyes and three cuts that resembled vents for a mouth. The creature's body was covered in odd designs, but Braim did not understand any of it, nor did he want to.

"By the Powers," said Fojak, looking up at the stone monster in shock. "It's a golem."

Braim's eyes widened. This was the first time he had seen the golems, though Raya had once described to him one she had seen shortly after she and Alira returned from Ruwa. This one matched the description Raya had given Braim, except it lacked the sword hand or saw hand. But that didn't quite matter, because the golem looked more than capable of crushing Braim beneath its fists without even thinking about it.

The only question now was where the golem had come from, but Braim pushed that out of his mind. He crawled away from the golem as quickly as he could, his fear of the stone monster forcing him to focus on escaping, while Fojak turned to face the golem, his hands now glowing with energy.

"I don't know how you got on World's End without anyone noticing, golem, but I am going to show you what happens when you invade the Throne of the Gods," said Fojak. He slammed his fists together. "I won't even need the help of my brothers and sisters to destroy you."

The golem, to its credit, didn't seem intimidated by Fojak's threat. It simply stepped forward, crunching the doors under its feet, and raised its fist, but Fojak was quick. He vanished and then reappeared on its back, grabbing its shoulders with his hands as the golem turned its head to try to look at him, although the movement of its head was limited.

"Now, golem, let's see what happens when you drop a rock from a very tall height," said Fojak. He grinned. "As in, ten thousand feet above ground."

But before Fojak could teleport the golem away, the back of the golem's head opened and a beam of energy fired out of it. The energy beam struck Fojak straight in the face, sending him flying backwards so fast that he broke through the wall above the entrance and out into the streets of World's End and out of Braim's sight.

Just when he vanished, however, Fojak reappeared inside the Stadium lobby, standing opposite the golem. His face was bruised from the blow, but he looked more annoyed than in pain. Rubbing his face, he said, "Good blow, golem. I admit I didn't see that coming. But never mind, because I—"

Fojak immediately stopped talking when he noticed that the golem was gone. Braim looked around the lobby, but didn't see the golem anywhere. It was like the golem had just up and vanished, which didn't make any sense, because as far as Braim knew the golems didn't have teleportation powers, nor could they turn invisible.

Fojak also looked around, turning this way and that as he tried to find the missing golem. "Damn it. How does something that big just disappear like that, without me even noticing? It was standing right in front of me, for the Powers's sake."

Just then, an ethereal portal exploded open behind Fojak. The god looked over his shoulder just in time to see the golem's fist fly into his face. The blow sent Fojak flying again. He crashed hard into the walls of the lobby, knocking down a few of the rules that had been pinned to the walls, and leaving an impression shaped like himself where he had hit. He fell to the floor and was very still.

Braim waited for Fojak to get back up, but the god didn't even stir. Then Braim looked over at the ethereal portal as the golem stepped out of it. The golem's expression had not changed at all, but with the way it looked at Fojak, Braim thought that it must have been quite proud of its accomplishment.

Crap, Braim thought. *Fojak's down. What the hell am I supposed to do now?*

At that moment, half a dozen Soldiers of the Gods dashed in through the open doorway. They carried swords and spears, looking ready for combat, but they stopped when they saw the golem standing not far from Braim. Braim didn't recognize any of these Soldiers, but he was glad to see them here anyway.

"Halt, invader!" said the lead Soldier, pointing his sword at the golem. "Stay where you are, or we will destroy you!"

The golem, again, showed no fear. It simply raised one of its massive fists, aiming it at the Soldiers like it was about to shoot them, even though the golem lacked a gun or any other projectile weapon with which to hit them.

"Very well, then," said the Soldier. He looked over his shoulder at the others behind him. "Men! Show this invader exactly why we are called the Soldiers of the—"

Without any warning whatsoever, the golem's fist shot off its arm and flew directly toward the assembled Soldiers. The lead Soldier only had enough time to look in the direction of the flying fist before it crashed into them with a *crunch*. It completely pulverized the lead Soldier, the fist's momentum making it crash into the Soldiers behind him, crushing them all underneath its weight as it went. It then came to a rather abrupt stop, allowing Braim to see that the fist was now covered in blood, while the Soldiers that it had crushed lay in its path looking dead or, at best, unconscious.

One of the Soldiers managed to stand up on his feet, however, even though his right arm appeared broken and his own broken chest armor was cutting into his stomach. He leaned against the fist for support, panting hard, blood running down the side of his face as he looked defiantly up at the golem.

"Is that … is that the best you've got, invader?" said the Soldier. He sounded surprisingly defiant despite standing among his dead fellow Soldiers. "Because my little sister has punched me harder than—"

Ka-boom!

The golem's fist that the Soldier had been leaning on exploded. Chunks of rock flew everywhere, almost hitting Braim, but he curled into a fetal position and kept as low to the floor as he could to avoid getting hit by the worst of it, though he was still showered by pebbles. But his fetal position couldn't save his hearing. The explosion was so loud in such a confined space that for a moment Braim couldn't even hear his own thoughts.

When the explosion passed, however, Braim looked up to see what remained of the Soldiers. And what he saw sickened him immensely.

The floor and doors were blackened by the explosion. What remained of the Soldiers were charred corpses and twisted weapons and armor. The stink of smoke and burned meat entered Braim's nostrils, made stronger by a gust of wind blowing in from outside. From what Braim could tell, not a single Soldier had survived the explosion.

He looked up at the golem. The golem still held its arm up, its non-existent face looking at the smoldering remains of the Soldiers. Its arm was now hand-less, but that hardly seemed to phase it. It merely lowered its arm and then looked at Braim. The slit that formed its eyes glowed, but Braim had no idea what that meant and wasn't interested in finding out.

So Braim got to his feet, despite the intense pain in his body, and faced the golem, which moved until it was now facing him directly. Braim glanced at Fojak, but the God of Teleportation was still out for the count.

Where are the other gods? Braim thought, biting his lip as he looked up at the dispassionate golem. *Guess it doesn't matter. I have to handle this on my own for now.*

The golem was so still that Braim thought it had simply stopped living and had returned to being little more than a glorified rock. Then it raised its hand-less arm again, allowing Braim to see that its forearm was hollow and empty.

Then a black hand shot out of the arm and grabbed Braim before he could move. The black hand's fingers wrapped around his body tightly, making Braim gasp in pain. They tried to pull him toward the golem, but Braim stood his ground. The black hand felt as cold as ice and felt far too familiar to Braim, but he didn't let it pull him toward the golem. Despite his best efforts, however, Braim did move a couple of inches, as the hand seemed determined to get him no matter what.

"No ... you ... don't ... you monster ..." said Braim as he struggled against the golem's black hand. "Not ... today ..."

Braim grabbed the hand and tried to remove its fingers, but it held onto him as tightly as a clamp. Then Braim heard a familiar feminine chuckle in his ear, one he had not expected to hear again. Braim looked down at the hand as he finally understood where the chuckling was coming from.

Hello, Braim, said the voice that had chuckled. **Did you miss me?**

Braim gasped. "The Void? What are you—"

Braim was cut off when the hand squeezed. He screamed in pain, while the Void said, **It doesn't matter why I am with this golem. What matters, Braim Kotogs, is that I am going to devour you and there is nothing you can do to stop me. And don't even bother praying to your precious gods, because there is no way that any of them can hear you now.**

Chapter Eight

I
T WAS THE largest wolf that Raya had ever seen in her life. It was much bigger than Raya, towering over her like a giant. Its teeth were longer than knives and looked twice as sharp. It had dark gray fur, with streaks of gold along its back and head, giving it a rather dignified look despite its ferocious snarling.

Raya didn't know how to react to it at first. She just stared at the wolf, which took up almost the entirety of the hall in which she stood, not sure if moving would give the wolf an excuse to pin her to the floor and rip out her throat or not. Then she remembered that she had to win the challenge and thus couldn't simply stand there in fear hoping that the wolf would ignore her.

Even so, Raya found that her legs were frozen where she stood. Her heart rate increased and she even started to sweat, but she didn't dare to wipe away the sweat because she was still afraid that making the wrong move would bring the wrath of the wolf down upon her.

Snap out of it, Raya, Raya told herself. *The longer you stand here, staring at this wolf, the more time you give the others to get to the Staff first. And if they get to the Staff first, then* you *lose.*

The thought of losing to anyone in this Tournament—

106

especially to Yoji—was enough to snap Raya out of her paralysis. She didn't walk nearer to the wolf, but she did fold her arms across her chest and glare at it in annoyance.

"And just what are you?" said Raya. "A dumb beast?"

The wolf shook its head. "No."

Raya almost yelped in surprise when she heard the wolf speak. She tried cleaning out her ears, just to make sure that her hearing wasn't clogged or anything, but her ears didn't feel clogged at all. Lowering her hands, Raya looked at the wolf with great unease.

"You can talk?" said Raya.

"Yes," said the wolf, nodding. "I'm a chimera created by Fojak to keep you from stealing his Staff. Call me Valfa."

"Valfa?" said Raya. "All right, then, Valfa, why don't you let me go past you?"

"Because I'm not supposed to," said Valfa, whose Divina was surprisingly good even though the thing wasn't human. "You have to get past me yourself if you want to go any further."

Raya scowled. She was tempted to complain, and indeed almost did, but then realized that complaining would do her no good in this challenge. After all, Valfa didn't seem likely to be sympathetic toward her complaints. He would probably just tell her that it was his job to make sure that she didn't get past him and that he wasn't going to let her past just because she complained.

"So that's how it is, then," said Raya. "You aren't going to make this easy for me."

"Why would I?" said Valfa. "But don't worry. While I have been given permission to attack you if you try to get past me, I don't have permission to kill you. So you won't have to worry about being ripped to shreds."

Raya grimaced. "That's reassuring."

Raya then started thinking about how she could get past Valfa. The chimera took up much of the hall, and even if he hadn't, Raya could tell that he was prepared to block her way no matter which way she went. He might even knock her down if she got too aggressive.

Think, Raya, think, Raya told herself, tapping her foot on the stone floor as she considered her situation. *How can you get around this chimera in a timely manner and without getting hurt too much?*

Raya looked at her artificial, slightly glowing bluish-white hand. Over the last week since she and Alira had returned from Ruwa, Raya had gotten a few moments to test out the full capabilities of the artificial hand. She could now make its fingers extend at will, as well as generate a barrier that protected her from most threats. That gave her a fairly good variety of defenses, but she wondered if any of it would be useful against the chimera.

Easy, Raya thought. *I'll just generate a shield and use it to go past the chimera. He won't be able to harm me at all and therefore won't be able to stop me from reaching the Staff.*

So Raya raised her artificial hand above her head and a spherical barrier glowing the same color as her hand appeared around her body. It covered her completely from head to toe, which caused her to smirk at Valfa, who was merely watching the barrier with interest.

"Well, Valfa, as you can clearly see, this barrier of mine will keep me safe from you," said Raya, gesturing at the barrier with her other hand. "Now I know you are a big, bad wolf, but even you won't be able to break it. I mean, you can try, obviously, but it will be a complete waste of time on your part, so I suggest that you don't."

With that, Raya walked forward, expecting Valfa to step out of the way and let her pass. After all, she had just explained that her barrier was unbreakable by normal means, and Valfa, despite being a chimera, clearly lacked any sort of magical or divine powers.

Valfa, however, did not move. He just stared at her as she approached, apparently completely unimpressed by Raya's barrier. Not that Raya cared, because she knew that it was only a matter of time before he moved out of the way and let her pass.

Then Valfa raised his front right paw and swiped at her. Raya kept walking, expecting the swipe to fail. That was why she was surprised when the paw cut through her barrier and slammed into her side.

The blow sent her staggering to the side and snapped her concentration, causing her barrier to vanish. But Raya didn't pay any attention to that, because she fell on her hands and knees, clutching her side where Valfa had hit her. The pain was awful. Not as bad as when the Void cut off her original hand, perhaps, but bad enough that Raya found it difficult to stand. She whimpered despite her best efforts to show no weakness in front of Valfa.

"How ... how did you do that?" said Raya, her breath ragged, looking up at the chimera, which looked as unimpressed as always. "My barrier is supposed to be impossible to break."

"But I didn't break it," Valfa pointed out. "I just swiped

through it."

"That shouldn't be possible, either," said Raya, shaking her head. "How did you do it?"

"When Fojak was designing this challenge, he had to take into account all of the abilities and powers of each individual challenger so he could make it equally difficult for everyone," Valfa said. "He learned about your hand's ability to generate a shield from Alira and so gave me an ability to ignore its existence."

"That bastard," said Raya through gritted teeth, because the pain in her abdomen where Valfa had hit her was still fresh. "Next time I see him, I am going to give him a stern talking to."

"Or you could come up with a new way to get past me," Valfa suggested. He then sat down. "Not that I expect you to. You don't seem particularly smart."

Raya jumped to her feet as quick as lightning and glared at Valfa. "Not smart? You don't know who you're talking to, Valfa. I am Princess Raya Mana, daughter of King Malock and Queen Hanarova of Carnag. I received a first class education from my parents in my younger years."

"None of that means anything to me," said Valfa, his large tail wagging back and forth in a bored manner. "Unless you think I care about fancy human titles, in which case you are very sorely mistaken."

Raya just huffed. She didn't need to explain herself to a chimera or a wolf or whatever this thing was. She just needed to think of a better way around it. She would outsmart it. After all, she was clearly far more intelligent than that chimera was. All she needed to do was give the matter some more thought and soon she would be on her way to achieving her destiny.

Thankfully, Raya didn't take long to come up with another plan this time. She held up her artificial hand, which Valfa's eyes followed, though it was less with interest and more with amusement, as if he was wondering what kind of prank Raya was going to play with that.

"All right, chimera, I am going to get past you whether you like it or not," said Raya.

"Actually, I'm pretty apathetic about the whole thing, to be honest," said Valfa with a shrug of his large shoulders. "I'm only trying to stop you because that's what I was created to do. I honestly have no idea why, but that's just the way it is."

"Well, getting past you will still be a sweet victory," said Raya. She pointed her hand at Valfa. "Did Fojak tell you everything that my hand can do?"

Valfa nodded. "He only told me about the barrier. Oh, and you can extend your fingers to make sword fingers that can cut through pretty much anything. He told me that that was all it could do."

And he was right, Raya thought, but aloud she said, "Actually, he should have told you that that was all *he* knew it could do. It's not like I've used all of its powers and abilities in public where everyone can see it."

"Oh?" said Valfa. He sounded slightly worried, but not by much. "Then what are the rest of its powers?"

Raya flexed her artificial hand's fingers. "Oh, they're quite extraordinary, I can assure you, but I won't tell you all of them because that would be giving away the surprise. Instead, I will only tell you the one most relevant to your situation."

"And what is that?" said Valfa.

Raya looked Valfa straight in the eyes, showing no fear or doubt as she said, "The ability to make any living being implode upon itself."

To her satisfaction, Valfa actually stood up and stepped back. It was only a step, but it was enough to let Raya know that her plan was working.

"What ... what does that mean?" said Valfa. He licked his lips, though it seemed more like a nervous habit than anything. "You don't literally mean you can make me implode, do you?"

"Of course I do," said Raya. She kept her tone and stance as confident as she could, although it was hard to do because she was still afraid of Valfa. "I did it on a small bird flying outside of my apartment window. It took me hours to scrap off its guts and feathers off the window itself, and I still didn't quite get all of it off even after I did my best."

"You're lying," said Valfa. "Fojak told me that you are in the running to become the Goddess of Deception, which means you're better at lying than most humans are. So I should take everything you say with a grain of salt."

Raya felt rather offended by the fact that Fojak thought she was a good liar, but then, she supposed he had a point and thus didn't argue it. Besides, arguing the point would waste precious time and she certainly could not allow that.

"It is true that my fellow challengers and I are rather good at lying and deception," said Raya, nodding. "But in this instance, I am telling the truth. With a single thought and a flick of my index finger, I could paint the walls, floor, and ceiling of this hall red with your own blood. It admittedly would be absolutely disgusting, but it would be a small price to pay to attain godhood and I am more than willing to do it if you keep standing in my way."

"Where is your proof?" said Valfa, though Raya detected fear in his voice. "I don't see any proof. Just baseless threatening assertions on your part. So forgive me if I am skeptical of your claims."

"Well, I can always show you by making you implode," said Raya, "although that would mean you wouldn't be alive to see that I was telling the truth. But clearly, you require proof, and I, for one, am not the kind of person to deny anyone the proof that they require in order to believe something." She smiled. "Although you are definitely not going to live long enough to see it."

Valfa's eyes were following Raya's hand. He was as still as a statue, which made it hard to tell what he was thinking, but Raya did not let that stop her. She raised her hand like she was about to snap her fingers.

"No, wait!" Valfa said, almost barked, causing Raya to freeze. "Please don't. I … I believe you. I don't need any proof of your claim. I am so sorry for doubting you."

Raya paused, looking at Valfa in surprise. "Really? Just like that, you're letting me through?"

Valfa nodded, sending its long hair waving back and forth. He stepped aside, giving Raya just enough room to walk by him without touching him. "Yes, yes, yes. Please just go. I promise not to touch you or try to stop you."

Raya looked at Valfa suspiciously, never lowering her hand the whole while. "How do I know this isn't just a trap on your part

113

to get me to lower my guard?"

"Because I don't want to risk imploding," said Valfa. "That's why."

Raya could tell that Valfa was telling the truth, because despite his obvious size and strength, he seemed more like a tamed dog than a wild wolf. Still, Raya kept her hand up the entire time as she walked by him, even brushing the tips of her fingers against his fur to scare him. As Valfa flinched when she did that, Raya was confident that he was indeed going to let her pass without issue.

Once Raya was past Valfa, she lowered her hand and turned to face the chimera. "Thank you for letting me pass. You truly are a good dog."

Valfa's ears twitched and there was a brief snarl at his lips, like he thought the term 'good dog' was an insult. But he stayed where he was and seemed unlikely to come after her. He just said, "You may have beaten me, but I am not the only obstacle lying between you and the Staff. There are others, others which are far more difficult to get past than me."

"Is that a threat?" said Raya.

"No," said Valfa. "It's a warning. A warning you can choose to ignore, if you want."

Raya nodded. "Very well, then. Anyway, I have to go. I have no time to waste talking to chimeras like you."

With that, Raya turned and resumed walking down the hall. She considered Valfa's warning, about how the other obstacles were far more dangerous than he, but she dismissed it without much thought. After all, Valfa had been an easy obstacle to trick. It wouldn't take much for other obstacles to be more difficult than him, and even if they were, that did not mean they were going to be *that* much more difficult than him.

Raya shook her head, still smirking. *And once I get past those obstacles, I will finally achieve my destiny.*

Chapter Nine

UPON EXITING THE Sanctuary, Carmaz saw nothing at first except for a large fallen tree that had only narrowly avoided crashing into the Sanctuary itself. The tree looked like it had been cut clean through at the base by a giant wielding a large ax, forcing Carmaz to climb over it in order to see what was on the other side.

There, Carmaz saw the Loner God and the Hermit battling against a trio of large golems. These golems did not look like all of the other golems that Carmaz had seen. For one, their appearances were far more humanoid, with human-like faces and fingers and even toes. They were slimmer as well, which allowed them to move with more fluidity and grace than other golems. They carried swords and shields, which made them resemble infantry, in a way.

The golems were fighting off the Loner God and the Hermit surprisingly well. The Hermit was waving his staff, causing tree limbs and vines to attempt to wrap around the golems' bodies, while the Loner God took the more direct route by punching or kicking any golem he could reach.

But despite the ferocious fighting styles of the Loner God and the Hermit, the golems did not seem likely to go down anytime soon. They cut through or dodged the tree limbs and vines sent after them, sometimes even jumped into the air to avoid certain attacks, and used their shields to block the Loner God's punching and kicking. Even stranger, the Loner God's blows did not destroy them in one hit, as though the golems were made of a substance that even the gods could not break.

That was when Carmaz noticed that the eyes of the golems were pitch-black. They also had black lines running along their bodies that reminded him of the Void. It might have been nothing more than a fancy paint job, but that seemed unlikely to Carmaz, because most of the golems he had seen so far had not had any paint on them at all.

If those black lines are what I think they are, then we're about to have a bad *day,* Carmaz thought with a shudder.

Even though there wasn't much Carmaz could do against the golems, he was about to jump off the fallen tree and rush into battle before an unfamiliar female voice to his right said, "Where do you think *you're* going?"

Before Carmaz could look at the woman who had said that, something large and thick slammed into the back of his head and he lost all consciousness right away.

-

When Carmaz awoke, the back of his head throbbed in pain. He tried to reach for the back of his head, but found his movement limited by thick and heavy stone shackles around his wrists and ankles.

Wait ... stone shackles? Carmaz thought. He blinked several times and raised his head to look down at his wrists and ankles,

117

which were indeed shackled together. *Where did* those *come from?*

Unfortunately, Carmaz could not see his shackles very well because of the low light he had to see by. There was a glowing stone in the ceiling above him, but it was very dim. He looked around to try to figure out where he was, but the area was so dark that he could not see anything beyond the stone bars to his right. He sat up, but it was hard, because the shackles around his wrists were very heavy and made movement awkward. So he gave up and just lay there, trying to remember what happened, which was difficult because the pain in the back of his head was sharp and made it hard to focus on anything else.

Last I remember, I was going to help the Loner God and the Hermit defeat those weird-looking golems, Carmaz thought. *Then someone was behind me and said something and something hit me, and next thing I know, I wake up here. Doesn't explain where 'here' is, though.*

From what little Carmaz could see, he was lying in a stone cell, possibly underground if the stale, dry air was a hint. A stone cell … he tried to remember where he had seen such a thing before, but then remembered that he had found Alira in such a cell not long ago.

Uh oh, Carmaz thought with a gulp. *If that means what I think it means, then—*

Carmaz suddenly heard the sound of stone moving to his right. He looked at the stone bars of his cell as the slab of stone that had been covering them moved away, allowing more light to shine in and causing Carmaz to squint to protect his vision. He tried to sit up again, this time succeeding, but he did not do anything else until the rest of the slab had moved away, allowing Carmaz to see what was outside of his cell. It took his eyes a moment to adjust, however, as they had been used to the dimness of the cell.

But even before the slab slid away, he heard that unfamiliar female voice from before, the one he had heard before he was knocked out, saying, "Here he is, Dia. I got him just as I said I would."

Carmaz blinked several times when the light from outside of his cell hit his eyes. He nonetheless leaned forward slightly in order to see what was on the other side of the bars of the cell.

Standing on the other side were three beings. Two he recognized right off the bat: Stalac, the golem general with a scorpion-like tail extending from his back, and Lady Dia, the leader of the golems, who had wings extending from her back. Standing alongside them was a human woman who Carmaz had never seen before. She had black hair tied in a ponytail and wore a green version of the uniform that all godlings wore, which surprised Carmaz, because that meant that she was also a godling, although again Carmaz was pretty sure that he had never seen her before. Her right arm was apparently missing, because she had a thick bandage around her elbow where her arm used to be, although it didn't seem to bother her very much.

But there was something else about that woman as well. Though she looked like an ordinary human, even Carmaz could sense that there was more to her than met the eye. She radiated power, the kind of power that Carmaz always associated with the gods, but that didn't make any sense because no human, not even the most powerful mage on the earth, was as strong as the gods.

He wondered if it was the blow he had taken to the head that was making him imagine things that were not there, but the power radiating from this woman felt too real to be a hallucination.

Whatever the case, Carmaz knew where he was now: Within the rock spire that the golems had marched out of, which he figured had to be the golems' base of operations now. He didn't see any other golems nearby, but that didn't mean they weren't here.

And if I am in here, then that means I am far away from the others, Carmaz thought. *And I probably will not be living much longer.*

Lady Dia folded her arms across her chest, looking at Carmaz with interest. "I see you were right, Tamra. That is indeed Carmaz Korva. I'm not always good at distinguishing between you mortals—you all look the same to me—but I never forget anyone who defeats me in such an embarrassing way."

Carmaz remembered shoving Lady Dia into the mud, but she looked shiny clean now, like she had taken a bath. Not that that made her look any less threatening than she was, of course.

The human woman—the one Lady Dia called Tamra, a name which seemed familiar to Carmaz, though he could not place it right away—smirked. "He wasn't hard to catch. I sneaked up on him and knocked him out before he even knew what was going on."

The pain in the back of Carmaz's head ached, but it didn't hurt quite as much as it did before. Still, Carmaz grit his teeth in order to avoid groaning, because there was no way he was going to show even the slightest sign of weakness in the face of these three.

Instead, he said, "How did I get here? What happened to the Loner God and the Hermit? How long have I been out?"

Stalac stepped forward, a fierce scowl on his face. Carmaz noticed Stalac's chest, which looked like it had been hastily repaired, though he stopped focusing on it when Stalac shot an ice bolt from the tip of his tail through the bars of Carmaz's cell. Carmaz just barely managed to dodge it, even feeling the cold air trailing it as it flew past his head. The ice bolt struck the wall of his cell behind him, freezing it solid in less than a second.

"Do you really think we'd answer any of your questions, human?" Stalac said. "We're only going to give you the knowledge that we think you need, and nothing more. So why don't you keep your mouth shut? Unless you'd like me to freeze it solid for you, of course."

"Stalac, please don't threaten the prisoner just yet," said Lady Dia, gesturing at Stalac to stand down. "And let him ask all the questions he wants. It's not like that is going to help him escape, after all. He will stay here inside his cell where he belongs until we are done with him."

"Done with me?" Carmaz repeated. "What does that mean? Are you going to torture me for information?"

"You'll find out soon enough," said Lady Dia. "For now, all you need to know is that you are far more important than you think you are."

"Very helpful," said Carmaz sardonically. Then he looked at Tamra. "And who is she?"

"Don't talk about me in the third person," said Tamra. She gestured at her chest. "I'm Tamra. Do you remember me, Carmaz?"

Carmaz shook his head. "No, but your name is familiar, like I've heard it somewhere before. Were you one of the godlings in the Tournament?"

Tamra frowned. "Well, that's not surprising, considering how we have never actually spoken to each other before. In any case, yes, I was in the Tournament, but not anymore."

Then Carmaz suddenly remembered where he had heard about Tamra before and he said, "Hold on. The Loner God told me about a godling who had stolen the souls of four gods. Are you —"

"The one and only," said Tamra, bowing briefly.

"But I don't understand," said Carmaz, looking from Tamra to Lady Dia and back again. "Why are you working together? I thought you golems hated humans."

"We've come to … an agreement," said Lady Dia, though when she glanced at Tamra, there was definitely some disapproval on her features. "In exchange for helping us attack the world, we will support Tamra's journey to become the Goddess of Martir."

"What?" said Carmaz. He looked at Tamra in shock. "But Tamra, these golems, they hate us Martirians. Why would you help them attack Martir?"

"Because I, frankly, don't really care who is living on Martir when I rule it, so long as there are some people on it," said Tamra. "What difference does it make, really, whether these people are golems or humans like yourself?"

"This is still insane," said Carmaz. He crawled forward across the floor of his cell, although he didn't get far due to the shackles around his ankles and wrists. "You don't realize what you're doing."

"Oh, shut up," said Tamra. She then looked at Lady Dia. "Now that you see that he's here, can I leave now? I want to make sure there aren't any other gods on Ruwa that I need to scare off."

"Go, then," said Lady Dia, gesturing behind her. "But do not go far from the base, because I still have future plans I wish to discuss with you."

"All right," said Tamra. She waved at Carmaz. "Bye, Carmaz. If you behave like a good prisoner, maybe I'll spare your life when I become the Goddess of Martir."

With that, Tamra vanished into thin air. As soon as she was gone, Lady Dia looked at Stalac and said, "You should leave as well. Check on the sentries and find out if there are any updates from the soldiers in the field. Then report back to me with what you learn."

"Yes, my lady," said Stalac, though he saluted her only with great reluctance. His eyes darted toward Carmaz suspiciously. "And what about the human?"

"I will deal with him," said Lady Dia. "Trust me, I will be fine."

Stalac looked like he wasn't convinced that Lady Dia was going to be fine on her own, but then he nodded and walked away out of sight. A minute later, Carmaz heard a door open and close, which was likely Stalac leaving to do what Lady Dia had commanded him to do. That left Carmaz alone with Lady Dia, who had her head bent as if in prayer.

Then she looked up at Carmaz with the oddest expression on her face. She was looking at Carmaz hesitantly, as if he was dangerous, even though there was nothing Carmaz could do to harm her right now even if he wanted to (which was to say that he *did* want to harm her, but unfortunately he had no way of doing so at the moment).

Carmaz sat back in his cell, ignoring the weight of his shackles around his wrists and on his lap as he glared at Lady Dia. "What are you going to do to me now? Torture me or just kill me outright?"

Lady Dia looked to the left and to the right. She then stepped forward. Her hands were shaking, which made no sense to Carmaz, as that implied that she was afraid of something happening, even though as far as Carmaz could tell, it was *he* who had reason to be afraid of something bad happening, not her.

This annoyed Carmaz enough for him to say, "What? Are you just going to stand there and stare at me like you've never seen a human before?"

Lady Dia then said the last thing he ever expected her to say:

"My husband … is that you?"

Chapter Ten

THE VOID'S VOICE was full of cold glee. It felt just like the shadow hand wrapped around Braim's body, the one that was currently squeezing the life out of him, despite Braim's best effort to fight it off. He wrestled against the Void's grasp, but it was like trying to fight your way out of quicksand. It seemed like the more he fought, the tighter the Void held him.

Why do you fight? the Void said. **You should rest. You are tired, tired after fighting against me for so long. Close your eyes. Embrace sleep. And never awaken again.**

"No … thanks," said Braim, though those two words were almost impossible to utter. "Not … tired …"

Now that wasn't exactly true, because the fact was that he could feel his energy being drained away and with it his alertness. Rest did sound good, sounded very good in fact, but Braim fought against it as hard as he could, because he knew that giving into rest would easily be the worst mistake of his life. He forced himself to keep his eyes open, doing the best he could to fight against the Void's seductive call.

If you will not sleep, then I will devour you anyway, the Void said. **It is the fate that awaits Martir and everything that**

lives upon it. Slowly but surely, I am eating away at the edges of this world. And before long, there will be nothing left of Martir, nothing left but the Void, and the Void alone.

Tell yourself that all you want, Void, but that doesn't change anything, Braim thought, although he could not say that aloud because the Void's grip on him prevented him from saying anything. He instead focused on trying to break free, as futile as that action may have been.

Braim Kotogs, do you remember how you told me, when we first met, that I was afraid of you? said the Void. **How you represented everything I fear the most?**

Braim nodded, but again said nothing. He tried to focus on that burning energy in his body from earlier, the energy he had received from Yoji during the ritual. He had a theory that he could use it to escape, but he needed time to test it before the Void decided to consume him.

I would rather not admit this, but you had a point, said the Void. **The Void does not feel fear or any sort of emotion, but the idea that I cannot consume everything ... that does fill me with ... dread? Unease? I don't know. The Void has never had need for such words in her vocabulary and so I don't know how to describe it.**

Braim decided that the energy in his body was similar enough to magical energy that he might be able to use it through normal magical means. He tried to focus on coming up with a spell, any spell, that he could use to break the Void's hold on him.

That is why I avoided fighting you directly again for so long, said the Void. **Your words—unlike the words of any other being I have ever faced—affected me. I lost my confidence, as**

you mortals might put it, and so avoided you in order to avoid thinking about my own weakness.

Even though the energy had been burning so hotly in Braim's body that he couldn't have ignored it even if he tried, now it felt like it wasn't even there. It was like the energy was hiding from him, which would have made him curse if he had had the energy to talk.

Then the Void's grip tightened once more. **But eventually, I came to the conclusion that I could not allow my fears to control me. In order to do what I want to do, I must not only face my fears, but *destroy* my fears. And that means destroying *you*.**

Braim's vision blinked in and out of focus. It was becoming more and more difficult to retain his consciousness. He felt like he was standing on the edge of a cliff, staring at the rocky bottom below, knowing that it was only a matter of time before he tripped and fell. Or before someone pushed him off.

So I am done playing games, Braim Kotogs, said the Void. **I am done playing nice. I will destroy you before I destroy anything else on Martir. By slaying the one who returned from death, I will be sending a signal to everyone else on this world, that not even returning from the dead can save you from the Void.**

Must ... not ... lose ... consciousness ... Braim thought, though he barely understood his own words anymore. His thoughts and words were starting to feel congealed and undifferentiated. He almost felt sick, but this wasn't mere sickness he was dealing with, but death itself.

Nonetheless, Braim forced himself to put both of his hands on

127

the fingers of the Void that were wrapped around his waist. He now felt the burning energy within again, only this time it was becoming stronger than ever. In fact, it was becoming so strong that Braim was almost afraid that he would lose control of it and kill himself, but then he considered the fact that he was going to die anyway and decided that he had nothing to lose at this point.

His hands lit up brightly all of a sudden, yet they also burned like he had placed them in the middle of a burning fire. But Braim didn't scream out in pain. He just focused more and more on sending this energy through his hands into the Void's hand, feeling it pour out of him like a river. He wasn't sure what was going to happen or if anything would happen at all, but he was willing to try anything now regardless of the consequences.

Before Braim's startled eyes, the dark hand of the Void started to disintegrate around his body. The disintegration started out gradually at first, but as more and more of this energy poured from Braim's hands, the disintegration of the shadow hand sped up.

What is this? said the Void. She actually sounded horrified. **I thought you couldn't use magic anymore. This is impossible.**

Braim would have agreed with her, but at the moment he was too busy trying to destroy her to pay attention to what she considered impossible. He increased the amount of energy he poured, which also increased the burning sensation on his hands. He smelled burning skin, which was likely his hands, but he didn't let that stop him, because the alternative was to let the Void consume him and he was not going to let the Void get him, not today.

Then, finally, the Void's hand disintegrated entirely around his waist. The constricting, devouring feeling suddenly vanished and Braim could breathe normally again. He gasped for air, almost fell on his hands and knees, but managed to retain his balance. He looked up at the golem standing before him, watching as the Void's darkness retracted back into the golem's hollow arm. He heard the Void's cursing, but he didn't care, because he now knew that he was safe.

Pathetic mortal, said the Void, whose voice now came from the golem. **So you pulled a silly trick on me that I did not see coming. No matter. I still control the body of this golem and I will use it to crush you like an ant.**

Braim stepped back, but stopped when he felt the burning sensation on his hands. He looked down and saw that the skin on his hands was red, raw, and shiny, even smoking slightly. He then looked up at the golem, which stepped toward him with the clear intent of smashing him to pieces.

Then, without warning, the golem's right arm—the one containing the Void's darkness—vanished, leaving an empty socket where its shoulder had been. The golem looked at its right arm in surprise, but a second later its left arm vanished as well, leaving it without arms.

What? said the Void as the golem's head rotated back and forth as it looked at the missing arms. **What is this? Is this another one of your tricks, Braim Kotogs?**

Braim shook his head, while a familiar voice said, "That would be one of *my* tricks, Void."

Braim looked over and saw Fojak standing up, one hand out. The god looked like he had been beaten up badly, but at least he wasn't unconscious anymore. Fojak glared at the Void as its golem body turned to face him.

You? said the Void. **I thought you were unconscious, deity.**

Fojak shook his head and wiped away a trickle of golden blood from the corner of his mouth with his other hand. "It will take far more than being thrown again a wall to defeat a god like myself. Now begone to the farthest corners of Martir, you foul creature!"

Fojak snapped his fingers several times in rapid succession. With every snap of his fingers, a different part of the golem's body vanished. First went its left leg, causing it to hop around on its right leg before that, too, vanished. Its body fell, but before it hit the floor, the body disappeared, causing the head—the only remaining body part—to crash to the floor with a loud *thunk*. The golem's head was only there for a second, however, before another snap of Fojak's fingers caused it to disappear as well.

Once the last of the golem was gone, Fojak lowered his hand and appeared next to Braim suddenly. He put one hand on Braim's shoulder and said, "Braim, have you been hurt?"

Braim nodded, although it was a weaker nod than usual. "Y-Yes. But I think I'll live."

"We need to get you to a healer," said Fojak. He looked up at the ceiling and cursed. "Why? How did that even happen?"

Braim thought that Fojak was probably talking about the appearance of that golem in World's End, but he didn't ask because he was so exhausted and hurting so much that he couldn't focus on anything else except for the pain.

"Never mind that," said Fojak, shaking his head. "Listen, I will have Atikos look you over and heal you while I tell my siblings about what happened. If this golem's appearance in the heart of our city means what I think it means ... then this war has just become *much* worse."

Braim nodded, but then a question occurred to him. It was hard to speak, but he managed to say, "The Tournament. What about the Tournament?"

"It will go on," said Fojak. "I'll inform Alira of what just happened as well. In any case, you should not worry about this. You just need to rest back in your room."

"All right ..." said Braim with a yawn. "I'll go and do that ..."

So Braim closed his eyes and, despite the pain, drifted into sleep right there and then, regardless of the fact that he was standing upright and nowhere near his bed.

-

"Braim Kotogs," said a kindly, feminine voice above him. "Please wake up and tell me how you feel."

Braim's eyes flickered open. The first thing he saw was the face of a grandmotherly-type woman looking down at him with concern on her old yet kindly features. She even smelled old, but at the same time, it was a comforting smell, which helped him to relax.

Still, Braim was curious about who this woman was, because he had never seen her before, or at least couldn't remember seeing her before. He glanced around the room briefly first, however, to ascertain his location.

He was lying on his bed in his room at the inn he stayed at. It looked the same as normal, except that he thought he caught a glimpse of movement outside the window. He wasn't sure what it was, but the kindly old woman sitting next to his bed didn't seem to notice it, or if she did, she didn't say so. She simply folded her hands over her lap and looked at Braim with the concerned eyes of a doctor looking after a patient that was recovering from a terrible illness.

Now that Braim was looking at her, though, he realized that she did indeed look like a healer. She wore pure white robes, which were the most popular colors among mages who specialized in healing magic, and her skin, though somewhat wrinkly due to her age, was rather smooth and clear, another common feature of healers, who often used their healing magic to get rid of physical deformities on their faces or bodies. Braim didn't see her wand anywhere, however, although he was starting to suspect now that this woman was no mage at all.

"Who ... who are you?" said Braim. His mouth was dry due to the fact that he had not drank anything in a while.

"I am Atikos, the Goddess of Healing and Steel," said the woman. She patted her chest armor, creating a tiny *chink* sound when she did so. "Please to meet you, Braim Kotogs. I have heard all about you, so when Fojak summoned me to heal you, I came as quickly as I could."

Braim nodded. "That's right. I was attacked by the Void controlling one of those golems."

"You remember," Atikos said. "Well, that's good. I have always found it harder to heal damaged memories than other parts of the body, but I suppose your memory was never really damaged at all, was it?"

"Yeah, sure," said Braim. He felt his body suddenly and then pulled his hands out from under the blankets to see that they were whole and without blemish. "Hey ... that pain is gone. And my hands look and feel better, too."

"I removed it," Atikos said. "As the Goddess of Healing, I can remove pain easily. I will admit, though, that in this case it was very hard, because the *cause* of the pain ... well, I had to leave that, because it is one thing that even I cannot remove."

"What *is* the cause of the pain?" said Braim, looking at Atikos. "That energy?"

Atikos coughed suddenly, like she was overcome with a bad fit. "Oh, er, um, it isn't really relevant to our current conversation. Anyway, don't worry about your fellow godlings, if you were. They have been informed of the attack, but are currently safe, because the gods have set up more Soldiers around and inside the Stadium, plus a handful of my siblings have taken up guard duty. I think they will be safe for now."

Braim scratched the back of his head. He knew that Atikos knew what that energy inside him was, but for some reason she wasn't telling him. He didn't know if Atikos was simply choosing not to tell him of her own free will or if the other gods had asked her to keep it a secret from him. In any case, Braim doubted he could trick a god into telling him what he wanted to know, so he decided to focus on other matters that she could tell him about for now.

So Braim said, "What about the Void? And have there been any more golems sightings in the city?"

Atikos shook her head. "Oh, heavens, no. There was only that one golem, although the entire city is on lock-down because my siblings are trying to find out how that golem even got in. We haven't seen or heard from the Void, either, but we are keeping an eye out for her nonetheless."

Braim nodded, although he didn't like the idea that no one had seen the Void. What that told him was that this attack by the golem had not been an actual attack, but a scout sent ahead of the main invasion, perhaps to scout out World's End for the actual attack. Of course, Braim could have been wrong about that, but right now that seemed logical to him.

"Do you know what I think this means?" said Braim, looking up at Atikos again. "I think this means that the Void is working with the golems."

"That's impossible," said Atikos. "The Void wants to destroy everything, while the golems want to take over Martir. Their goals are too different for them to be allies."

"I don't know about that," said Braim. "The Void worked with Uron for a while there, didn't she? At least that was what I was told."

"True, the Void has had a history of allying with other beings if she thought it would help her destroy the world, but I thought she was done with that after being betrayed by Uron," said Atikos. "Nonetheless, it is very much a possibility we will have to consider. It would certainly explain why she was controlling that golem, as well as how it got here."

Braim propped himself up on his elbows and looked Atikos straight in the eye. "What do you mean, 'how it got here'? Do you know what's going on?"

Atikos looked away from Braim, like she was trying to keep a secret. "There is still a lot about this attack that we gods do not know, but I suppose I can share with you some of our current theories. Just be aware that they may not be correct, although all of the evidence points toward them being the most likely and obvious explanations."

"I'm listening," said Braim. "Go on."

Atikos looked at Braim again, except now with a far more serious look in her eyes. "We believe that the Void is allowing the golems to travel the ethereal to enter World's End. It is the only explanation for how that golem could have gotten into the city without any of us noticing it."

Braim nodded. "Yeah, that makes sense. The golem did use an ethereal portal during the battle, but it never occurred to me that the Void might have allowed that. Of course, the Void does control the ethereal, so it's pretty logical."

"And unfortunately," Atikos continued with frustration in her voice, "there isn't anything we can do about it, because we have been unable to retake control of the ethereal from the Void."

"Can't you just close it?" said Braim. "There's supposed to be a spell that can lock the ethereal, isn't there?"

"There is, but the Void will simply break it," said Atikos with a sigh. "The best we can do is prepare for the inevitable invasion of the golems. I think we will be able to defend our city against them, but there are no guarantees in war, especially if the Void is aiding them with her power."

"Dang," said Braim, scratching the back of his head. "That's tough. Is there anything I can do to help?"

Atikos shook her head too fast for Braim's tastes. "No, no. You just need to rest and then, later today, participate in the final challenge in your bracket. You and the other godlings do not need to fight or participate in this battle. Leave it to the gods and the katabans."

"All right," said Braim, although secretly he wasn't so sure that he could trust the gods to beat back the Void and golems by themselves. "Anyway, I noticed that you changed the subject earlier, when I asked you about the energy in my body that almost killed me."

"I said it isn't relevant," said Atikos, again too quickly for Braim's liking. "It doesn't matter. You just need to rest and heal."

Braim shook his head in disagreement. "No, it *does* matter and you are trying to avoid talking about it because you don't want me to know what it is. I may be mortal, Atikos, but that doesn't mean I'm stupid."

Atikos looked at him with uncertainty. He thought she was going to deny it again, but then Atikos sighed and said, "All right. I will tell you about the power within you, even though my siblings would not be at all happy about my doing this. Still, I trust you, Braim, because I have been watching your actions and I believe that you are a good mortal who can be trusted with this information."

"Great," said Braim. He sat up and stretched his arms. "Let's hear it, then. I'm all ears."

Atikos folded her hands over her lap, looking like she did not know where to start. That seemed odd to Braim, because he had never known the gods to have a hard time talking about anything.

"The power within you, Braim, is not magical power, at least not what you are used to," said Atikos. "It is the kind of power that mortals are not supposed to have at all. In fact, it is the kind of power that would normally destroy a mortal's body and their life, yet somehow your body is handling it without too much trouble. I suppose it is due to the fact that you are not a normal mortal."

"I know, I know," said Braim. He put a hand on his chest.

"But you still haven't explained *what* it is, exactly. If it's not magical power, then what is it?"

Atikos looked Braim in the eyes. "It is divine power; that is, the power of the gods."

When Atikos said that, Braim felt a burning sensation in his stomach and chest. It was the same burning sensation from before, only it didn't hurt quite as much as it did before, although it was still uncomfortable.

"The power of the gods?" said Braim. "What … what does that mean?"

"It means that you have power similar to—though not exactly the same as—us," said Atikos, gesturing at herself. "You are now more powerful than most mortals, perhaps even more powerful than those mortals who are known as the Limitless. In any case, you are powerful enough to defend yourself from the Void, so that is one thing you have going for you."

Braim looked down at his body. It looked the same as it always did, but it did feel a little different. It was that burning sensation flowing through his veins that made it feel different. Again, it was not quite as painful as before, but he could no longer ignore it, despite his best efforts to do so.

"But how?" said Braim, looking up at Atikos again. "How did I gain the powers of the gods? Wasn't the ritual supposed to merely restore my original magical powers, not give me new ones?"

"That may have been what the ritual was *supposed* to do, but your friend Yoji made a mistake," said Atikos. "He misread one or more of the steps that the book describes as necessary for the ritual to work and was hasty in applying them. You are lucky that

137

you weren't killed, because that was one of the things that could have happened if he had messed up too badly."

Braim shuddered at the thought. "But if I got this power, what did Yoji get?"

"Nothing," said Atikos. "Except he lost quite a bit of his own magical power during the ritual. But I'm sure he has already regained most of it by now."

Braim breathed a sigh of relief. "Good. I was worried about him for a moment there, but I guess if he's going to be all right then I shouldn't worry about him."

"Agreed," said Atikos. "You should instead be worrying about yourself."

Braim looked at Atikos in confusion. "Why? After all, if I have the power of the gods flowing through me like you said, then I'm even better off than I was before. Sure, it isn't exactly what I was looking for, but I'll take it."

"You should worry about yourself because your body is still mortal," said Atikos. She frowned. "And mortal bodies cannot handle this kind of divine energy for long. While we gods can grant mortals temporary boosts in power, we never allow the power boosts to last very long because mortal bodies cannot handle even a fraction of our power for very long. It is like trying to fit an ocean into a wineglass."

"What will happen to me, then?" said Braim. "Can't be anything too bad, right?"

"You will die," said Atikos simply. "At some point, the power will completely overwhelm your mortal body and you will die. Your body will likely burn up completely, but we don't know that for sure."

Braim suddenly felt cold, even though the temperature in the room was rather warm at the moment, especially with the rays of the sun streaming in from the window. He was thinking about what the Mysterious One had told him, about how, if he died, then not even his soul would survive. How he would end up just like Uron, as pure nothingness from which he would never recover.

Up until this point, Braim had thought that he was going to remain safe so long as he stayed in the Stadium and participated in the Tournament. But now, he was looking at dying far sooner than he expected no matter how careful he was.

He looked at Atikos again. "When will I die?"

"I don't know," said Atikos. "None of us do. As you are a godling and a resurrected mortal, you might live longer than normal mortals, but not by much I think. Perhaps until the end of the day or until tomorrow morning."

"Has this ever happened to any other mortal?" said Braim. "Anyone else at all? If so, how long did they last?"

Atikos seemed uncomfortable about his questioning, but Braim didn't stop. He leaned forward, ready to listen to whatever Atikos said.

Finally, Atikos said, "Ten minutes. He took on our power and lasted only ten minutes."

"Has it been ten minutes since I gained this power?" said Braim.

"More than ten," said Atikos, nodding.

Braim sighed in relief again. "Hey, I'm still alive. I guess that's good, isn't it?"

"Yes, but your chances of dying are still very high," said Atikos. "Like I said, the fact that you are different from other mortals means that your body probably has a stronger tolerance for our power than most, but that still doesn't mean you will live. You will still die, and when you do, none of us will be able to bring you back to life again."

Braim lay back down on the bed, staring up at the ceiling. He didn't feel like he was dying, but he had no reason to doubt that Atikos was telling him the truth. It explained the intense pain he had felt before, which had likely been his body dying. His body was probably still dying, in fact, and he had no idea when it would go from 'dying' to 'dead.'

"I am sorry to be the one to tell you this, Braim, but I think it is better for you to hear the truth from me than from one of the other gods," said Atikos. She sounded genuinely sorry, which surprised Braim, as he had never known any of the gods to sound genuinely sorry about anything. "As a healer, I have always disliked telling people they are dying and there's no way to save them."

"Can't you heal me?" said Braim, looking at Atikos once more. "Or at least remove the divine power inside me?"

"I can't," said Atikos. "None of us gods can. It is part of the balance that the Powers built into us. If we could take away divine power from mortals, then we could also take it from ourselves, which would upset the already fragile balance among the gods. Even if we could, it might not make a difference, because divine power often leaves irrevocable scars on those who use it and you might die anyway."

Braim gulped. He rested both hands on his chest, not sure what to say. He didn't want to die, but if Atikos was telling the truth, then there was nothing he or the gods or anyone else could do to save his life. He was going to die whether he wanted to or not.

"Again, I am sorry to have to be the one to tell you this, but this is the way it is and there is nothing I can do about it," said Atikos. "The only possible way you could survive beyond the end of the day is by winning the Tournament and becoming the God of Martir. If you do, your body will be transformed into the body of a god and thus will be able to handle the divine energy within."

"What if I don't live long enough to win the Tournament?" said Braim. He put one hand on his forehead and shuddered. "There's no guarantee I'll live until even the next hour. It is looking more and more to me like my life is just about up."

"I don't know what we will do if you die before the Tournament is over," said Atikos. "All I know is that if you have survived this long so far, then you will probably live until the end of the day. But again, I don't know for certain and I could always be wrong."

"Then I need to go back to the Stadium," said Braim. He sat up again and tossed the covers off of his legs. "If winning the Tournament is what I need to do in order to survive, then I don't want to be any farther away from the Stadium than I need to be."

"Do you feel well enough to go?" said Atikos. "After all, you were in very bad condition when I was summoned to heal you. And even after I healed you, your body is still not fully healed."

"I'll be fine," said Braim, swinging his legs over the side of his bed. "It's not like there's much worse that can happen to me, after all. I just need my shoes. Where are they?"

Atikos reluctantly pointed at the dresser, where Braim's shoes stood. "Right there."

Braim nodded in thanks, slid off the bed, and walked over to his dresser. When he reached the shoes, he started pulling them on, although he was aware of Atikos behind him looking at him with disapproval.

Once Braim got his shoes on, he stood up to his full height again and turned to face Atikos. "All right. I'm going to go back to the Stadium now. Are you coming with me?"

Atikos shook her head. "No. I must return to guard duty with the other gods. I would like to come with you to protect you, but you will instead be escorted by a group of elite Soldiers who have been tasked with protecting you on your way there. They are the best of the best and will do everything they can to protect you from anyone who tries to harm you."

Braim glanced at the window and saw the helmet of one of the Soldiers pass by, which probably explained the movement he had seen outside the window earlier. He then looked at Atikos again, who had not moved from her chair.

"All right," said Braim. "But can you be sure I'll be all right?"

"I see no reason why you wouldn't," said Atikos. "After all, there are not any other golems in the city and, as I said, these Soldiers in particular are elite. You will be safe."

"Okay," said Braim, nodding. "Guess I'd better go, then. Wonder if anyone has won the Hollech Bracket Challenge yet."

"I am not sure," said Atikos. "But anyway, we will all learn soon enough. Good bye, Braim Kotogs. I hope that you live long enough to win the Tournament and survive this awful curse cast upon your body."

With that, Atikos vanished in a flash of light, leaving Braim alone in his room. Then Braim felt hungry and thirsty and decided to get something to eat before he returned to the Stadium. Just something small and quick, however, because he did not want to waste what was probably going to be his last day on this world eating.

Chapter Eleven

RAYA LOOKED AT the large gap in the floor of the hallway, frowning. She had come upon this gap quite suddenly not long after she got past Valfa. She had been walking down the hall, keeping her eyes and ears open for any other traps, when without warning she had come across this massive gap—more like a pit, really—in the floor. It split the hallway neatly in two, with no bridge, rope, or anything else she could use to cross it. Nor could she jump the gap, either, because it was too far for her to jump even if she got a running start.

But I don't have all the time in the world to figure this out, Raya thought, playing with a few loose strands of her hair as she looked from her side to the other side and back again. *Yoji or the others are definitely not going to sit back and wait for me to catch up, even though it would be polite of them to do so.*

Raya looked around the hallway just to make sure that she hadn't overlooked anything she could use to escape. The walls were smooth, lacking any sort of handholds or footholds she could use to climb across them. The pit between her side and the other side seemed as bottomless and dark as the Void, which made Raya keen to avoid it.

If only I could open an ethereal portal to get to the other side, Raya thought. *Then this challenge would be a piece of cake.*

As it was, however, Raya could not open an ethereal portal, because the Void currently controlled the ethereal and Raya had no interest in going anywhere near the Void right now. She decided to come up with a better way of getting across, but she wasn't sure how.

Raya looked down at her artificial hand. She wondered if it could get her across, but then dismissed that thought right away. As amazing as her artificial hand was, she knew its limits and its powers and it could not create a bridge or some other way for Raya to across the gap. That simply wasn't what it did. It was good for self-defense purposes, but for travel it was just as useless as her other hand.

So Raya folded her arms across her chest and looked to the other side of the gap again. The hall continued down quite a ways from that side until it met a sharp corner and turned out of sight, but that didn't matter to Raya because it didn't help her figure out how to cross it.

Come on, think of something, Raya, Raya told herself, tapping the floor with her foot as she looked around, searching for anything that could give her an idea she could use to get across. *The longer you stand here, thinking of a plan, the more likely it becomes that someone else will beat you to the Staff and to godhood.*

Raya knew all of that, but that still didn't bring any plans to mind. She wondered if there might be some kind of secret panels or buttons on the walls that might create a bridge of some sort that would allow her to cross easily, but a quick search of both walls

145

on either side of her revealed nothing out of the ordinary. As far as she could tell, there was no way to cross this pit.

But if she couldn't pass, then that meant she would lose. And she could not accept that, not when she was so close to godhood that she could practically taste it.

That was when Raya got an idea. She looked down at her artificial hand again, and then at the hall on the other side of the pit. The plan didn't seem likely to work—it could easily end with her falling to her death—but it was the only plan she had and at this point she was willing to try anything to succeed.

So Raya took several steps backwards until she was far enough back that she was confident that she had enough room to build up the momentum she would need to cross the gap. She then prepared herself to run, situating her feet so she could get a good start.

All right, Raya, let's do this, Raya told herself.

With that, Raya ran as fast as she could toward the edge of the pit. Fear rose within her as she drew closer to it, but she ignored it, focusing instead on what she would need to do next after she made the jump. Because if she let fear get the best of her now, then she would almost certainly die.

When Raya got right to the edge, she jumped. She wasn't a good jumper, but she put all of her strength into her legs, hoping that it would be enough to propel her across the gap before she needed to do the next part of the plan.

And indeed, Raya did fly across the gap, flew across it quite a bit farther than even she expected, but as soon as she felt herself peak, she stretched out her artificial hand. Its fingers immediately extended, shooting through the air and striking the floor on the other side of the pit. They dug themselves deeply into the floor, but despite that, Raya fell anyway. She screamed as she fell until she came to an abrupt stop in midair, causing her to bounce up and down briefly. Panting in fear, Raya looked up and saw that the elongated fingers of her artificial hand had saved her from falling. They had managed to dig themselves into the stone floor on the other side deeply enough to keep Raya from falling to her death, which was a miracle. They didn't even look like they were going to break, but Raya did not waste any time in testing that theory. She then started retracting her fingers, which pulled her up.

In a few seconds, Raya was on the other side of the pit. She was still shaking and panting because of the near fall, but she was also quite satisfied with herself for coming up with such a great move. She looked over her shoulder at the pit and smirked at it.

Dumb pit, Raya thought. *Valfa was harder to get past than that. If Fojak designed that pit, then I'm shocked that his Staff hadn't been stolen by someone before the Tournament.*

Raya gave herself only a few seconds to sit there and catch her breath. When she felt better, she stood up and dusted herself off, brushing strands of hair behind her ear and wiping the sweat off her face. Because she seemed to be in good condition, Raya decided to keep going forward. She was surprised at how quickly she had gotten past that obstacle, but then, she reflected, of course it made sense, because it was her destiny to win the Tournament and become a goddess, so why wouldn't she be able to get past the obstacles quickly?

So Raya walked down the next hall with a confident stride, but then she heard skittering movement above her. Raya stopped and looked up at the ceiling, but did not see anything. Yet she was certain that she had heard something move, even though she did not know what it was.

Can't be Valfa, Raya thought, looking around, but still not seeing anything. *Did Fojak create another chimera? Or is it something else?*

Raya stayed still for a few seconds, but did not hear anything. She shook her head, deciding that the stress of the Tournament was getting to her and making her hear things, and took another step forward.

As soon as she did, she heard more skittering movement above and looked up again just in time to see a large, ugly spider-like creature materialize above her. It clung to the ceiling with its four legs, staring down at her with its many eyes, but there was something about the creature that told Raya that it was far more intelligent than it looked.

Raya attempted to run forward, but before she could get far, the spider creature fell down to the floor in front of her, cutting off the path. It rose to its full height, putting its head level with Raya's. The creature smelled like dirt and blood and it snapped at her with its pincers, causing Raya to walk backwards to avoid getting bitten. She had no idea whether this spider was poisonous or not, but she wasn't going to find out the hard way.

But Raya could not back up very far, because soon she reached the edge of the pit that she had just crossed. She almost fell over backwards into it, but caught herself and regained her balance, standing upright and facing the spider creature, which still advanced on her with hungry eyes.

"Go away, you stupid spider!" Raya said, shaking her fist at it.

"I don't have time to play with you. I'm on my way to fulfill my destiny and I cannot do that if you are in my way."

Unfortunately, the spider creature didn't seem to be a chimera like Valfa and so didn't seem to understand her, because it simply kept advancing toward her with a purple, poison-like substance dripping from its mouth. Raya decided that she would not spare its life.

Extending the fingers of her artificial hand, Raya swung her sharpened fingers at the spider. The spider creature blocked the fingers with its pincers, however, holding back against them with surprising strength. Still, Raya pushed back against it, putting all of her effort into making it getting her fingers past its pincer.

But then the spider creature shoved Raya back without warning. Raya staggered backwards and fell off the ledge into the pit below.

In panic, Raya reached out and grabbed the ledge with her normal hand. As soon as she did, however, the spider creature was above her, snapping its pincers. It stepped on her hand with one of its large legs. Actually, it was more like it smashed down on her hand, like it was trying to make her let go and fall to her death.

Raya, however, did not scream out in pain. Biting her tongue, Raya retracted the long fingers of her artificial hand and then aimed it at the spider creature's face. The spider creature only had a second to look at her hand before her fingers lengthened again, this time stabbing the creature straight through the face.

The spider creature roared in agony, taking its leg off Raya's hand. It yanked its head off of the fingers and staggered back, but then it collapsed onto the floor, twitched a few times, and stopped moving entirely.

Breathing and sweating hard, Raya retracted her fingers again and pulled herself back up onto the floor. She looked at the dead spider creature, at the spots on its face where her fingers had pierced. An ugly green liquid that smelled absolutely putrid leaked out of the holes in its head, which was either blood or maybe bits of its brain.

Raya looked down at her artificial hand. The tips of her fingers were covered in the awful green stuff. Although it didn't seem poisonous or dangerous, it was so foul-smelling and icky that Raya walked over to the spider creature's corpse and wiped off her fingers on its hairy back. She could have wiped it off on her clothes, but even though her uniform was hardly the most fashionable piece of clothing in the world, she did not want to get this crap stuck on her clothes.

Once her hand was clean, Raya looked around again just to make sure that there were no other giant monstrosities awaiting her. She didn't see any, but considering how she had not expected to run into this massive spider creature, she decided to be even more careful on her way to the Staff than before.

So Raya turned and walked down the hall as quickly as she could, hoping that she had not wasted too much time fighting this creature. She doubted that any of the others had gotten to the Staff just yet, because Alira likely would have announced a winner if there was one, but that just made Raya walk faster because there was no way that she was going to let Yoji or any of the others get there before her.

Turning the corner, Raya found herself standing before a locked door. Its surface was shiny and metallic, looking brand new. It was reflective as well, allowing Raya to see her own

150

fabulous appearance and the stray hair poking out from the side of her head rather awkwardly. Pushing the stray hair back, Raya then grabbed the doorknob and tried to turn it.

Unfortunately, the door was indeed locked, as she suspected. Letting go of the doorknob, Raya stepped back and observed the door. It didn't seem to have any special magical properties that she could tell, but that did not mean it would be any easier for her to open than if it did. She looked at the area around the door quickly to see if she could find a hidden key, but of course there was nothing that she could use as one.

It would be far too easy if Fojak had left a key for me, Raya thought. *As the next Goddess of Thieves, I should be able to pick this door's lock easily.*

'Should' was the operative word, because Raya frankly knew next to nothing about the art of lock-picking. So she decided to take the direct approach and struck the doorknob with the lengthened fingers of her artificial hand, but unfortunately that did nothing. Whatever the door was made out of, it was too strong for her artificial finger blades to cut through. That meant she needed to figure out a different way of opening the door, although she wasn't sure how.

Raya walked up to the door and leaned in closer to look at the lock in an attempt to understand how it worked. Not that that helped, seeing as she didn't know much about locks, but she thought that if she studied it then maybe she would see something that she could use to break the lock and get in. She also briefly wondered about what was on the other side of the door, but dismissed that thought from her mind so she could focus instead on the problem at hand.

Then Raya noticed that the lock on the door was roughly the same size as the fingers on her artificial hand, at least when they were elongated. An idea popped into her mind, but she wasn't sure if it would work. She decided that she would give it a shot anyway and see what happened. At the very least, she didn't think it would cause her any harm.

So Raya elongated her index finger, sticking it directly into the keyhole. Her finger fit perfectly and, with a twist to the side, she heard the lock *snap*, which meant that she had likely broken it.

Withdrawing her finger, Raya grabbed the doorknob again and turned it. To her satisfaction, the door opened quite easily, so she stepped through eagerly to see what was on the other side.

The room Raya stepped into was wide, round, and circular. Running along the walls were metal doors very similar to the one that she had just opened, except in different colors, such as red, blue, green, and yellow. She supposed that those doors were the ones that the other challengers would emerge from, assuming they made it past whatever obstacles they ran into on their way here.

But to her delight, the room was completely empty of any other living being besides herself. The reason she was delighted was because she noticed the object floating silently in the center of the room in a glowing cocoon of blue energy. It was long and stiff, with a knife on the tip, and had to be at least twice as tall as her. It was also made of a shiny, reflective metal that reflected the light from the ceiling.

Although Raya had never seen this particular object before, she knew that it had to be the Staff of Teleportation. She again looked around the room, just to make sure that there were no guards or traps or other godlings to get in her way, but as far as she could tell, the entire room was completely empty. That meant that the Staff was hers for the taking.

Oh my gods, Raya thought, hopping up and down on the balls of her feet. *I can't believe it. I thought for sure that one of the other godlings would get here before me, but I guess it really* is *my destiny to become the next Goddess of Deception, Thieves, and Horses. Yay!*

So Raya confidently strode across the shiny marble floor, her boots clicking against its smooth surface, toward the Staff. In less than a minute, Raya was before it. She looked at the Staff with reverence for a moment, because she wanted to savor this final moment before she won.

It's so pretty, Raya thought. *And powerful. I wonder if I will get my own object like this when I become a goddess? Will I get a Lock Pick of Theft or something? I guess I'll find out.*

Just as Raya reached for the Staff, the door on the opposite end of the chamber burst open. A second later, Yoji dashed through the open door, followed shortly by a large, slimy black tentacle that tried to grab him. He zapped it with a spell from his wand, however, making the tentacle screech in pain and then retract back into the room. As soon as the tentacle was gone, Yoji waved his wand at the door and it slammed closed with a ringing *boom.* Even then, Raya could hear the sounds of that tentacle beating against the door on the other side, although it was thankfully not strong enough to break down the door on its own.

Panting, Yoji looked over at Raya, noticed that she had almost touched the Staff, and said, "Oh, no, you don't!"

Yoji raised his wand and thrust it forward like a sword. Raya felt a powerful gust of wind strike her, sending her tumbling backwards onto the floor and messing up her hair. The fall did not hurt, but it did jar her a little.

Raya recovered her senses in time to see Yoji standing right in front of the Staff. He reached for it as greedily as a thief, but Raya wasn't going to let him get it. She thrust her arm forward, elongating her fingers faster than she had before.

Her fingers struck the Staff and knocked it out of its glowing blue aura. The Staff tumbled across the floor several feet away from both of them, but neither Raya nor Yoji waited to run toward it. As Yoji was nearest to the Staff, he almost reached it first, but Raya caught up with him and shoved him to the side out of her way.

Now Raya reached for the fallen Staff, but then Yoji grabbed her wrist and pulled her back. Raya swung her other fist at him, but Yoji just dodged it and then pointed his wand at the Staff.

The Staff suddenly flew toward Yoji. He let go of Raya's hand and held out his open hand, but at the last second, Raya rammed into him with her shoulder. Yoji staggered to the side, but so did Raya, and as a result the Staff flew past both of them and clattered across the floor again.

Again, neither Raya nor Yoji stopped. They ran toward the Staff, side by side, but Raya was just a little bit ahead of Yoji. She realized, however, that Yoji was going to get there before her anyway, because he was gaining on her and had his spells and magic to stop or slow her own progress.

So Raya elongated her fingers again and slammed them into Yoji's chest as hard as she could. The blow sent Yoji staggering backwards, but Raya knew that he would recover soon.

Not that it mattered, because Raya reached the Staff, bent over, and grasped it with both of her hands. It was heavy and thick, but she grasped the Staff tightly against her chest like it was her firstborn child and turned around to face Yoji, who was now staring at her with a dumbfounded expression.

Raising the Staff above her head, Raya cried out, in the most gleeful voice she could muster, "I did it! I got the Staff! I, Princess Raya Mana, daughter of King Malock and Queen Hanarova, won the Hollech Bracket Challenge! I have finally fulfilled my destiny! I will become the next Goddess of Thieves, Deception, and Horses! At long last, victory is *mine!*"

"All right, all right," said Yoji, who looked and sounded quite annoyed, covering his ears with his hands. "You're the winner. I heard you. I'm not deaf."

Tears formed in Raya's eyes when she thought about how proud her parents would be when they learned about her victory. She also imagined how happy Carmaz would be for her when he heard the good news. In fact, she decided that her very first action as the Goddess of Thieves, Deception, and Horses would be to go and visit Carmaz.

Lowering the Staff, Raya wiped the tears from her eyes and said, "Oh, how I have been waiting for this day ever since I learned that I was chosen to participate in the Tournament of the Gods. It was a long journey, one full of happiness and sorrow in equal measure. I fought every step of the way and many times, I was certain that I was going to lose, but it was my destiny to win, so I could never really lose at all."

"Can you save your victory speech for later?" said Yoji, lowering his hands from his ears, although he still looked annoyed. "There's no one here to listen to it but me."

"You're just jealous because *I* won," said Raya, hugging the Staff to her chest again and smiling at Yoji in triumph. "Don't worry, Yoji. I won't forget about you when I ascend to godhood. Perhaps I will even grant you immortality. That's what Hollech could do to his followers before he died, right?"

"No," Yoji said. "He couldn't."

"Well, in any case, you can rest assured that I will be a much better Goddess of Deception, Thieves, and Horses than you would have been," said Raya. "This isn't just bragging on my part, either. After all, if I was not going to be better than you, how could I have won the Tournament? It must have been my destiny to win."

Yoji rolled his eyes and sighed heavily. "Sure, Raya. You keep telling yourself that."

Raya decided not to push the subject any further, mostly because she saw no reason to let Yoji's obvious jealousy put a damper on her victorious feelings.

So Raya looked up at the ceiling and said, "Alira? Can you come and get me now? I won the Tournament, so I am ready for the next step, which is ascension to godhood."

Raya then waited patiently. She knew that Alira must have heard her, but the longer she stood there with no response, the more worried she became. She looked at Yoji, who was also looking at the ceiling with confusion on his face.

Raya looked up at the ceiling again and said, in a raise voiced, "Alira, are you there? Can you hear me? I'm ready for my prize. Are you going to come and get me? Alira?"

Again, no response. It was like Raya was talking to a ceiling, which she supposed she was, but that did not make her feel any better. She looked at Yoji again and said, "What in the name of Grinf is going on here? Why hasn't Alira announced my victory yet and ended the challenge? What is she waiting for?"

Yoji shrugged. "No idea. Maybe she's getting the others first."

"That can't be right," said Raya. "Doesn't Alira always come to get the victor first?"

"Normally, yes," said Yoji, nodding. "But those last obstacles were difficult. I mean, not so difficult for me, obviously, because of my training and practice, but they were definitely a step above the last challenge, so it wouldn't surprise me if the others are stuck in dangerous situations that they need to be rescued from."

Raya shook her head. "What could possibly be more important than getting me and announcing to the whole world that I won the Hollech Bracket? I mean, for the gods' sake, I'm going to be the first of the new gods. That is far more important than rescuing a bunch of losers who couldn't even make it past the first obstacle."

"You do have a point," said Yoji. "Maybe something is wrong. Maybe the Void or something attacked."

Raya shuddered. "Oh, I most certainly hope that that is not the case. The last time the Void attacked the Stadium was very scary. I barely escaped alive."

"Just a theory," said Yoji. "But I think it a very likely—Watch out!"

Raya frowned and looked over her shoulder in time to see a large stone fist come out of an ethereal portal and fall down on her. With a yelp, Raya jumped forward, avoiding the fist's fall just in the nick of time. The gigantic stone fist crashed into the floor, followed by another fist as a massive golem rose from the ethereal portal.

Raya backed up as fast as she could until she was standing next to Yoji, keeping her eyes on the golem that had emerged from the portal the whole while. This golem was tall enough that the tip of its head almost scraped the ceiling, its fists as big as boulders. The ethereal portal then closed behind the golem with a *pop*, at which point Raya knew that there was no way that they were getting out of this one alive.

"By the gods' names," said Yoji, holding out his wand before him defensively as the golem looked down upon them both. "What *is* that thing?"

"A golem," said Raya, unable to hide the fear in her voice. "A really big golem that I am absolutely certain is going to crush us both."

Chapter Twelve

Husband?" Carmaz repeated. He stared at Lady Dia in confusion. "Did you just call me your *husband*?"

"Yes," said Lady Dia, nodding. She stepped closer to the cell. "Are you him?"

Carmaz looked down at his fleshy human body and then back up at Lady Dia's stone body. "No. I'm Carmaz Korva, a human being. I have always been a human being and I've certainly never been married to anyone."

Lady Dia rubbed her hands together, which seemed like an unconscious habit to Carmaz. "Can you be absolutely certain of that? You may think that you have always been a human, but perhaps there is more to your life than you think."

"No, I'm pretty sure I've always been human," said Carmaz, shaking his head. "I don't even know how you could possibly even confuse me with your husband. Granted, I've never seen him before, but if he's a golem, then he probably looks nothing like me."

"My husband ..." Lady Dia's trailed off, as if she was distracted by her memories of her spouse. "He looked nothing like you, yes, but there is something about you, something in your eyes, that makes me think you are him, but reborn."

"Reborn?" said Carmaz. "I have no idea what you're talking about. Are you trying to trick me or something?"

"It's no trick," Lady Dia insisted. "I should start at the beginning, because you clearly don't remember. Maybe if I explain to you what happened to my husband and who we are, it will jog your memory."

Carmaz had no real interest in listening to Lady Dia tell him anything, but as he had nothing else to do, he decided to listen. Maybe he would learn some useful information that he could use against the golems later on, or at least get some information he could use to escape if nothing else.

Lady Dia rubbed her hands together, looking like she was trying to decide where to start. It was very strange to see her looking so confused and worried, because Carmaz had come to believe that she was a much stronger and deadlier person than she appeared. It could have been—in fact probably was—all an act, but perhaps it wasn't. After all, if Lady Dia truly believed that Carmaz was her husband, then her behavior toward him right now was probably genuine.

Finally, Lady Dia said, "Do you know who we golems are? Where we come from? Our origin?"

Carmaz shook his head. "No, I don't."

That made Lady Dia look quite depressed, as if his admitting that he didn't know where the golems came from had confirmed all of her worst fears. Nonetheless, she said, "You think of us golems as an alien force, as some kind of 'other' that you can safely kill. Like demons rising from the pit, you humans view us as foreign invaders who are trying to take over your world."

"Isn't that what you are?" said Carmaz. He glared at Lady Dia. "You killed my fellow Ruwans who did nothing wrong. You destroyed my home village and you aren't even sad about it. Forgive me if I'm not stupid enough to believe that you're actually a good person."

"But that is where you are wrong," said Lady Dia. She put one of her hands on her chest. "We golems are not some foreign force that holds only malicious intent for the world. We are creations of the Powers, just as you and the gods and everything else in this world is."

Carmaz's eyes widened. "Impossible. None of the legends state that the Powers ever created another sentient race like yourself. There are only humans, gods, aquarians, and katabans."

"Your legends may state that, but legends are not always right," said Lady Dia. "The Powers created us golems to be separate from the rest of Martir. They made us different, made of stone, in order to test their own abilities as creators. And they succeeded quite admirably, in my opinion."

"What happened after they created you?" said Carmaz.

"They placed us beneath the earth," said Lady Dia, gesturing at the ground upon which she stood. "Deep, deep, deep beneath the surface of Martir, to regions where even the gods do not venture. They cast us into a deep slumber from which we were never supposed to awaken."

"Why?" said Carmaz. "Because you're a bunch of murderous monsters?"

"Because there was no room for us on Martir," said Lady Dia. "The Powers did not design Martir with us in mind, seeing as we had been designed as prototypes of the other sentient species that would inhabitant this world. When they finished the world, there was no place for us, but they still wanted to keep us alive. So they kept us safe and out of sight miles beneath the surface, where no one except the gods would find us, but even the gods would not dare to awaken us without knowing what we are and what we do."

There was a hint of bitterness in Lady Dia's voice, bitterness as sharp as a sword. It almost made Carmaz feel sorry for her, but then he remembered who she was and what she did and all the sorrow he felt for her vanished in an instant.

"Why do you want to conquer the world, then?" said Carmaz. "What do you hope to gain from it?"

"Justice," said Lady Dia, her hands clenching into fists. "Weren't you listening to my tale? We golems, unlike every other Martirian species, never received the opportunity to live our lives and create our own cultures. We were forced to live beneath the earth, to sleep eternally. Our right to form our own communities and cultures were denied us, all because the Powers didn't design the world to accommodate us as well."

"So your answer is to attack and kill everyone, because you're angry at the Powers?" said Carmaz in disbelief. "That doesn't seem logical to me."

"We need land," said Lady Dia flatly. "And in order to get that land, we need to do what you and every other species on this planet has done since the dawn of creation: Conquer it through war. If any innocents die because of this, that is of no great concern to me or to the others. It is simply one of the consequences of war and not worth losing any sleep over."

Lady Dia certainly sounded like she had slept well. She spoke as casually as if she were speaking of the weather, which told Carmaz all he needed to know about her character.

"All right, then," said Carmaz. "So why do you think I'm your husband? I didn't even know you golems even *had* the concept of marriage."

"It isn't exactly the same as the human concept of marriage," said Lady Dia. "But it is close enough that I am comfortable describing it that way. Besides, you humans were not the ones who created marriage, so it isn't like you have some sort of monopoly on the term anyway. As for my husband, well, I have a few reasons for believing that you are him, only reincarnated."

"Reincarnated?" said Carmaz. "Reincarnation doesn't exist."

"You humans may believe that, but we golems differ," said Lady Dia. "It is our belief that when someone dies, their soul returns to Martir eventually in a new body that often has little to do with their old one. Reincarnated spirits can even jump into new bodies that are from a different species entirely, such as a golem reincarnating into a human."

"Is that what you believe about me, then?" said Carmaz. "You believe that I am your golem husband reincarnated into a human?"

"Yes," said Lady Dia, nodding. "That is what I believe."

"What happened to your husband, then?" said Carmaz. "Did he die?"

Lady Dia looked down, as if Carmaz had shouted at her, even though he had asked the question in a normal voice. "It was ages ago, at the beginning of Martir, shortly after the golems were created and the Powers left Martir to go onto other projects. They put me, my husband Basan, and Stalac in charge of our resting peers."

"You mean that you weren't cast into sleep like the rest of them?" said Carmaz. "Why?"

"Because we were different," said Lady Dia. "In case you haven't noticed, most golems lack the sort of intelligent minds that you and I have. Because the Powers did not put as much effort into them as they put into us, the other golems are little more than machines that do what they are told, though that does not make them any less valuable than the rest of us. The Powers gave Basan, Stalac, and me individuality so we could better protect our fellow golems while they rested."

"Then what was stopping you from awakening them and leading them to invade the surface?" said Carmaz.

"We didn't want to, at first," said Lady Dia, shaking her head. "We didn't see any need to. We only did what the Powers wanted us to do, which was to oversee and protect our sleeping siblings from any threats. We were happy that way for a while, but then a few hundred years ago, that all changed."

"How?" said Carmaz.

"When Basan died," said Lady Dia. Her voice became harder. "Basan told me and Stalac that it was not fair that the Powers had condemned us and the golems to an eternity below ground, away from the surface. He told us that we should lead the golems to invade the surface and take what was rightfully ours."

"Where did he get that idea from?" said Carmaz.

"Basan was always an independent thinker," said Lady Dia. She sighed in happiness. "He never accepted anything on the surface of it. And he eventually came to the conclusion that we were being treated unjustly, that our entire species was being mistreated, and that the only way for us to correct this error was to attack the surface, whether the Powers wanted us to or not."

Carmaz looked around and said, "Then where is Basan? How did he die?"

Lady Dia turned away. "Basan was killed when he left for the surface by himself. Neither Stalac nor I followed him because we thought that the Powers would kill us if we left. Basan disagreed, but there was nothing we could do to convince him to stay and he couldn't convince us to go with him."

"Who killed him?" said Carmaz.

"I don't know," said Lady Dia, shaking her head. Her voice sounded strained, like she was trying to keep her emotions under wraps. "When Basan left for the surface, he vanished completely. But it is obvious that he must have been killed by someone, although who and why, I don't know."

Then Lady Dia turned around again. This time, there was anger in her blue eyes, a murderous anger that made Carmaz wish that his wrists and ankles were free, because he was afraid that she might just attack him even though he wasn't in any position to harm her.

"But I think it is likely that the Ruwans killed him," said Lady Dia. Her voice shook with anger. "It is the only logical explanation. They killed him, killed my husband, and did away with the body. I have my men searching for it, but he's been dead for so long that I doubt they will have any luck in finding it, especially if it sank into the Swamp."

Carmaz tried to remember if he had ever heard any stories of a golem being killed, but he could not recall ever hearing anything of the sort. He wondered if maybe Basan had instead fallen into the swamp water somewhere and sunk to the bottom and was unable to surface, but he kept that theory to himself, because the exact circumstances of Basan's death did not change the fact that the golems were the single biggest threat to Ruwa and its people today and needed to be stopped.

Lady Dia stepped up to the cage and wrapped her fingers around the bars. Her eyes were focused on Carmaz now, focused to an obsessive degree, which made Carmaz feel very uncomfortable. He leaned back, even though there was no way Lady Dia could touch him even if she stuck her arm through the gap between bars in the cell and reached for him.

"But maybe not all is lost, if you are him," said Lady Dia. "We golems don't have a very complicated belief system, but we've always believed in reincarnation. And I think that it is likely that *you* are him, because your personality is similar to his. You just don't remember, perhaps because the reincarnation process went wrong at some point or you have been through other reincarnations between your first death and the birth of your human body."

"Listen, Dia, you are seriously misguided if you think I am him reincarnated," said Carmaz. "If your husband is dead, then he is dead and there is no way to change that, not even through reincarnation, which doesn't even exist anyway."

"What about Braim Kotogs?" said Lady Dia. "He came back to life, didn't he?"

Carmaz bit his lip when he thought about Braim. "Braim is a special case. The fact is that the vast majority of creatures and beings in the world stay dead when they die. They don't come back, don't even reincarnate."

"You say that, but I don't believe it," said Lady Dia, shaking her head. "I see too much of Basan in you for it to be a coincidence. The man I loved is in you somewhere. Your eyes look like his and you even speak somewhat like him."

"The man you love is dead and you need to come to terms with that," said Carmaz. "I'm Carmaz Korva. I've always been Carmaz Korva and I will die as Carmaz Korva. Sorry to burst your bubble, but that's the truth and you just have to accept it."

"I don't need to accept any 'truth' from you," said Lady Dia. "I just need to find some way to reawaken your memories from your past life. If I can do that, then you will stop saying such foolish things. We could even live together, ruling the golems as we march across Martir and conquer every land we arrive on."

"I don't want to rule with you or anyone else," said Carmaz. "I want you to stop destroying Ruwa and to leave us alone. We have done nothing against you and so you have no case against us."

Lady Dia removed her hands from the bars and stepped back. She looked at Carmaz with disappointment in her eyes before shaking her head and said, "You will remember at some point. Maybe I should help you to remember."

Lady Dia touched her forehead with her left hand. Her hand glowed blue, and then a blue beam of energy shot from her forehead and struck Carmaz in the face. It was like getting punched in the face by a sledgehammer, causing Carmaz to yell in pain, but then he was forced to shut his mouth by the energy itself. It stuck to his own forehead like spider web, forcing him to look at Lady Dia, who with her closed eyes and hand on forehead appeared to be meditating.

But Carmaz didn't see Lady Dia for long. The world he saw

melted away quickly, until soon he was no longer sitting inside the dark, cramped cage. Now he found himself standing in another cave, only this one was much larger and open than the other one.

Carmaz stood on an outcropping overlooking what appeared to be an entire sea of golems, all resting in neat rows. It was an absolutely massive sea, with thousands, perhaps even tens of thousands, of golems spreading out for as far as the eye could see. If Carmaz hadn't noticed the gigantic stone walls on all sides, he would have assumed that he was actually outside somewhere, rather than deep underground, which was where he most likely was.

Then Carmaz heard movement behind him and, looking over his shoulder, he saw Lady Dia walking up to him. She looked pretty much the same as always, except a lot happier and more content, which made Carmaz wonder why she looked that way.

Nonetheless, Carmaz felt a smile appear on his lips, even though he didn't want to smile. And when Lady Dia stood by his side, he actually draped an arm around her shoulders. That was when he realized that he was not in his normal body at all, because the arm draped around Lady Dia's shoulder was made out of a thick, sand-colored rock, like a grotesque mockery of an actual human arm.

"Dia, I am so glad that you are here with me," Carmaz heard himself saying, even though he didn't want to talk. His voice sounded strange, too, much deeper and gravelly. "I thought you were asleep."

Lady Dia shook her head. She was still smiling. "I wanted to see what you were doing. Can't sleep anyway with Stalac's snoring."

Carmaz heard himself chuckle. "Well, I was just looking at our resting siblings and thinking about how much I cared about them and their safety. I sometimes wonder what they dream about, if they dream about anything at all."

"The Powers said that they don't dream about anything," said Lady Dia, looking out over the resting golems as well. "Remember? They said that they do not think or feel and have no reason to dream. They're little more than puppets."

"Maybe, but what if they developed souls on their own?" said Carmaz. "Maybe the Powers made them better than they think. It's impossible to tell. I sometimes wish we could awaken them just to see what they would say."

Lady Dia rested her head on Carmaz's shoulder and sighed. "Oh, Basan, I love your speculations, even if I don't always agree with them. I could listen to you talk forever and ever and never get bored, even if most of it is nonsense."

Carmaz grinned, again despite the fact that he did not want to. "Oh, most of what I say is nonsense, so I think you've already been doing that."

Lady Dia playfully punched him in the side. The punch didn't hurt at all and in fact Carmaz wouldn't have even noticed it if he hadn't seen her do it. "Oh, stop saying that. You're always so hard on yourself."

"Someone has to be," Carmaz said. Then he looked at the golems again. "Maybe one day, when they awaken, I will ask each and every one of them what they dreamed about. That's what I will do."

"That sounds nice," said Lady Dia with another sigh. "You are always so kind and thoughtful, Basan. That's why I love you so."

Carmaz wanted to retch at her sugary words, but unfortunately he was unable to do that. Instead, he said, "And I love you, too, Dia. And I hope that we will always be together no matter what."

Quite abruptly, the entire scene around Carmaz melted away and he gasped for air. Blinking rapidly, Carmaz noticed that he was sitting back in his jail cell again. The stone shackles around his wrists and ankles were still attached and made his wrists and ankles ache, while Lady Dia stood on the other side of the cell bars, lowering her hand from her forehead as she looked up at him.

"What … what was that?" said Carmaz. He was sweating a lot more now than before.

"I shared some of my memories with you," said Lady Dia. "Did it help you remember your original self?"

Panting, Carmaz shook his head. "No. Didn't trigger any memories in me at all. It just freaked me out."

Lady Dia actually looked hurt when he said that. She sighed once more and said, "Perhaps you need more time, then. Time to think about what I showed you. And then maybe you will remember who you are."

Carmaz doubted that he would 'remember' that he had been Basan even if he had a thousand years in which to do it. He did, however, have a few more questions for Lady Dia that he needed answering.

"What are you going to do to me?" said Carmaz. "Are you going to torture me now?"

"No," said Lady Dia. "Of course not. If you are my husband reincarnated, as I suspect, then torturing you would be an unforgivable sin. Instead, I am going to leave you here, where you can think about the memory I shared with you and understand who you really are."

Carmaz opened his mouth to again state that he was not Basan, but before he could say anything, the floor of his cell suddenly shook. And it wasn't just the floor of his cell, either, but the entire cavern, because Lady Dia was trying to maintain her balance as the ground shook under her feet.

"What's that?" said Carmaz. He gulped and looked at the ceiling of his cell, hoping it would not fall in and bury him alive. "An earthquake? On Ruwa?"

"Impossible," said Lady Dia, looking around. "And this most certainly is not the work of one of my golems, but I'm not sure what—"

Abruptly, two green fists broke through the ground several feet behind Lady Dia. Lady Dia whirled around as the hands tore a large hole into the ground, allowing the owner of the hands to pull himself out of the earth and stand on the ground. The ground stopped shaking after he pulled himself out; even so, Lady Dia stepped back until she was up against Carmaz's cell. Carmaz couldn't see her facial expression, but he figured that she had to look absolutely terrified at the short, fat green-skinned man who was now dusting himself off.

"Ah," said the Loner God, grinning at Carmaz and Lady Dia as he dusted off his shoulders. "There you are, Carmaz. I was looking for you. Looks like I'm going to have to save you again, eh?" He chuckled. "Now if I'm not careful, I could make this into a habit."

"How ... how did you get in here?" said Lady Dia. She

171

sounded absolutely terrified of the god, which made sense, because the Loner God was far above her in terms of sheer power. "You're not supposed to be here."

"As a god, I can be wherever I want regardless of what some dumb rock like you says," said the Loner God. "But it doesn't really matter how I got here, because I came here to end your entire invasion by myself. So my last suggestion to you, lady, is that you should curl into a fetal position. Won't actually save your life, of course, but it should make your death a little less painful than it otherwise would be."

Chapter Thirteen

WHEN BRAIM ARRIVED at the Stadium again, this time with the Soldiers assigned to protect him, he swore as soon as he saw all of the other godlings standing outside of it in a large group, along with an even larger number of Soldiers blocking off the streets and sending away anyone who shouldn't be there. Fojak also stood near the destroyed entrance of the Stadium, although Alira was nowhere to be seen.

Braim walked up to Tashir and Malya, who were standing a little away from the rest of the godlings, as his assigned Soldiers went over and started speaking with their fellow Soldiers. Malya waved at him as he approached, while Tashir just looked relieved to see him again.

"What's going on?" said Braim, glancing at the Stadium entrance, where several Soldiers entered. "Another attack?"

"Yes," said Malya, nodding. "The good news is that Raya got the Staff of Teleportation and thus won the Hollech Bracket. The bad news is that a golem appeared in the room where the Staff was kept and is now alone in there with both Raya and Yoji."

"Dammit," said Braim, rubbing his forehead in frustration. "Why haven't any of the gods gone in there and saved them?"

"The ethereal is closed off and a spell is preventing them from teleporting inside and saving them," Tashir said. He sounded even more worried than Malya, especially when he glanced at the Stadium. "Alira ordered the Soldiers to evacuate us from the building so we would be safe from any other golems that might try to attack."

"How much luck have they been having?" said Braim.

"Not much, I am afraid," said Tashir. "Nor have we heard from either Raya or Yoji. They might not even be alive anymore, but we don't know for sure. The Soldiers are trying to rescue them and Alira is supervising the rescue attempt."

"Is there anything any of us can do to help?" said Braim. "Anything at all?"

"They told us to stay outside and not get involved because we could be killed," said Malya. She folded her arms across her chest in worry. "Oh, I hope Raya is all right. You know how delicate she is. I don't even want to think about what that golem will do to her."

"She has Yoji to protect her," said Tashir. Then he looked at Braim. "Braim, you were just attacked by a golem earlier, were you not? What would you say are the chances that Yoji can defeat it?"

Braim remembered how the Void-controlled golem had been about to kill him before Fojak teleported it away in pieces and frowned. "Unless he gets divine help, very low, I'm afraid, especially if it's controlled by the Void."

"That's just awful," said Malya. "I never expected this to happen so quickly. I thought that World's End was the only island in the world that was truly safe from the threat of the golems, but if they can send two of their own here, right now, without anyone noticing until it's too late, then are any of us truly safe?"

"No," said Tashir, shaking his head. "And unfortunately there's not much we can do about it except hope that the Soldiers, the gods, and Alira manage to rescue them. I only wish I knew how likely that was."

Braim nodded and looked around at the other godlings. Most of them were standing around talking among themselves, although a handful had bowed their heads in prayer. A handful of Soldiers patrolled the edges of the group, probably to make sure that all of the godlings were where they were supposed to be. Although Braim knew that the Soldiers had only their best interests at heart, he nonetheless felt a little disturbed whenever he saw them walking around the group, looking almost like prison guards in a way.

Then Braim looked at the Stadium. He remembered what Atikos had told him earlier, about how he had divine power flowing within him now. He could still feel it burning in his soul, slowly killing him just as Atikos said it was. He still didn't know how to control the energy completely, but because he already had some experience with it, he figured that he had some control over it.

Maybe I can help save them, Braim thought. *Might as well try, seeing as I don't have much longer to live anyway.*

So Braim said to Tashir and Malya, "Stay here," and then walked away from the group toward the Stadium entrance, where Fojak was standing by himself.

But when Braim got only a few feet away from the group, a nearby Soldier shouted, "Hey!" and stepped in his path. This

Soldier carried a crystalline sword in both hands, his steely eyes looking at Braim through the holes of his helmet.

"Go back and stand with the rest of the godlings," said the Soldier, his tone firm. "Lord Fojak ordered all godlings to remain together and in one place until the golem is dealt with and the hostages freed."

Although Braim was unarmed, he didn't fear the sword-bearing Soldier very much. He met the Soldier's steely gaze and said, "I don't care what Fojak said. Two of my friends are in there and may or may not already be dead. I'm going to go help them whether you want me to or not."

The Soldier, however, did not move an inch from where he stood. "No. Go back to the group or else."

Braim sighed. "Listen, bub, I'm not in the mood to argue. Get out of my way."

"Or what?" said the Soldier. "You will attack me? I know who you are. You are Braim Kotogs and you lack magic. If you tried to attack me, you'd—"

Braim interrupted the Soldier by shoving him to the side hard. Although Braim had been intending to knock the Soldier over, even he was surprised at how much strength he put into the blow. The force of the shove knocked the Soldier flat off his feet, even causing him to drop his sword clattering to the street, a stunned expression on his face.

But Braim didn't stand around to see if the Soldier was okay. He just walked up to Fojak, who looked up when Braim approached. The god's face didn't look as bloody or bruised as Braim remembered it being after the first golem attack, although that did not make him look any friendlier, especially when he scowled.

"Braim Kotogs, what are you doing here?" said Fojak, not bothering to hide the annoyance in his voice. He pointed back at the others. "Go back and stand with the rest of the godlings. It is too dangerous for you to be anywhere near here, especially after what you have just been through."

Braim stopped before Fojak and shook his head. "No. I want to help. Raya and Yoji are my friends and I don't want to abandon them."

"How do you intend to get in there and help them when even I cannot?" said Fojak. He glanced over his shoulder at the interior of the Stadium with a scowl. "If it hadn't been for whatever spell the Void has cast, I would have teleported in and gotten them out already."

"I can still do it if you'd let me," Braim said. "I *want* to help. I'm in a better position to help than any of the other godlings are."

Fojak looked at Braim again. His features twisted with anger and he pointed again at the rest of the godlings. "How many times must I tell you to go back with the others before you finally listen?"

"Why don't we find out?" said Braim, folding his arms across his chest and planting his feet. He stared defiantly up at the god, meeting Fojak's harsh gaze.

The two stared each other down for what felt like an eternity before Fojak looked away. He sighed. "Fine. You may go in and see how you can help. I don't expect you to be able to do much, however, because—"

Fojak was interrupted by a series of popping sounds that echoed off the buildings all around them. Braim at first thought that the popping sounds were guns being fired before he realized that there were no guns in the area.

Then he spotted ethereal portals opening all around them, at least a dozen, and from within these portals came massive golems, all armed to the teeth with swords, spears, hammers, and any other weapons they could carry. The sudden appearance of so many golems at once caused some of the other godlings to shout in fear, while the Soldiers of the Gods protecting them quickly formed a loose but secure circle around the remaining godlings, their weapons pointed at the golems that were now on all sides and blocking off every street exit.

"What the hell?" said Fojak, looking around at the golems in shock. "Where did all of these golems come from?"

"No idea," said Braim, also looking around at them all. "But I am pretty sure that it doesn't matter because they are going to slaughter us all anyway."

"No, they won't," said Fojak. "At least they won't get the godlings, anyway."

Fojak thrust his fist toward the godlings. As one, they all vanished into thin air, except for Braim, who was now the only godling still in the area.

"Where'd you teleport them to?" said Braim.

"To the Temple," said Fojak. "They will be safe there. In the mean time, we must destroy these golems before they can cause any serious damage to the city."

"But why didn't you send me away, too?" said Braim, putting his hands on his chest. "Not that I'm complaining, but I was just curious."

"Because we will need every bit of help we can get if we are going to stop these golems and you've already offered to help," said Fojak. "Do you have a weapon?"

Braim shook his head. "No, I don't."

Fojak sighed and then pulled out a sword from behind his back. It was a long black blade that looked wickedly sharp. He then handed it to Braim and said, "Take this. It is a powerful blade, one that I don't usually entrust to mortals, but if you are going to fight, then you will need it."

Braim took the sword, which felt heavy but perfectly natural in his hands. "What's it called?"

"Devourer," said Fojak. "It is one of two swords I use. It can cut through stone and channel divine energy. Should be useful against the golems."

Before Braim could ask any more questions about Devourer, Fojak drew another blade, this one white as snow, from his back and held it in both hands. "Now, we must fight."

He then shouted to the rest of the Soldiers, "Show these golems what happens to those who invade the Throne of the Gods!"

The Soldiers all cheered in unison and ran to battle the golems.

The golems—which had briefly paused their march when they saw the godlings vanish—resumed advancing toward the Stadium. They did not get far, however, before the Soldiers were upon them, running around their legs and slashing at their ankles and thighs. Unfortunately, the Soldiers' blades did little to harm the golems, who began swatting them aside like they were nothing more than minor annoyances.

Fojak teleported before a particularly large golem, which

raised its hammer to squash him. But then he slashed the golem's ankle with his sword, cutting straight through it like butter. As Fojak's sword cut through the golem's leg, the golem's leg vanished, causing the golem to stagger around before it fell on its side with a loud *crunch*. And before the golem could do anything else, Fojak slashed it several times in multiple places, each hit causing more and more of its parts to vanish into thin air until soon all that was left of the golem was its head, which Fojak then crushed under foot with one powerful stomp of his boot.

Seeing Fojak destroy that golem was quite satisfying to Braim, but then he heard a golem to his right and looked over to see a golem approaching him. He raised Devourer and charged at the golem, even though the golem was twice his size and more than capable of squashing him like a bug.

The golem raised its sword and brought it down on Braim as he approached. But Braim jumped out of the way just in the nick of time, allowing the golem's own sword to smash into the street. Braim then jumped forward and slashed at the golem's leg, but his blade, unlike Fojak's, only left a minor cut rather than cutting straight through it.

So Braim had to run away out of the golem's reach in order to rethink his plan of attack. The golem, meanwhile, raised its sword again and turned to face him.

Why did Fojak give me a useless sword? Braim thought, walking backwards as he held Devourer before him. *Does he want me to die or something?*

Before Braim could do much else, a huge fire erupted between him and the golem. Braim started as the fire disappeared, leaving Grinf, the God of Fire, Justice, and Metal, in its place in his full golden armor and glory.

"Grinf?" said Braim. "What are you—"

Braim was interrupted by the sudden appearances of several other gods, whose entrances weren't quite as flashy as Grinf's. They all appeared in the spot where the godlings had been standing before they had been teleported away before immediately dispersing, each god going to take down a different golem. The few Soldiers of the Gods left cheered the appearance of so many gods, which seemed to renew their morale, because they then started fighting harder than ever against the invading golems.

"We came as soon as we got word that the golems were invading," said Grinf, looking over his shoulder at Braim. "We will not let others fight for us, not when this threat is at our doorstep."

"That's great," said Braim. "But what am I supposed to do?"

"Stay alive," said Grinf.

He turned to face the golem, which was advancing toward him, and then flew toward it with his gavel's head out. Grinf swung his gavel back and slammed it into the face of the golem, crushing the golem's face and sending the golem staggering backwards. Grinf, however, did not give it time to react, instead pounding away at it with vicious blows from his gavel.

Braim looked around at the battle raging on all around him. The gods were busy with fighting and destroying the golems and did not look like they needed his help. Yes, the golems were actually holding their own against the gods fairly well, but it was clear to Braim that the gods were going to win this battle even if Braim did nothing to help.

Then what should *I do?* Braim thought, feeling disgruntled. *And 'staying alive' isn't really 'doing' something, if you ask me.*

Then Braim realized that there was no one in the Stadium, except for Alira, and that this was the perfect opportunity to try to help save Raya and Yoji. He looked around to make sure that none of the gods were near enough to stop him and then he ran into the Stadium, Devourer at his side, hoping that he was not too late to rescue his friends.

Chapter Fourteen

THE GOLEM DID not have eyes. That was probably the most disturbing thing about it to Raya. Instead, it had a single slit in its face where the eyes should have gone, from which a green light glowed. It was impossible to tell what the golem was thinking, because it didn't have any facial expressions, but that did not make it any less terrifying to Raya.

"We can deal with it," said Yoji. He was sweating and looked even more terrified than her, but he held out his wand like a sword. "Nothing to be afraid of. Just a big, lumbering rock creature."

"You haven't seen them before, though," said Raya, shaking her head. "They're huge. And they can't be killed easily, either."

"How do you know?" said Yoji, looking at Raya in annoyance. "Anyway, it's not like we can just run and hide. There's nowhere to run to or hide. Let me deal with it."

"All right," said Raya, though she was anxious about Yoji's safety anyway. "But please be quick about it. I don't want to take any chances with this thing."

Yoji nodded and looked at the golem again. The golem hadn't moved from where it had appeared, but now it seemed to be ready to attack, because it started to advance toward her and Yoji at a slow pace. Every step sent minor tremors through the floor, although they were thankfully not strong enough to knock Raya or Yoji over.

"All right, you dumb rock," said Yoji. "Why don't you take a bath?"

Yoji thrust his wand forward and a burst of water shot out of it and struck the golem in the chest. It looked like a devastating hit, but the golem kept advancing like it hadn't been hit at all. In fact, Raya thought that the golem looked more annoyed than anything, even though it had no real facial expressions to speak of. That meant it was probably just her imagination thinking that. Even so, the fact that the golem was still coming toward them made her feel more than a little panicky.

"Not to fear," said Yoji. "That is not the only trick I have up my sleeve. Observe."

Yoji slashed his wand down, sending what looked like a slash of green energy flying through the air toward the golem. The energy slash struck the golem dead on, actually cutting into its rock hard skin, but the golem still kept advancing. Raya was starting to think that this golem was incapable of even feeling pain, which would certainly explain a lot.

"That was an energy slash," Yoji explained to a rather exasperated Raya. "Very difficult to do, one of my best attacks, but—"

"But clearly *useless*," Raya finished for him. "Come on, don't you know some geomancy or something? Can't you make it fall apart, maybe?"

Yoji shook his head. "No. Geomancy has never interested me.

It always seemed like a pointless magical discipline to learn, so I never learned more than the basics. Geomancers tend to not be very bright."

"What other spells do you have that could possibly stop or destroy the golem?" Raya asked.

"Let's try this," said Yoji.

Once more, he thrust his wand at the golem. Immediately, thick ice formed around its feet, causing the golem to stop its progress toward them. The golem looked down at its feet and tugged at them, but the ice was too thick around them for it to break free.

"Amazing," said Raya. She looked at Yoji and smiled. "Oh, Yoji, I am sorry for doubting you. I promise you that, when I become the Goddess of Thieves, Deception, and Horses, that I—"

Raya was interrupted by the sound of ice shattering. She looked back at the golem, which had successfully managed to break free from the ice around its feet, and was now walking toward them again, except this time at a faster pace than Raya thought possible for a creature of its size and weight. If Raya hadn't known any better, she would have thought that the golem was angry at them now.

Yoji whipped out his wand again, but before he could cast another spell, the golem threw its sword at them. The sword flew through the air like an arrow, heading straight for them. Yoji and Raya separated right before the sword struck the floor, its blade sinking into the marble and sending up chunks of the floor around it into the air.

Raya, still clutching the Staff, ran until she was as far away from the sword as she could be. Then she stopped and looked at it and saw Yoji standing on the other side of the blade, looking freaked out by that sudden attack.

The golem, on the other hand, had not halted its advance at all. It had simply changed its direction and was now walking toward Raya even faster than before, meaning that it would be upon her within seconds.

Yoji immediately started shooting lightning and fire bolts at the golem's back, but the golem didn't seem to notice his assault at all. Its focus was entirely on Raya, causing her to back up as quickly as she could until she was right up against the wall and had nowhere else to go.

The golem reared back its fist and swung it directly at Raya. Raya yelped and jumped to the side just as the fist crashed into the wall. Raya, however, did not jump well, and ended up stumbling across her own feet, almost tripping. As a result, she could not dodge the golem's next attack, which sent its fist flying toward her body.

All Raya could do was brace for the impact. When the fist slammed into her, it sent her flying. She landed hard on the marble floor, almost cracking her skull open on the floor, and lay there, her whole body wracked with pain that she had not felt since losing her hand. Her chest in particular was aching, as it had taken the brunt of the attack, the pain making it almost impossible to think clearly.

"Raya!"

The next thing Raya knew, Yoji was kneeling by her side. He grabbed her head and forced her to look at his boyish features, the light from the ceiling reflecting off his bald head.

"Raya, are you all right?" said Yoji. "Raya, can you still talk?

186

Tell me where it hurts and I'll do my best to heal it."

Raya couldn't speak. She just shook her head and moaned, gesturing at her chest, but she was really trying to communicate that it felt like every bone in her body was broken.

"Your chest?" said Yoji. "All right, I'll deal with that. Just give me a moment to—"

At that moment, the golem suddenly appeared behind Yoji and Raya. Raya wasn't sure how neither she nor Yoji had heard it, but she pointed up at it anyway, causing Yoji to look over his shoulder and say, "How the hell did that thing sneak up on—"

The golem simply grabbed Yoji in one of its massive hands and threw him across the room. Raya watched in horror as Yoji flew through the air and struck the wall on the opposite side of the room, which he then slid off. His impact had left a splatter of blood on the wall, the red liquid visible even from Raya's position, while Yoji himself did not so much as stir where he lay.

"Yoji!" Raya shouted, although shouting that word hurt her lungs, which seemed to have been damaged from the golem's attack. "Yoji, no!"

The golem, which seemed satisfied with what it had done to Yoji, then bent over and grabbed Raya. It lifted Raya off the ground until it stood upright again. Raya struggled weakly against its grip, but the golem didn't even seem to be trying to hold her. It just looked at her with its blank expression, making it impossible to tell what it was thinking.

"Let me go," said Raya. She punched its hand with one of her fists. "Let ... me ... go ..."

The golem simply stared at her and then started to squeeze. Raya gasped, but she couldn't scream because the golem gripped

187

her so tightly that all of the air had been pushed out of her lungs. The golem was trying to squeeze her to death, but there was nothing she could do about it.

This ... is ... the end, Raya thought, her vision turning blacker and black as the golem tightened its grip. *And just when I fulfilled my destiny ...*

Then, out of nowhere, a loud, familiar voice shouted, "Unhand her, you monster!"

A blast of white energy hurtled out of nowhere and struck the golem's arm. The golem actually dropped Raya, like it had been hurt, and Raya fell to the floor where she landed with a *thud*. Air suddenly returned to Raya's lungs as she gasped for breath, although she still felt too weak to get up and run.

The golem looked to the right, like it was wondering who had attacked it, and then another blast of white energy struck it in the face. The blow sent the golem staggering backwards and a second later Alira was at Raya's side, bending over her with a concerned expression in her eyes.

"Raya, are you all right?" said Alira. "I got here as fast as I could. Can you still hear me?"

Raya blinked, which was about all she could do at the moment. Although she did have enough strength to nod to show that she could indeed hear Alira.

"Oh thank the gods," said Alira with a sigh. "I thought I was going to be too late."

Then Alira stood up and glared at the golem. Raya also looked at the golem and saw that it had recovered from Alira's surprise attack and was coming toward them again.

"Let me destroy this monstrosity," said Alira. "I will then get you and Yoji to the nearest healer."

With that, Alira ran up to the golem and, raising her hands, fired more energy blasts from her hands at it. The blasts struck the golem head on, but unlike Yoji's spells, they actually seemed to be hurting the golem, causing it to stagger from the blows. Nonetheless, it continued forward, looking ready to smash Alira into pieces like it had beaten Yoji.

Raya tried to sit up, but the pain from the golem's squeeze on her body made it impossible. So she lay there, watching as Alira unleashed energy blast after energy blast at the golem, which could not get close enough to smash Alira with its fists. It tried to hit her, but Alira kept out of its range, forcing the golem to stay on the defensive. Chunks of its stone skin got blasted off, which gave Raya hope that the golem might get destroyed after all.

But then the golem stopped defending against Alira's attacks. It raised its right fist and aimed it at Alira, ignoring her energy blasts, which endlessly struck it. Alira didn't seem to care, probably because the golem's lack of active defense made it easier for her to attack it.

Then the golem's fist exploded off of its arm and hurtled toward Alira. Alira only had enough time to see the incoming fist before it struck her head on, sending her flying through the air. Alira crashed onto the floor, rolling across the ground until she came to a stop on the other side of the room, where she lay as still as death.

Raya gasped, but there was nothing she could to help. Still, she managed to gather enough strength to stand up, although she had to lean on the Staff in order to avoid falling back down. She looked at the golem, which lowered its empty arm and stared at

Alira's prone body for a moment before looking back at Raya again.

And then, as before, the golem advanced toward Raya. It had returned to its original pace, like it believed that there was nothing else to stop it from killing her. Raya tried to walk away, but even with the Staff for support, Raya found it impossible to move more than a couple of steps. Her body was still in extreme pain from being crushed in the golem's hand earlier, which made every step hurt.

Can't run, Raya thought. *Looks like I have no choice but to fight.*

Raya turned to face the golem, even though she knew that there was no way in hell that she could ever hope to defeat it. She was too weak, too small, and the golem too big. It was even worse knowing that both Yoji and Alira were likely dead trying to defend her, but she stood anyway, ready to fight.

"Come on, you stupid boulder," said Raya, though her voice was too weak to intimidate the golem. "Come and fight me. Or are you afraid of a girl like me?"

The golem, of course, did not answer. It merely continued to stomp over to her, its focus never wavering.

No way I can beat it in a straight fight, Raya thought. *Even if I wasn't wounded as badly as I was, I still wouldn't be able to fight it. The golem will destroy me unless ... unless I use the Staff.*

Raya looked at the Staff of Teleportation, which provided her sole support. She didn't know how it worked, but if this had belonged to Fojak, then that meant that it probably had magical powers all its own. And if Raya could simply access those powers, then she might stand a chance of escaping alive.

190

Unfortunately, Raya didn't know *how* to access the Staff's powers. She knew very little about Fojak and his abilities or how they worked, as she had been raised to worship Grinf and none of the other gods. Still, Raya was desperate enough at this point to try anything, so she gripped the Staff even tighter than before and focused on connecting with its divine energy so she could use it to get herself, Yoji, and Alira out of here alive.

Please, Fojak, let me use your Staff, Raya prayed silently, even though she wasn't sure that Fojak could even hear her at the moment. *I may have never been a follower of you, but I need your power in order to get me and my friends out of here alive. Please grant it to me, even just for this moment.*

Raya looked up and saw that the golem was still walking toward her. In only a few seconds, Raya knew, the golem would be upon her and then she would die. She closed her eyes anyway, however, and focused on accessing the Staff's power. She imagined using its power to escape, to teleport away, to teleport anywhere at all. She focused on teleporting to the Temple of the Gods, which seemed like the safest place to be at the moment.

Soon, however, the golem stood above her and raised both fists above its head. Together, its two fists were twice as thick as Raya's body, if not thicker. Raya had no doubt that those fists would completely crush her, so she closed her eyes so she wouldn't have to see her death coming toward her.

Just as she did that, however, Raya felt a sudden spike in energy that she had not expected to feel. She opened her eyes and was surprised to see three energy tendrils rising from the Staff. They glowed a golden color and extended all over the room. One of them touched Raya's head, while the other two went over to the

191

prone forms of Alira and Yoji.

Even the golem looked surprised by this sudden turn of events, because it had not yet brought its fists down upon Raya's head. But then the golem shook its head, like it was clearing its thoughts, and then brought its fists smashing down on Raya at a frightening speed.

But the fists never hit Raya, because in an instant the entire chamber vanished from around her. In another instant, Raya landed on a sandy floor, collapsing the minute her feet touched it. She had tried to lean on the Staff, but the teleportation had taken even more energy out of her than she had already lost, which made it impossible for her to stand.

Then Raya heard someone say, "Raya? Alira? Yoji?"

Raya looked up and saw that she was not alone. Samvan stood before her, as did the other godlings in the Tournament, who were all staring at her, Alira, and Yoji in shock. As for Alira and Yoji, the two of them were still out cold, lying as still as stones, but Raya could not tell whether or not the two of them were even still alive.

"Please ..." said Raya, her voice weak, reaching up to Samvan. "Help ... Alira and Yoji. They're harmed even worse than I am."

Unfortunately, the godlings all looked too confused to help, which made Raya despair that her teleportation had been for nothing at all.

But then an elderly female voice called out, "Make way. Let me see them. Move!"

The godlings parted to allow an elderly-looking woman to approach. Raya had never seen this woman before, but she didn't care because the woman seemed to know what she was doing. The elderly woman came to Raya first and, bending over, said, "Raya, what happened?"

"Golem … attacked," said Raya. "Almost killed us. Used the Staff to escape."

"I see," said the woman. "Yes, that fits with Fojak's warning about the golem attack outside the Stadium."

"Please heal them," said Raya, who didn't really understand what the woman meant about some golem attack outside the Stadium. She gestured weakly at Alira and Yoji. "I don't think they're going to make it."

"Yes, yes, I will heal them, Raya, I will," said the woman. "But you need to be healed yourself first. I will cast you into a deep sleep for a little while, okay? It will be easier for your body to heal if you are unconscious."

Raya didn't see any reason to argue with that, so she nodded weakly to show that she agreed.

"Very well," said the woman.

The woman waved her hand over Raya's head and Raya drifted into sleep immediately.

Chapter Fifteen

S O THIS IS your lair, huh?" said the Loner God, looking around the cavern with an unimpressed expression on his face. "I've seen better."

"Guards!" Lady Dia cried, pointing at the Loner God. "Kill the god before he kills me!"

As soon as the words left Lady Dia's lips, two huge golems stepped into view, both carrying massive stone hammers that looked more than capable of turning a normal person into mush. The Loner God noticed their approach with annoyance and sighed.

"*More* dumb rocks?" said the Loner God. "I've already crushed several of them, but I guess I can't expect anything better from a bunch of golems."

The Loner God jumped toward the nearest golem guard. He landed on its head, but as soon as he did, the second golem guard brought its hammer down on the head of its brother. At the last second, the Loner God hopped off and the guard's hammer smashed the head of its ally into pieces. The first golem guard fell backwards onto the floor, while the second golem guard looked around for the Loner God, who had seemingly vanished.

Then the Loner God appeared on the golem guard's back and smashed in the back of its head with his fist. The golem guard collapsed immediately, while the Loner God jumped off with a smirk on his face. Landing exactly where he had been standing when he attacked the golems, the Loner God crossed his arms over his chest and looked at Lady Dia with a satisfied smirk.

"Now, lady, why don't you let the human go?" said the Loner God. "I don't really care for him, to be honest, but since he's here anyway, I might as well save him while I also save Martir from you and your minions."

"How … how did you get here?" said Lady Dia. She sounded close to panicking. "No one is supposed to be able to get into here without my permission or knowledge."

"As I said, I am a god, and gods can generally do whatever they want," said the Loner God. "How many times must I explain that concept before it drills through your thick skull?"

"Why are you here?" said Lady Dia. "To save Carmaz?"

"No," said the Loner God, shaking his head. "The Hermit told me that this was where the invasion started. I decided that destroying this place would end the invasion or at least slow down its progress long enough for my brothers and sisters to get their act together and come up with a more permanent way of dealing with you stupid rocks."

"But the Void-controlled golems that we sent after you," said Lady Dia. "They should have destroyed you or at least prevented you from getting here."

"They were tough, yeah, but I dealt with them easily enough," said the Loner God, waving off that thought like it was irrelevant to the current situation. "I mean, sure, I didn't see an alliance between you and the Void coming, but—"

"Hold on," said Carmaz, looking at Lady Dia. "You mean to tell me that you golems are working with the Void, too? Why?"

"Because she knows that the golems aren't strong enough to kill we gods on their own," said the Loner God, before Lady Dia could respond. He chuckled. "But I probably should have seen it coming, because the Void is pretty much the only thing in Martir that can give us gods a real challenge if we're not careful. Still, Void-controlled golems are not really that much more difficult than normal ones, if you ask me."

"How is the Hermit?" said Carmaz. "And Frissa and Herune?"

"They're all fine," said the Loner God. "Hiding in fear of their lives, but alive. I told them to stay put where they are because I didn't want them getting in the way of my destroying this place."

Carmaz breathed a sigh of relief, while Lady Dia gulped and said, "So you are not going to spare me or the lives of my fellow golems, then."

"Of course not," said the Loner God. "This is war, and in war, you don't stop fighting until you destroy every last enemy on the battlefield. I am going to turn you and your followers into dust."

Lady Dia suddenly no longer looked quite as terrified as she had before. She stood up to her full height, with her wings out, and then said, "Very well. I will fight you myself, since it is clear that none of my men are strong enough to destroy you."

"That's pretty cute," said the Loner God with another chuckle. "Pretending you are strong enough to destroy me … if I wasn't in such a bad mood today, I might be willing to laugh at your arrogance."

Carmaz didn't understand where Lady Dia's sudden courage

came from until he spotted Stalac sneaking up behind the Loner God. The golem general's tail was glowing with suppressed ice energy, which helped Carmaz understand what was about to happen.

"Loner God!" Carmaz shouted. "Behind you!"

The Loner God looked over his shoulder, while at the same time Stalac unleashed a beam of ice at the Loner God. The ice bream struck the Loner God in the back, immediately coating him in a thick layer of ice, but Stalac didn't let up. He kept pouring more and more ice energy onto the Loner God, creating a larger and larger ice dome around the Loner God until soon the god was completely lost in the thickest and coldest dome of ice that Carmaz had ever seen in his life.

Then Stalac stopped shooting the ice from his tail. He walked around the ice dome, a satisfied smirk on his face, as he looked at the Loner God's new prison.

Then he looked at Lady Dia. "My lady, are you all right?"

Lady Dia nodded. "Yes. The god did not harm me, although he did frighten me. But I think I will be okay."

"Good," said Stalac. "I was worried that he might have harmed you in some way, but I see that I got here in the nick of time. What a re—"

Without any warning at all, the Loner God's ice prison suddenly exploded, sending chunks of ice flying all around the room. Stalac and Lady Dia had to duck to avoid getting hit. Carmaz fell to the ground as well, but mostly out of habit, as the stone bars that held him in his cell blocked most of the ice chunks. Still, a few bits of ice got through the gaps between the bars and slid across the floor to Carmaz's feet.

Then Carmaz looked up and saw the Loner God standing where he had always stood, but now looking far angrier. Chips of ice lay on his shoulders, while his grassy hair was covered in icicles, although he hardly seemed to notice that as he marched up to Stalac, who was now cowering in fear before the Loner God.

"You little shit," said the Loner God, the anger in his voice even more obvious than the anger on his face. "Did you really think that freezing me would work?"

Stalac didn't answer. He just tried to jab the Loner God with his stinger tail, but the Loner God caught Stalac's tail and snapped it off easily. Stalac let out a howl of pain, but his howl was cut off by the Loner God smashing in his jaw. Then the Loner God literally punched a fist through Stalac's chest and, pulling his fist out, pushed Stalac over. Stalac fell onto the floor with a small *thud* and did not move again. He was clearly dead.

"Stalac!" Lady Dia shouted. "No!"

Lady Dia did not get a chance to do much else, however, because the Loner God was suddenly in front of her. He grabbed her by the neck and lifted her off the earth, his red eyes blazing with anger. He tightened his grip around Lady Dia's neck, making audible cracking sounds from his fingers as the golem struggled to break free of his grasp.

"I am done playing with you golems," said the Loner God, venom and hatred in his voice. "Good bye."

With a final, ringing *crack*, Lady Dia went limp in the Loner God's hands. He then dropped her at his feet. She landed on her back, but her head and face were pointing toward Carmaz. She, too, was dead, but the expression of terror on her face made her look almost alive. For some reason it bothered Carmaz, even though he was happy that Lady Dia was dead. Maybe it had to do with the way she had died: alone and afraid, at the hands of an angry and violent god.

In any case, Carmaz looked up at the Loner God, who was now walking toward him like nothing out of the ordinary had just happened.

"Well, I'm not sure if killing their leaders will do the trick, but I'm pretty sure that that is going to seriously mess up their invasion plans," said the Loner God. "I can't wait to see the looks on the other gods' faces when they see what I did. I singlehandedly ended the invasion all by myself, just as I said I would."

Once he was in front of Carmaz's cell, the Loner God reached up and ripped the door of the cell off its hinges. He hurled it away and then jumped into the cell, where he walked over to Carmaz and broke his stone shackles with two swift taps of his powerful hands. Carmaz rubbed his wrists and ankles when his shackles fell off, because they were quite sore.

Looking up at the Loner God, Carmaz said, "I don't know how to thank you for everything you just did."

"Don't," the Loner God said, holding up one finger. "Unlike my insecure northern siblings, I don't need your praise and gratitude. It is enough that the golems are no longer a threat to Martir."

"But I still must thank you," said Carmaz. "I mean, maybe I was wrong about the gods. Maybe you aren't as bad as I thought."

"Nah, my siblings are twice as dumb as you think they are, although I am pretty great myself, I agree," said the Loner God, nodding. "Anyway, I'm going to go and kill as many golems as I can find now, so—"

A sudden, sharp decrease in temperature caused the Loner God to shut up. He looked around suddenly, like he had heard something that Carmaz had not.

"What's the matter?" said Carmaz. He shivered. "Why did the temperature drop?"

"Not sure," said the Loner God. "But it feels familiar. Too familiar."

Then, beyond the bars of the cell, Carmaz saw the blackest darkness he had ever seen in his life moving toward them. It flowed as rapidly and naturally as water bursting from a dam, until it washed over the corpses of both Stalac and Lady Dia. The Loner God whirled around to face it, but then a black tendril shot out of the darkness toward him. The Loner God managed to deflect it, however, and the tendril returned to the darkness.

But the darkness did not retreat. It came up to the very edge of the cell, but did not actually enter the cell itself. Still, Carmaz could feel the coldness emanating from the darkness like a powerful gust of wind. And it was in that moment that he recognized the darkness for what it was: The Void. And it was going to kill them both.

Chapter Sixteen

UPON ENTERING THE Stadium lobby, Braim saw several
Soldiers of the Gods running toward him. Before Braim
could ask them where they were going, the Soldiers
dashed past him and out of the Stadium to the battle between the
gods and the golems in the streets, which was sounding louder
and more dangerous than before, as if more golems had arrived
(which was probably the case, as Braim had heard several *pops*
from other ethereal portals when he ran into the Stadium).

Even so, Braim didn't know why the Soldiers were running
out into the streets when Raya and Yoji were still stuck in the
Stadium. He was just about to yell at them to come back when a
voice behind him said, "Braim Kotogs, what are you doing here?"

Braim turned around to see Captain Garvan running toward
him. The katabans looked tired as he approached Braim, yet
Braim could tell that the captain was still ready to lead his men
into battle regardless of how worn out he might be personally.

Stopping before Braim, Captain Garvan looked Braim over in
confusion. "You should be with the rest of the godlings, not here
in the middle of the battlefield."

"It's fine," said Braim. "Fojak said I could stay and fight the golems alongside the gods."

Garvan shook his head. "Sometimes I don't understand what the gods are thinking, but I suppose it isn't any of my business. In any case, you need to come with us out of here, and right away."

"Why?" said Braim. He pointed toward the entrance to the Stadium's field. "Aren't Raya and Yoji still trapped in there?"

"Not anymore," said Garvan. "We received a gray ghost a minute ago from Atikos. She said that Raya, Yoji, and Alira used the Staff of Teleportation to teleport to the Temple, where they are currently being healed."

"So they're safe?" said Braim. He sighed in relief. "Thank the gods. I was really worried about them for a while there."

"Atikos has confirmed they are safe," said Garvan. "That is why my men and I were running into battle. We wanted to go help the gods fighting the golems outside."

"Then I guess I'll join you," said Braim as he rested Devourer on his shoulder. "Ready?"

"Always," said Garvan as he held his own crystalline sword up.

Garvan ran past Braim toward the exit. Braim turned to run after him, but then he suddenly sensed a powerful spike of energy in the room. He paused and looked around, wondering if perhaps one of the gods had entered, but when he didn't see anyone in the ruined lobby except for himself and Garvan, Braim figured he had simply mistaken the power of the gods outside for being in here.

So Braim was about to run again, but then he felt that energy spike again and had to stop. Garvan must have noticed it as well, because he also came to a stop about halfway to the exit and looked around the lobby like he was trying to locate the source of some annoying sound.

"Do you feel that?" said Braim, looking at Garvan in confusion. "That energy?"

"Yes …" said Garvan. "It feels like the power of four gods combined, but that doesn't make any—"

Without warning, Tamra appeared behind Garvan. The Captain of the Soldiers whirled around, swinging his sword at her neck, but Tamra jabbed her wand into his mouth and twisted it.

Garvan suddenly froze. Literally. His skin turned blue, his clothes became icy, and his armor became shinier than normal. His crystalline sword stopped an inch from Tamra's neck, but Tamra didn't look bothered by that at all. With a vile smirk on her face, she pushed Garvan forward. The frozen katabans fell onto the floor and shattered into a million pieces upon impact.

"Garvan!" Braim shouted in horror.

"What a silly little katabans," said Tamra, shaking her head. "I will give him credit, though, for at least trying to take my head off my shoulders. He would have been a fine Soldier under my rule, but I guess he was too loyal to the gods to even think about sparing me."

"Tamra, what are you even doing here?" said Braim. He pointed Devourer at her. "I thought you had left World's End."

"You mean you really haven't figured it out?" said Tamra. She laughed. "I'm working with the golems now. I came here to provide them with some support, seeing as the gods are still far more powerful than the golems. But that doesn't mean I can't take a few moments to kill my favorite person in the whole world: You."

Braim gritted his teeth, but then noticed the stump where

Tamra's right arm used to be, and smiled. "Still haven't healed your arm, eh?"

Tamra scowled and looked at her stump. "I'm not very good at panamancy, and even if I was, the rebound permanently affected my arm in a way that even divine energy can't heal. But it isn't really as bad as it looks. I am still far more powerful than anyone else and am still in line to become the Goddess of Martir, as is my rightful destiny."

Although Tamra sounded as arrogant as usual, there was something about her appearance that seemed off to Braim. Her skin was slightly grayer, her veins were more visible, and she seemed to sweat more. Maybe it was just the stress of recent events was getting to her, or maybe there was something else affecting her.

Whatever the case, Braim said, "Not unless I stop you."

"Stop me? How?" said Tamra with a laugh. "You are just a normal mortal, even if you did come back to life. I don't even want to fight you, not even to get revenge for what you did to my arm, because killing a mortal like you would just have no sport to it at all."

"I'm not just an ordinary mortal anymore," Braim said. Devourer glowed in his hands as he channeled divine energy through it. "I have divine energy flowing through me, divine energy which will give me enough strength to stop you for good."

"Where did you get *that* from?" said Tamra, sounding genuinely surprised. "The Tournament isn't even over yet."

"Doesn't matter where I got it," said Braim, shaking his head. "What matters is that I am going to use it to stop you."

"You can believe what you like, but that doesn't change the

fact that I am still far more powerful than you will ever be," said Tamra. "After all, I have the souls of four gods coursing through my veins. You aren't even a god, despite your power. So why don't you just give up? If you do, I might keep you as a pet when I become the Goddess of Martir."

Braim shook his head. "Nah. I'd rather die free than live as your slave. Not like I have much time left on this world anyway."

"Are you dying, then?" said Tamra. "Then maybe I don't need to fight you at all. I just need to stand back just out of your reach and let whatever is killing you run its course. It would certainly be easier than killing you myself, though probably not as quick."

The divine energy was burning through Braim again, only this time it wasn't nearly as painful as before. Instead, it gave him strength he had never felt before. His muscles became stronger and his senses sharper. The sword in his hands felt less like an artificial metal weapon and more like an extension of his very body, as if he and Devourer had become one.

"But you know I'm not just going to stand aside and let you get away with your plans," said Braim. "So long as there is even one breath left in my body, I will fight you to the end."

Tamra rolled her eyes. "Sure. Keep telling yourself that. Maybe it will make death a lot less scary for you than it is for most people."

Tamra suddenly jerked her wand in Braim's direction. An ice bolt hurtled through the air toward him, which Braim dodged by jumping to the side. The ice bolt struck the back of the lobby, instantly covering the back wall in a thick sheet of ice, while Braim himself charged at Tamra, Devourer's blade glowing with divine energy.

He swung Devourer at Tamra's head, but Tamra jumped backwards to avoid it. She then pointed her wand at Braim again and this time materialized and shot a massive boulder at him, which Braim dodged by rolling underneath it. Rising back to his feet, Braim stabbed at Tamra with Devourer, but Tamra jumped to the side and avoided the blow. She thrust her wand at him, but Braim dodged the ice bolt that fired out of it and grabbed her wrist, jerking the wand up and leaving her body exposed.

With a yell, Braim stabbed at her again, but before his sword could strike her in the stomach, Tamra vanished. Braim looked around for her before spotting her standing several feet away outside of his reach, scowling and aiming her wand at him again.

"You're a fast one, aren't you?" said Tamra, breathing hard and sweating harder than ever. "Well, let's see how fast you are in the rain."

Tamra waved her wand above her head and a large rain cloud suddenly appeared at the ceiling above them. Thick, gray, and heavy, the rain cloud started pouring rain, causing Braim to raise his arms above his head, but it did little good, because he still got soaked through completely.

Even worse, the heavy rain obscured Braim's vision. He could barely see Tamra—who seemed to stay dry somehow—through the pouring rain. Nonetheless, Braim slashed his sword at her, sending an energy beam flying toward her.

But he did not hear the beam hit her, which meant that she must have dodged it. Braim looked around, trying to spot her in the rain, before he suddenly felt the temperature drop around him and realized what was about to happen.

Braim leaped forward. And just in the nick of time, because as soon as he jumped, a thick block of ice appeared where he had been standing. Braim again looked around, trying to find Tamra, but it was almost impossible to see anything in the thick rain. His soaking clothes clung to his body, which made movement far more difficult than it had been mere moments ago.

Gotta get rid of the rain, Braim thought, squinting as the rain poured even harder on him. *But how?*

Then Braim heard a rumbling in the ground over the sound of the heavy rain. It sounded like something was coming toward him from behind, forcing Braim to whirl around to see a huge boulder rolling toward him at an insane speed.

Without even thinking, Braim brought his sword down on the boulder, cutting it in half and causing both halves to roll around him. Then, for a split second, Braim saw Tamra, who was illuminated by the glow of her wand, before her wand stopped glowing and she became impossible to see again.

But Braim wasn't going to let her get away. He dashed at her, but then suddenly slipped on the wet floor. He staggered forward, almost tripping over his own feet, but managed to regain his balance before he could fall.

Just as he did that, however, Braim felt the tip of Tamra's wand jammed into the back of his head. Without thinking, Braim spun to the side, just as a freezing beam of ice shot out of Tamra's wand and flew through rain. Braim saw Tamra standing there with a surprised look on her face, but he didn't even think about his next move.

In one smooth motion, Braim slashed at her hand with Devourer. The black sword's sharp blade, shining with green energy, cut through her wrist like butter. Tamra screamed as her hand, still holding her wand, fell to the floor, but Braim followed it up by stabbing her in the chest as hard as he could. She gasped in pain as Braim's sword pierced through her heart and out her back, and then immediately collapsed after Braim pulled his sword out of her chest.

As soon as Tamra collapsed, the rain stopped and the rain cloud itself suddenly dispersed. Panting hard, Braim looked down at Tamra's corpse. Blood leaked out of the stump where her hand had been and from the hole in her chest where Devourer had stabbed her. The blood mingled with the rain water, causing it to become discolored and ugly, although Braim didn't care. He looked at Devourer, which was now stained red with Tamra's blood, but rather than be disgusted by it, he felt quite happy about this turn of events.

Looking down at Tamra, Braim said, "That's for Garvan, bitch."

He kicked her body, although that didn't do anything. Then a sudden exhaustion overcame him, causing Braim's shoulders to slump. The burning divine energy in his body returned full force, causing Braim to grab his chest with one hand. He wondered briefly if the energy was now finally going to kill him, but then the pain subsided and he felt normal again.

At that moment, Grinf appeared in the Stadium's exit. He looked beaten and bloody, but at the same time still quite powerful and ready to fight, with both of his hands holding his gavel like a sword. When the god spotted Braim, he immediately ran over to him, ignoring the wetness all around them.

"Braim, what happened here?" said Grinf as he approached Braim. He glanced at Tamra and his eyes widened in surprise. "Is that Tamra?"

"Yes," said Braim, nodding, although he found it difficult to say that word. "I killed her. She's not a threat anymore."

Grinf's mouth actually fell open, but then he shook his head and his serious expression returned. "That is amazing. I never expected you to be the one to kill her. I thought for sure that it would be one of us."

"Does it matter?" said Braim. He gestured at Tamra's corpse. "She's dead. Martir is safe once again."

"And the golems that invaded World's End are also dead," said Grinf. "My siblings and I, with help from the Soldiers, managed to kill them all. I came in to help you, but I can see that you do not need my help here."

"Thanks," said Braim. Then he frowned and looked at Tamra again. "But what about the souls of your siblings? Are they going to return to their bodies, now that Tamra is dead?"

"They might," said Grinf. "But I am not sure. Did you see anything when you killed her?"

"No," said Braim, shaking his head. "I saw nothing."

Grinf looked down at Tamra's corpse again. "I am not sure if that is a good thing or a bad thing. I think it is likely that their spirits cannot be seen, so they have probably returned to their original bodies now. I will send some Soldiers to check on their bodies and confirm that my siblings have their souls again."

"They probably do," said Braim. "Don't see any reason why they wouldn't, seeing as Tamra isn't alive any more to hold them in her body."

"I agree, but we must confirm it anyway," said Grinf. "Now, let us go back to the Temple and inform everyone of Tamra's death. After that, we will resume the Tournament."

Braim nodded. "Sounds good to me."

The two of them walked away from Tamra's corpse, but they managed to walk only a few feet before Braim heard movement behind them. Braim and Grinf looked over their shoulders at Tamra's corpse, which was still for a moment ... before it twitched.

"What the hell?" said Braim as he and Grinf whirled around. "Did you see that?"

"Yes, I did," said Grinf, nodding. "Her corpse moved. But how can that be possible if she is dead?"

Before Braim could respond, Tamra's skin suddenly turned as black as the night. Darkness flowed down both of her arms and then morphed into the shapes of crude hands, which had fingers that were more like claws. Then Tamra pushed herself up and looked at both Braim and Grinf, but her eyes were nothing more than empty black pools which showed no life in them at all. Then she blinked and her eyes suddenly became red, a dark, sinister red that was all too familiar to Braim.

"No ..." Braim said. "It can't be ..."

But it is, said the Void, her voice issuing from Tamra's mouth. She stood up in the puddle of rainwater and blood, but her chest no longer had the bloody hole from where Braim had stabbed her. She spread her arms. **I am back once again, but this time, I am going to destroy you all myself.**

"The Void?" said Grinf. He held his gavel at his side, looking ready to swing it at her face if she got too close. "What are you doing here? I thought Fojak already dealt with your golem."

The Void chuckled, which sounded disturbing coming from

210

Tamra's mouth. **Oh, Grinf, it is not that simple to get rid of the Void. You see, I had placed a part of my darkness in Tamra. When she died, I took over her body, because I don't like letting good things like this go to waste. Of course, I will consume it eventually, but it will suffice for my current needs.**

"So were you and Tamra working together this entire time?" said Braim. He took up a defensive position, even though he wasn't sure if he could defeat the Void even with Grinf at his side.

Yes, said the Void. **I promised her that I would help her become the Goddess of Martir if she would just let me use her body. She didn't seem to understand, of course, that I never intended to let her survive longer than I needed her, but Tamra never struck me as a particularly intelligent mortal anyway, so I never worried about her realizing what I was actually doing.**

"I see," said Grinf. "You worked with her because of the souls of the gods she had in her body. You hoped she would eliminate we gods so you wouldn't have."

Yes, said the Void. **But it appears that I will have to do things myself, as always seems to be the case. I should stop relying on manipulating mortals and others like them to do my dirty work. It is getting me nowhere.**

"You should return to whence you came and never harm us again," said Grinf. "But if necessary, we will force you to go back to the hole you crawled out from."

Do you really believe that you can stop me? said the Void. **I am the Void. My power is beyond the power of any god. And it has only grown as the boundaries separating me from Martir have weakened. It won't be long now before I am**

211

strong enough to consume all of Martir, and there is nothing you gods can do to stop me.

"We will still fight you," said Grinf. "It is the job of the gods of Martir to protect this world from monsters like you. We have beaten you before and we will beat you again."

So arrogant, but that is no surprise coming from you, the most arrogant of all of the gods, said the Void. She raised her clawed hands. **Allow the darkness to consume you, as is the fate of all who defy the Void.**

Six thick tendrils shot out of the Void's body and hurtled through the air toward Grinf and Braim. Braim held his sword, ready to slash them, but then Grinf looked over his shoulder and said, "Braim, watch out!"

Before Braim could look to see what the god was talking about, Grinf shoved him to the side. Taken by surprise, Braim lost his balance and fell onto the floor. At the same time, the tendrils wrapped around Grinf's body, capturing him in their grasp, and then even more tendrils appeared from behind and also wrapped around Grinf. The god struggled against the Void's tendrils, but he was unable to break through them. Grinf's whole body blazed with fire for a moment, but when the flames cleared, the Void's tendrils still held him as tightly as ever.

"What?" said Grinf. There was actual fear in his voice now, which Braim had never thought he'd hear from Grinf. "What is this? Why didn't my flames destroy your shadows?"

As I said, I am getting stronger, said the Void, a smirk on her lips. **What once worked against me now no longer does. Your chances of survival are now less than zero.**

Braim scrambled to his feet and lifted Devourer in order to

help Grinf, but then Grinf shouted, "Braim! Get out of here! You cannot help me or defeat the Void. Go and tell the other gods about what has happened!"

"But I—"

"Go!" Grinf bellowed.

Braim was tempted to ignore Grinf's commands and stay and fight, but he realized that if Grinf couldn't beat the Void, then he probably could not, either. So Braim turned and ran toward the exit, but as he did so, the Void's tendrils chased after him. But Braim slashed at the tendrils, forcing them back, and giving him enough time to reach the exit.

Before Braim left, however, he looked over his shoulder one last time to see Grinf still struggling against the Void's tendrils. The tendrils, however, were slowly covering his form, until soon only Grinf's head was left visible, and in a second, that, too, was gone, disappearing beneath the shadows of the Void.

Braim then looked back ahead and ran outside of the Stadium, a sense of dread and despair falling over him again. And this time, he knew it would not be easy to shake.

Chapter Seventeen

RAYA AWOKE SUDDENLY, the back of her head pounding. She yawned and squinted, but was not sure where she was and for a moment could not even remember why she had been sleeping at all.

But then she remembered. She remembered how the golem had attacked her and Yoji, how it had dealt with Yoji and Alira as easily as if they were insects, and how it nearly crushed her to death between its massive fingers. Even now, she could still feel its stone fingers wrapped around her body, crushing her in its grasp, her lungs tightening as the air was pushed out of them.

Raya sat up, rubbing her forehead, and looked around at the chamber. It was not her apartment, that was for certain. It was a simple, square room with stone walls, floor, and ceiling. It looked like the same stone used in the Temple of the Gods, which she recalled teleporting to earlier via the Staff of Teleportation. She didn't remember teleporting onto this bed, though, but perhaps someone had brought her here after she passed out.

The bed itself was soft, but it didn't seem to be made out of any sort of material she recognized. It actually reminded her of the white stone used in the streets of World's End and in the

214

ethereal, but it was softer and more comfortable than that, which made her wonder exactly what this material was and where the gods and katabans got it. She decided that Carnag would be a lot better if its streets were made out of this material. At least it would be a lot more comfortable, anyway.

Another thing Raya noticed was how she no longer hurt nearly as badly as she did before, after the golem crushed her in its hands. It was like she hadn't been nearly squeezed to death at all, which was amazing. She assumed that magic was the cause, though who exactly healed her, she didn't know.

But a far more pertinent question came to mind: Where was everyone else?

Tossing the covers off her legs, Raya swung her legs over the side of the bed, put her shoes back on (which she found lying right next to her bed), and then stood up. It was a little hard at first because she was still tired, but she succeeded after a couple of seconds. She was then about to make her way over to the door before the door opened suddenly and an elderly woman entered.

Raya recognized the elderly woman as being the one who had cast Raya into a deep sleep in the first place. The woman looked almost like Raya's grandmother, except Raya could tell right off the bat that this woman was no normal grandmother.

"Ah," said the woman. She smiled kindly. "Hello, Princess Raya. I didn't expect you to be up so soon."

"Are you Atikos?" said Raya.

"Yes, I am," said the woman, nodding. "I'm surprised you recognized me."

"Part of my royal education involved learning the names and traditional appearances of the main gods," said Raya. "You look

215

just like the statue of Atikos I was shown once, so I assumed that that is who you are."

"It sounds to me like you received a fine education, then," said Atikos. She gestured toward Raya's bed. "Now, why don't you go back to bed? You were severely injured back there and I believe that you still need a lot of rest."

"I don't, but thanks for your concern," said Raya, waving off Atikos's concern like it didn't matter. "I'm feeling fine. What about Alira and Yoji?"

"They are both recovering well enough due to my magic, though not nearly as well as you," said Atikos. "They are in their own separate rooms resting, so I suggest that you do the same."

"Why?" said Raya. "I don't need to rest. I just want to find out how long I have been out and what's been happening."

"You were out for fifteen minutes," said Atikos. "But really, you don't need to stress yourself."

"Yes, I do," said Raya. "I won the Hollech Bracket Challenge. That means I am going to become a goddess. I want to ascend as soon as possible."

"You are correct that you won the challenge, but it may not be possible for you to ascend just yet," said Atikos. She rubbed her hands together anxiously. "Recent developments make it unlikely that you will get to ascend to godhood anytime soon."

"What recent developments?" Raya said. "What happened?"

"Golems are invading the city," said Atikos. "They are coming through the ethereal and they are led by the Void. The gods are currently using all of their strength to stop them, but the Void is much stronger than we anticipated and it is becoming harder if not impossible for us to focus on anything else."

"How are the other godlings?" said Raya. "Are they safe?"

"They are all here, in the Temple of the Gods, which the golems have yet to reach," said Atikos. "So yes, they are safe. But unless we can end the golem invasion quickly, I am not sure how much longer they will all be safe."

Raya bit her lower lip. She didn't like hearing this bad news, but she supposed it was better than not knowing it at all. Still, a part of her almost wished that she could go back to bed and ignore all of this, even though she knew that that was a silly thought with no basis in reality.

"Now, will you please go back to bed?" said Atikos. "You were very badly wounded when I found you and I would feel much better if you were resting."

"Resting, sister?" said a familiar voice above them. "This is no time for anyone to be resting, especially Princess Raya."

Raya and Atikos looked up to see the Ghostly God's pale and strange face sticking out of the ceiling. The rest of his head and body soon floated down, until his entire, slightly transparent form now floated in the room with them. Raya stepped away from the Ghostly God, who she did not trust due to how his actions had resulted in Carmaz getting kicked out of the Tournament not long ago.

"Brother, what are you doing here?" said Atikos. Raya was pleased to see that Atikos looked just as disgusted by the Ghostly God's appearance as Raya felt. "I thought we had banished you from World's End."

"I was given permission by Tinkar to stay on World's End and help, seeing as every god is needed in order to fight off the Void and her army of golems," the Ghostly God said, though the smirk

217

on his face told Raya that he was pleased at annoying his sister with his presence. "But I don't need your approval to be here. I came for the royal brat."

"Why?" said Raya. "Are you going to experiment on me like what you did to Braim?"

"No," said the Ghostly God, shaking his head. "I was sent by Tinkar to get you for your prize for winning the Hollech Bracket: The Ascension Ceremony."

"The Ascension Ceremony?" said Atikos in surprise. "But I thought we were going to wait to do it until after the Tournament was over and all of the winners were announced."

"That was the original plan, sister, but Tinkar says that we need as many gods as possible to defeat the Void, so we might as well go ahead and make Raya into one now," said the Ghostly God. "Especially after the report from Fojak, who claims that the Void consumed Grinf."

"Grinf?" said Raya with a gasp. "You mean Lord Grinf himself?"

"The very same," said the Ghostly God. "A pity, really, as Grinf was one of our best fighters. It makes me wonder what chance the rest of us gods have if Grinf couldn't beat the Void."

Raya put a hand over her mouth. She had been happy to hear that she was going to get to go through the Ascension Ceremony so soon, but hearing that Grinf was gone had almost completely eradicated those happy feelings. She was now not sure what to feel, because their chances of defeating the Void and saving Martir seemed a lot lower than they had just seconds ago.

"Are you certain that Tinkar said we should go ahead with the Ceremony?" said Atikos. "Our older brother doesn't always mean what he says, you know."

"He was quite clear this time, sister," said the Ghostly God. "And for once, I agree with him, because we do need as many gods as we can get, even if that means ascending mortals."

"Then what are we waiting for?" said Raya. She held out her hand. "Take me to the Ascension Ceremony right away."

"But Raya still needs to rest," Atikos argued. "She has not yet fully recovered from the golem's assault."

"As I said, Atikos, I am *fine*," said Raya, rolling her eyes. She then addressed the Ghostly God, saying, "Please don't listen to her. She doesn't know what she is talking about."

"My sister never does," the Ghostly God said in agreement.

"Hey!" said Atikos in annoyance, but neither the Ghostly God nor Raya noticed.

"Then we will go to the Ascension Ceremony right away," said the Ghostly God.

He wrapped his large, cold metal fingers around Raya's arm. A second later, Raya found herself standing inside yet another stone chamber, but this one was completely different from the last chamber, so Raya had to look around to see what it was like.

Unlike the room she had been resting in, this chamber was shaped like a dome. It had no windows or even entrances, which made Raya wonder how anyone got down here (perhaps they teleported, like how she and the Ghostly God had). It was also a lot larger and more wide open than the last room, although Raya could still tell that it was underground, as the air was somewhat stale.

But what caught Raya's eye were the carvings on the walls. Hundreds and hundreds of carvings depicted an equal number of figures, which Raya quickly recognized as the gods of Martir, because she saw a carving of Grinf that was very accurate to his appearance. Each one of the carvings was highly detailed and a faithful representation of the god they were based upon, but there were so many of them that Raya found it almost impossible to focus on any one individually.

The carvings ran along the walls, completely covering them. As for the floor, it had markings and words in Godly Divina, which Raya found as impossible to read as ever. In the center of the room was a pedestal made of intricately carved marble that went up to Raya's waist. It stood in the center of the elaborate carvings and markings in the floor, which appeared to be an important part of some kind of ritual.

But Raya and the Ghostly God were not alone in this place. Tinkar stood near the pedestal, leaning on his clock-topped staff as he always did. While he still gave off an aura of authority and power, he appeared tired to Raya, like he hadn't gotten enough sleep over the last day or so. It made him look more like an elderly man and less like a powerful god, which worried Raya.

"Ah, Raya," said Tinkar, nodding at her. "I am glad to see that you are here. Are you ready to ascend?"

Raya tugged her arm out of the Ghostly God's hand and stepped toward Tinkar. "Of course. I have always been ready, ever since I first entered the Tournament."

"Well, she certainly has the attitude of a goddess," the Ghostly God said sardonically. "She will make a good sister."

Raya glared at the Ghostly God, while Tinkar said, "We shouldn't fight. Now more than ever, we gods must stand together regardless of our differences. The real threat is the Void and her army of golems, which are even now destroying our city."

"Then what are we waiting for?" said Raya, looking at Tinkar again. "I'm ready to ascend."

Tinkar nodded. "Then please come and join me in front of the pedestal. Then we can begin the Ceremony."

Without hesitation, Raya walked toward Tinkar until she stood only a few feet opposite him. She looked at the pedestal between them and noticed that it had a depression in the center of it that looked like the place where the bottom of a small stone statue would go, although she saw no statue on top of its surface at the moment.

"So what do we do now?" said Raya, looking up at Tinkar. "Do you cast a spell that will ascend me to godhood?"

"It is somewhat more complicated than that," said Tinkar. He frowned. "It has been centuries since we did the last Ascension Ceremony, though I remember quite clearly that Niham was the last mortal we ascended. I never thought we'd do it again, but here we are."

"Yes, yes, Lord Tinkar, that's very interesting, but also very irrelevant," said Raya, not bothering to hide the impatience in her voice. "Can we get on with it now? Please?"

"All right," said Tinkar. "Ghostly God?"

The Ghostly God floated next to Raya, a bored look on his face. "Yes, brother?"

"You are needed for the Ceremony, so you should stay here with us," said Tinkar.

The Ghostly God sighed in annoyance, but nodded and said, "Very well. It isn't like I have anything better to do at the moment, anyway."

"Good," said Tinkar. He looked at Raya again. "Now, Raya, listen carefully, because a successful ascension depends on the correct behavior of the gods and mortal involved. It isn't a terribly complicated process, but it has been known to fail if not done correctly."

"What happens if it fails?" said Raya. "Has that ever happened before?"

Tinkar and the Ghostly God exchanged dark looks, like Raya had just asked a question that had brought bad memories back to their mind.

"Once, a long time ago, the Ceremony did fail because the mortal we were trying to ascend made a mistake," said Tinkar. "Let us just say that it isn't something that will be pleasant for either gods or mortals and leave it at that."

"But—" said Raya, before the Ghostly God interrupted her.

"What that mortal did or didn't do isn't relevant to the current situation," said the Ghostly God. "Now, do you want us to go on with the Ceremony or are you just going to keep asking us these dumb questions that have nothing to do with anything?"

Raya glared at the Ghostly God, but she had enough sense to realize that neither of the two gods were going to elaborate on what happened to the mortal who messed up their own Ascension Ceremony. She decided that she would ask the other gods about that after she became a goddess herself.

So Raya nodded, albeit grudgingly, and said, "All right. I'm listening."

"Very well," said Tinkar. He gestured at the stand. "First, you will have to put your hands on the pedestal. Then the Ghostly God and I will place our hands on top of yours. Once we are all standing in the correct positions—which we are, so don't worry about it—the Ghostly God and I will call forth from the well of divine energy located deep underneath World's End, which will then flow into your body and turn you into a goddess."

"That's it?" said Raya. "There's no elaborate dance or chants I need to repeat or anything?"

"None at all," said Tinkar. "As I said, it isn't a complicated process, but it can be messed up if you are not careful. I am confident, however, that nothing will go wrong."

"Because you can see into the future?" Raya asked.

Tinkar shook his head. "Oh, no. I can't see any of our fates, due to the limitations placed upon my powers by the Powers, but I believe that all of us here will not allow ourselves to make any mistakes during such an important process."

"Agreed," said the Ghostly God. "Though I must say, brother, that I am less confident in Raya's abilities to handle the immense amount of divine energy we will pump into her than you are."

"She will handle it because she is a godling," said Tinkar.

"Will it hurt?" asked Raya.

"It will, but not very much," said Tinkar. "Most mortals who ascend usually do not expect to receive so much energy at once, so I am telling you this so you will be able to mentally prepare yourself for the power that will be flowing through your body very shortly."

Raya nodded. "All right. But you know, I don't need to prepare that much, because it is my destiny to ascend. Other mortals might need to, but I need only the minimum amount of time to prepare because I will be able to handle it without any trouble."

"Her ego is already godlike and she hasn't even ascended," said the Ghostly God, sarcasm dripping from his words. "Amazing."

Again, Raya glared at the Ghostly God, but Tinkar said, "Enough. Now Raya, please place your hands on the pedestal."

Although Raya wanted to say something witty and sharp to the Ghostly God, she decided that she would rather ascend to godhood first than waste more time arguing with a god who wasn't, in her opinion, very godly.

So she placed her hands on the pedestal. Then Tinkar placed his old and cold hands on top of hers and the Ghostly God placed his on top of Tinkar's. Their hands were not very heavy on Raya's, but Raya could not move hers regardless.

"Wait," said Raya. "Why do we need two gods for the Ascension Ceremony?"

"Because two gods are necessary to draw upon the power beneath World's End," said Tinkar, nodding at the pedestal. "And it has to be one northern god and one southern god. It cannot be two northern gods or two southern gods, as the Treaty forbids it."

"The reasoning behind that particular rule is that the Powers did not want either Pantheon upsetting the balance of power in Martir by ascending as many mortals as possible to join their ranks," said the Ghostly God. "The Powers believed that it would be hard for a northern god and a southern god to work together and that any god created from such a unity would have a real choice of which Pantheon they wanted to join, rather than being drafted into one or the other upon creation."

"I see," said Raya. "I guess it must have worked, then. But what is this 'well of divine energy' you mentioned?"

Tinkar looked rather impatient at her questions, but he said, "Deep beneath Martir, down in a cavern that even we gods cannot reach, is a well of divine energy placed there by the Powers at the beginning of time. Its sole purpose is to be used to ascend mortals such as yourself to godhood. And it is constantly regenerated by the divine energy that we gods constantly produce from our bodies, so it is never in danger of drying up."

"Oh," said Raya. "What would happen if someone were to plunge directly into it?"

"No one knows," said Tinkar. "But I think that if they were mortal, they would instantly die, while a god might simply receive an immense power boost for a short while."

"Does it really matter?" said the Ghostly God in annoyance. "I thought you were eager to ascend, Raya, not stand around and ask irrelevant questions all day."

Raya took offense to the Ghostly God's tone, but she realized that he had a point, so she said, "All right, all right. I was just asking."

"Good," said Tinkar. "Now, please be quiet. The Ascension Ceremony will require our utmost concentration, which we cannot achieve if we are busy talking with one another."

The Ghostly God nodded in agreement, but said nothing. So did Raya, even though she still wanted to yell at him for his rudeness toward her.

"Concentrate," said Tinkar, addressing Raya. "Focus. And when you feel the divine energy burning through you, do not panic, but let it run its course."

Then Tinkar went silent and focused entirely on the pedestal in between them. Raya also focused on it, even though she wasn't

225

sure what was going to happen next. Still, she didn't divide her focus even for a second, because she didn't want whatever happened to the last guy to happen to her.

A second later, Tinkar's hands felt warm over hers, like he had placed them over a hot, blazing fire. The pedestal started to glow, even shake a little, but neither Tinkar nor the Ghostly God seemed surprised or worried about that. They simply continued to stare at the pedestal like it was the most important object in the world, which, in a way, it was, at least to Raya.

Even so, Raya didn't really feel anything overwhelming or difficult to handle until a second later. What felt like a hot, burning fire—like the forges of Grinf—shot through her hands, up her arms, and into her body coursed through her without warning. She wanted to scream in pain, but she remembered what Tinkar had said about not losing her concentration and so she kept her mouth shut.

But oh, it was so, so hard. Her entire body felt like it was on fire, like she had swallowed a burning forge. Her body wanted to rip her hands away from the pedestal and step back, but her mind told her body to keep her hands on the pedestal until Tinkar gave her the signal to pull them away. There was no way in hell that she was going to mess up the Ceremony, not when she was so close to godhood that she could practically taste it.

And taste it she did. In addition to the burning fire that was melting her organs and her skin, Raya tasted flaming coals in her mouth. It was almost like eating smoke, but far worse. Her lips dried out and her tongue became like sandpaper and there was nothing, nothing she could do about it except try not to lose consciousness or pull her hands away and make things that much worse.

A part of her prayed to the gods, even though she doubted that any of the gods would dare to intervene during such an important Ceremony. Still, her prayer was instinctive, and she prayed to Grinf, despite the Ghostly God claiming that Grinf had been consumed by the Void and therefore likely couldn't even hear her. Still she prayed, because it was the only thing she could do.

But through the pain, Raya also felt something else. Her body suddenly felt ... stronger, like she always felt after a good exercise session back on Carnag. Her hands—always rather small and weak—suddenly felt strong enough to shatter stone. Her vision became clearer, so clear that she could see the tiniest of details in Tinkar's face and robes, details that she normally would never have seen or noticed before. It was like she was seeing a brand new world, a world that she had never even known existed until this very moment.

This sudden increase in strength was almost addictive, despite the horrible pain that came with it. Raya wanted to keep it flowing into her forever and ever, wanted to stay here forever in this chamber, never leaving for any reason whatsoever. She didn't care if the Void consumed all of Martir in the process as long as she had access to this intense power that never seemed to end.

But a part of her feared that the power was going to burn her up from the inside out. This fearful part of her wanted to let go and run, despite her best efforts to remind herself of Tinkar's warnings. Still, it was hard to ignore that unconscious, instinctive fear of pain, even though she was aware that neither Tinkar nor the Ghostly God would let her die here.

Then, a few seconds later, a sudden power surge hit her like a ton of bricks. She gasped and her fingers trembled, like she was going to let go, but then Tinkar and the Ghostly God pressed their own hands down further on her own, keeping her where she needed to be. Still, Raya's heart beat had increased when she felt that boost of power, which she had thought was going to kill her.

And finally, after several more tense seconds passed in silence, the flow of power going into Raya's body slowed down to a trickle. And then, in another second, it cut off completely, although Raya still felt the power in the pit of her stomach, in her very soul, that she had never felt before, but which she understood to be the power of the gods themselves deep inside her.

The Ghostly God and Tinkar removed their hands from Raya's. Raya removed hers as well and looked at her hands, although they didn't look very different from how they always looked.

"There," said Tinkar. He sounded exhausted and had bags under his eyes, as if that ritual had taken a lot out of him. "Welcome, Raya, Goddess of Deception, Thieves, and Horses."

A smile crept along Raya's lips, but she didn't smile all the way just yet. "Did you just .... did you just call me the Goddess of Deception, Thieves, and Horses?"

"Yes," said Tinkar, nodding. "The ritual is complete. Everything went exactly as it was supposed to. You are now no longer a mortal, but a powerful goddess, on the same level as I, the Ghostly God, and every other deity in both Pantheons."

Raya's mouth fell open. She looked up at the Ghostly God, who had crossed his arms over his chest, looking unimpressed.

"Did you hear that?" said Raya. She smirked. "I'm now as

powerful as you. How does that make you feel?"

The Ghostly God shrugged. "All I can say is that I am glad that your power level now matches your ego. It is always embarrassing to see mortals with egos far larger than their own puny forms."

Annoyed, Raya punched the Ghostly God in the arm. Much to her surprise, the Ghostly God actually pulled his arm away, rubbing the spot where she had punched it.

"Oh my gods," said Raya, looking at her hand in surprise. "Did I actually *hurt* you?"

"Mildly," said the Ghostly God, rubbing his arm. "I was not prepared for it, probably because I still think of you as a mortal and not a goddess."

Raya's face burst into the largest smile she had ever smiled. She put her hands on her body and could feel the difference already. She hadn't realized it until just now, but as a mortal, her body had felt rather weak and fragile, while as a goddess, her body now felt like a solid brick wall, impenetrable to all but the strongest of weapons.

Her senses, too, were far more intense. She could smell the ancient stone of the chamber, even make out the subtly different scents between the Ghostly God and Tinkar, one which smelled like death, the other like an old wooden clock. It was almost too much, but Raya enjoyed every second of her enhanced senses.

"I feel *amazing*," said Raya, running her hands down her body with a sigh. "Is this how you gods *always* feel? Powerful? All-knowing? Highly confident? Unafraid of anything?"

"Most of the time, yes," said Tinkar. "We gods are, after all, the strongest beings on Martir. It is only natural that we would tend to have limitless confidence and courage."

"Oh, yes," said Raya, nodding. "I cannot wait to see exactly what kind of powers I have. It will be—"

Raya was interrupted when she felt movement in her chest. Her hands flew to her chest immediately, but then she noticed something odd about her hands: They were changing. They were growing short, brown fur, while her fingers were becoming harder and sturdier.

"What … what is this?" said Raya with a gulp. "What is happening to—"

Then Raya felt her head starting to change shape as well. Her nose became elongated, her eyes shrunk back, her hair became messier, and the gap between her eyes grew. She gasped and tried to stop it, but her head and hands kept changing.

And it wasn't just her head or hands, though. Her entire body felt like it was growing larger and hardier. She could feel her skin being replaced by fur, the same short, brown fur on her hands, which she discovered when she pulled her shirt open to see her chest. Her feet, too, were changing, her toes becoming hardier and grittier, just like her fingers.

It was not painful, but it made Raya fearful. She staggered backwards, while Tinkar and the Ghostly God watched, Tinkar with disgust, the Ghostly God with amusement. Neither one moved to help her.

"You two …" said Raya. Even her voice sounded different, almost like the whinny of a horse. "Why aren't you helping me?"

"There is nothing *to* help you with, my new sister," said the Ghostly God, the amusement in his voice obvious. "It is all part of the ascension process."

Raya wanted to cuss out the Ghostly God, who was obviously taking great pleasure in watching the transformation taking place on her body, but she was too distracted by the transformation to be able to speak. She fell down on her hands and knees, groaning as her body continued to shift and alter in ways she couldn't even comprehend at the moment.

But soon, it was over, and Raya could think clearly once again. She looked down at her hands, which now closely resembled horse hooves mixed with human hands. She then felt her head, which was longer and larger, but because her body had grown larger as well, it didn't feel unnatural on her neck.

Then Raya looked up at Tinkar and the Ghostly God. "Mirror. I need a mirror."

The Ghostly God produced one from a compartment in his armor, a smirk still on his face. He sent the mirror floating through the air toward Raya, which Raya grabbed and looked into quickly. She screamed when she saw the face of a horse—with brown fur and frightened eyes—looking up at her from the mirror, with her own beautiful face nowhere in sight.

Without thinking, Raya threw the mirror aside. The mirror flew across the room and smashed into one of the walls, shattering into a million pieces as Raya covered her face with her mutated hands.

"Hey," said the Ghostly God, who now sounded annoyed. "That was my favorite mirror. I didn't give you permission to break it."

Raya, however, didn't pay him any mind. Touching her face, she just said, "What in the name of the gods was *that* thing? Was that ... was that *me*?"

231

"Yes," said Tinkar. "That horse face you saw in the mirror was indeed your own face, staring right back up at you. There was no trickery or deception involved there."

"But … why?" said Raya, still without looking up at either of her two new brothers. "It doesn't make sense. Why do I look like a *horse*?"

"Because you are now the Goddess of Horses," said Tinkar. "Hollech, when he was still alive, resembled a humanoid horse. Your own body has simply changed to better reflect your new role."

"But … but it's *hideous*," Raya said with a shudder. "It's ugly. I want my beautiful face back. I don't want to look like a dumb animal."

"It is possible for gods to change our appearances at will," said Tinkar. "So you do not necessarily have to look like that forever."

Raya immediately looked up at Tinkar, hope rising in her heart. "Really? How do I do that?"

"It requires training and effort," said Tinkar. "You will not be able to do it right away. So I am afraid that you are stuck with that appearance for now."

Raya smashed her fist into the floor, creating a crack where she punched it. "No! I want to change it back *now*."

"We don't have time to teach you that *now*," said the Ghostly God in annoyance. "What we need to do *now* is return to the Temple and inform everyone else of your successful ascension. Then you will be able to help us defeat the Void and her army."

Raya stood back up. She considered forcing them both to teach her how to change her appearance—after all, she was a goddess herself now, so she had the power to make anyone do anything she wanted.

But then she reconsidered it. Both Tinkar and the Ghostly God were far older than her and had far more experience as gods than she did. They could probably beat her easily if she tried to force them to teach her how to change her appearance, and the last thing Raya needed to do as a goddess was get beaten by her older brothers (she found it weird to think of them as such, even though it was technically accurate).

Anyway, she supposed it wasn't entirely bad. It could be worse. Carmaz could be here and he could see her new hideous face and be completely turned off by her forever. That didn't quite make her feel good about her appearance, but it at least made her feel a little better about herself.

So Raya's shoulders slumped and she said, "Fine, fine. I guess I'll ... learn to live with this for now. But—"

Unfortunately, Raya did not get a chance to finish her sentence, because at that moment a gray ghost entered the chamber from the ceiling and landed on the floor. The gray ghost resembled Atikos, which meant that she must have sent it, and it had an urgent look on its face.

"To Tinkar and the Ghostly God," said the gray ghost that resembled Atikos. "Urgent news: The Loner God has returned. And he brought Carmaz Korva with him."

Chapter Eighteen

THE DARKNESS OF the Void hovered before the jail cell without making a sound. The Loner God raised his fists, like he was going to punch the Void, which didn't make sense to Carmaz. Still, Carmaz also rose to his feet and took a fighting stance, even though he knew that there was absolutely no way he could ever hope to even touch the Void.

"What are *you* doing here?" said the Loner God to the Void. "I thought you were more interested in what was going on in World's End than what was going on in Ruwa."

That I am, God of Solitude, that I am, said the Void, her voice as dangerous and vile as ever. **But I never pass up an opportunity to destroy my enemies. Especially the ones who escaped me in the past.**

Carmaz was under the impression that the Void was referring to him, because he had once escaped her some time ago. That only made him feel slightly less confident about his chances of survival.

"So you're going to try to destroy us, eh?" said the Loner God. He laughed. "Sure, you can try, I guess. Don't know how successful you'll be, seeing as you've never actually killed a god before, but—"

A shadow tendril shot through the bars of the cell, which the Loner God blocked with his arm. But the tendril shot straight through his arm, stabbing through it like a sword and making him swear in surprise. Then the Void pulled her tendril back through the bars, allowing the gold blood of the gods to leak from the Loner God's arm and drip onto the floor.

Gripping his arm, the Loner God looked at the Void, a look of bewildered shock on his face. "How did you hurt me?"

I am growing stronger, Loner God, said the Void, her voice full of malicious glee. **The barriers keeping me from consuming Martir have grown weaker, allowing more and more of my essence to enter this world. And it will not be long before all of Martir is consumed by my darkness, including you gods.**

The Loner God stepped back, scowling. "Well, you don't scare me. I can still defeat you, because I am a god, and not a weak one, either."

So you think, Loner God, but you fail to understand that soon there will be no one in the world who can stop me, said the Void. **It won't be long now before my shadows consume World's End. And without the gods to stop me, there will be nothing standing between me and complete consumption of all of Martir and everything within it.**

"Then we'll just escape," said the Loner God. He closed his eyes, but then opened them immediately. "Why can't I teleport out of here?"

Because I am keeping you from doing that, said the Void. **I am not going to let either of you leave here alive. My shadows**

will suffocate you both and you will not live long enough to see your world destroyed.

The darkness of the Void began creeping into the cell, forcing Carmaz and the Loner God to walk backwards until they reached the back of the cell. There was nowhere to go from here, no other exits for the two to take. All they could do was watch as the Void's consuming shadows slowly but surely filled the cell, inch by inch, as if the Void was taking her sweet time.

"Any ideas?" said Carmaz, looking at the Loner God.

"No," said the Loner God, shaking his head. "Well, we *could* try fighting our way through, but frankly if the Void can cut me like that, I have a feeling neither of us would last very long against her power."

"For a god, you sure are useless when you are needed most," said Carmaz.

The Loner God glared at Carmaz. "Says the mortal who isn't even a mage."

Carmaz rolled his eyes and looked at the darkness of the Void that was drawing closer and closer to them with every passing second. In seconds, the Void's shadows would be upon them, and there was nothing that Carmaz could do about it. He kicked at the Void's shadows, but his foot hit nothing and he succeeded only in looking foolish.

But just when the Void's shadows were perhaps less than an inch from the tips of Carmaz's boots, the Void suddenly let out a cry of pain and surprise, followed by a blinding burst of light that forced Carmaz to cover his eyes to avoid being blinded permanently. The Loner God didn't cover his own eyes, however, probably because as a god his eyes were stronger than Carmaz's, but based on how surprised he looked, he clearly hadn't expected the light, either.

"What's going on?" Carmaz shouted, causing the Loner God to look at him. "Where did this light come from? One of your fellow gods?"

The Loner God shook his head. "No idea. Could be anything."

Then the light faded enough for Carmaz to lower his hands from his eyes and look out the cell to see who had created the light. He was surprised by what he saw.

Standing in a hole that looked like it had been carved out of the Void's darkness itself was the Hermit. He looked as old and tired as ever, but there was a fierce look in his eyes, with the tip of his staff glowing a brilliant white light as he waved it back forth, driving back the Void's shadows with every swing of his staff. Despite his fierce appearance, every swing of his staff seemed to tire him out, because his swings became slower and slower with every movement.

"Away with you, you shadows!" the Hermit cried as he swung his staff around. "Away! Let the light of magic drive you back to whence you came!"

The Hermit made his way through the cave, every swing of his lighted staff clearing the way until he was just outside of the cell. He then looked at Carmaz and the Loner God while still swinging his staff back and forth.

"Hermit?" said Carmaz in surprise. "What are you doing here?"

"The Loner God told me where he was going, but I wanted to come and help him because I believed that he might need my help," said the Hermit. "It appears that I was correct in that

237

assumption."

The Loner God scowled. "How are you holding off the Void when I couldn't?"

"Took her by surprise," said the Hermit. He glanced over his shoulder at the darkness of the Void, which still hadn't restored yet. "But if the Void is as powerful as you say, then she will recover quickly enough. In the meantime, we must escape before she strikes back."

"Will you come with us?" said Carmaz.

"I will try," said the Hermit. "But I cannot guarantee that I—"

A shadow tendril shot out of the darkness and stabbed straight through the Hermit's heart. He gasped in pain, but still managed to swing his staff and make the tendril dissipate into nothingness, but it was obvious now that the Void's shadows were beginning to recover from the Hermit's surprise attack.

The Hermit himself fell to the ground, his staff falling at his side. Nonetheless, he must have had enough strength to keep the light shining, because it still shone even with the blood leaking out of his chest, but how long that would last, Carmaz didn't know.

"All right," said the Loner God. He grabbed Carmaz's arm. "Let's get the hell out of here while we have an opening."

"But what about the Hermit?" said Carmaz, gesturing at the Hermit's prone body. "Can't we bring him with us?"

"No time," said the Loner God. "Now hold on. We're getting out of here *now*."

Before Carmaz could say anything else, the cell became as black as night, although this time it was due to the fact that they were teleporting and not because of the Void's own shadows. For a moment, Carmaz couldn't breathe, but then the darkness vanished and Carmaz landed on the soft and sandy floor.

The sudden impact almost made Carmaz fall over, but he caught himself quickly enough. He looked around at his surroundings, wondering where the Loner God had teleported them.

Carmaz had never seen this place before. It was a wide-open room with hundreds of thrones of varying heights standing around the room's perimeter, like stands in a coliseum, with sand covering the floor in the middle where Carmaz currently stood. Through the clear ceiling, he saw the blue sky, except it was partially covered in shadows that were all too familiar to him by now.

Then Carmaz heard someone gasp and he looked down to see that he and the Loner God were not alone. Standing several dozen feet from them were a group of mortals who Carmaz recognized as the rest of the godlings, although they were a much smaller group than the one he had been a part of before being sent home. They were all standing together, apparently talking among one another, but now they were pointing at and whispering about him and the Loner God, like they had never seen either of them before. It occurred to Carmaz that his and the Loner God's appearance here must have taken them all by surprise, seeing as they had not actually announced their arrival beforehand.

Then a handful of Soldiers of the Gods, clad in their crystalline armor, marched up to Carmaz and the Loner God. In the lead was a katabans with red hair who Carmaz didn't recognize, who looked just as surprised as the godlings did at their sudden appearance.

"Lord Loner God," said the katabans—who was apparently the Captain of this group of Soldiers—in surprise. He and the other Soldiers quickly bowed before the deity. "We did not expect you to return so quickly. We thought you were on Ruwa fighting the golems."

"I was," said the Loner God in annoyance. He gripped his bleeding arm and scowled. "But I decided to come back because I got bored of smashing rocks."

The Captain nodded, but then finally took notice of Carmaz, who he frowned at. "Is this Carmaz Korva? What is he doing here? Wasn't he kicked out of the Tournament for cheating?"

"He's with me," said the Loner God, waving at Carmaz. "I brought him with me for a reason, so don't touch him unless you want to spend the next few years of your life having to be fed like a baby."

The Captain again nodded, but much more hurriedly this time. "Yes, yes, Lord Loner God, I, of course, was not questioning your decisions, but—"

"What's going on here?" the Loner God cut him off. He gestured at the other godlings. "Why are the godlings here in the Temple?"

"The Stadium of the Gods was attacked, sir," said the Captain. "The Void has taken it over and we had to move the godlings here for safety reasons. Not only that, but the Void is using the ethereal to drop golems directly into the city, which are currently destroying it even as we speak."

"That little bitch," said the Loner God. He shook his head. "Tell my siblings that I have returned and that I have brought a ... friend, if you want to call him that."

"Yes, sir," said the Captain, saluting the Loner God. He then turned to the Soldier on his right. "Go and tell Atikos about the Loner God's return. Tell her that he brought Carmaz Korva with him as well."

The Soldier nodded and then ran off toward the nearest exit, but he didn't get far before Atikos suddenly appeared out of nowhere and walked over to the Loner God. The Soldier—who looked a little disappointed at not getting a chance to go and tell Atikos—nonetheless stopped where he was and rejoined his fellow Soldiers without complaint.

"Brother, I thought I sensed your return," said Atikos as she approached the Loner God and Carmaz. She glanced at Carmaz. "And you brought the rule-breaker with you?"

Rule-breaker? Carmaz thought. *Is that all I am known for now? Breaking the rules?*

But he did not say that aloud. Instead, he merely watched as the Loner God said, "Yeah, I brought him with me because I thought he might be able to help us somehow. Anyway, what's this I heard about the Void attacking World's End with an army of golems?"

"It just happened," said Atikos with a shudder. "Luckily we have only lost a few Soldiers, but the Void's power is growing and she is helping more and more golems invade the city itself. We don't have much time."

Then Atikos looked at the Loner God's arm. "Brother, what happened to your arm?"

"The Void," said the Loner God. "And it isn't healing on its own for some reason."

"Let me heal it for you," said Atikos, raising her hands over

241

the Loner God's arm.

The Loner God looked like he'd rather than she didn't, but surprisingly, he held out his arm, which still bled gold blood. A flash of light emitted from Atikos's hands and the wound was healed, although there was still some dried blood on it.

The Loner God pulled his arm back and looked it over, though as far as Carmaz could tell, there was absolutely nothing wrong with it at all. "Well, thanks, sister. Looks as good as new."

"You're welcome, brother," said Atikos. "What should we do now?"

"Now?" said the Loner God. "I think—"

The Loner God was interrupted by the sound of the doors to the Throne Room opening. Carmaz turned around to see someone who he hadn't expected to see again: Braim Kotogs, who staggered through the door, panting and sweating, looking like he had run a mile. He had a strange black sword at his side that Carmaz had never seen before, although Carmaz didn't think much about it at the moment.

"Braim Kotogs?" said Atikos, looking at him in astonishment. "Where have you been?"

"The Stadium," said Braim, his hands on his knees as he panted. "The Void got it. And Grinf, too."

"We know," said Atikos, shaking her head sadly. "Are you all right?"

"Yes," said Braim, nodding. "Just tired is—"

Braim abruptly stopped speaking when he saw Carmaz. Carmaz, of course, knew why, but he didn't look away from Braim's confused stare. He just met Braim's gaze with his own, even though he didn't want to look at Braim at all.

"What the ..." said Braim. "Is that Carmaz?"

"Yes," said Carmaz. He gestured at himself. "This is indeed me, in the flesh."

Braim's confusion quickly turned to anger. Seemingly forgetting all about his exhaustion, he marched up to Carmaz, his long black sword in his hands, and said, "Just what the *hell* are you doing here? I thought you had been sent back home for breaking the rules.

"It wasn't *my* idea," said Carmaz. He pointed at the Loner God. "The Loner God took me here."

"And the reason you did that is ...?" said Braim, glaring at the Loner God.

The Loner God snorted. "Since when did I, a god, ever have to explain myself to a mortal? And don't act like the fact that you came back to life makes you an exception, because it doesn't."

Braim opened his mouth, probably to continue to argue, but then Atikos said, "Please, let us not fight. The real enemy, as always, is the Void. We should be glad that we are all here and that we are all alive. We need to gather the rest of the gods together and unite to save Martir."

"Sure, sister," said the Loner God, though he tossed a nasty glare at Braim as he said that. "I was just about to suggest that same thing. I have an idea that I want to suggest to everyone anyway, a way to beat the Void."

"Really?" said Atikos. "What is that?"

"I'll tell everyone once they're here," said the Loner God. "For now, summon the others. I'll be back in a minute."

With that, the Loner God vanished, which made Carmaz wonder where the god had gone. He looked at Atikos, who shrugged like she had no idea where her brother had gone.

Then Atikos held up her hand and a stream of smoke leaked from her fingers until it formed a shapeless cloud before her. She then spoke into it a quick message to Tinkar and the Ghostly God, of all people, and then the gray ghost took her form and flew down through the floor of the Temple.

When the gray ghost was gone, Atikos looked at Carmaz and Braim. She gestured at the other godlings and said, "You two should go stay with the others. I am going to gather the rest of the gods, but will be back soon, so do not worry."

With that, Atikos turned and, like the Loner God, vanished into thin air, leaving Carmaz and Braim standing next to each other awkwardly. Carmaz glanced at Braim's sword, which he was afraid Braim might stab him with, but Braim, thankfully, seemed to have gotten better control over his temper, because he kept the sword by his side and did not seem likely to attack Carmaz with it.

"Well," said Braim, looking at Carmaz. "Guess we should go and do what she said."

Carmaz nodded, albeit awkwardly, and the two walked over to the other godlings. As soon as they reached the others, Braim was immediately greeted by pretty much everyone, who seemed to have missed him a great deal based on all of the hugs and back slaps he got. Carmaz, on the other hand, just stayed back and was ignored by the others, which was fine by him, because he didn't know most of them all that well and didn't feel very comfortable interacting with them either.

After a while, however, the others returned to their original gossiping and talking, though now they seemed to be talking about what the Loner God's plan was. Then Tashir and Malya approached Braim and Carmaz, the two of them looking the same as Carmaz remembered seeing them last.

"Oh, Braim, we're so glad you're all right," said Malya. She grabbed his face and looked it over with the concern of a mother. "Did the Void or any of those golems hurt you?"

Braim gently removed Malya's hands from his face and said, "No, I'm fine. But Grinf isn't. The Void consumed him."

"Exactly what happened?" said Tashir. "Everyone has been speculating about what the Void did back there, but no one actually knows anything."

Braim quickly explained what had happened back at the Stadium. Tashir and Malya listened, and so did Carmaz.

When Braim finished, Malya rubbed her hands together anxiously. "If Tamra is dead, then does that mean that the souls of Xocion and the others were freed and have returned to their bodies?"

"I don't know," said Braim, shaking his head. "I didn't see their souls leave her body, but maybe they did. I think the Void might have taken them in order to keep them from returning to their bodies, but again, I don't know."

"What about you, Carmaz?" said Malya, looking at Carmaz. "Do you know anything about the Void or the golems?"

Carmaz remembered Lady Dia's story about the golems' origin, although as he didn't think it would help, he shook his head. "I don't know anything that could help us stop either of them. All I know is that the Void is getting stronger and that soon not even the gods will be able to stop her."

"That's what she said back at the Stadium," said Braim grimly.

245

"If so, then I think we can safely say that we are screwed."

"We mustn't give up just yet, though," said Tashir. "I am certain that the gods will come up with some way for us to defeat the Void. We must continue to fight no matter how bleak things may look."

"I agree," said Carmaz. He looked around suddenly when he realized that someone was missing. "Now that I think about it, where is Raya? I thought she would be the first to greet me."

"She, Yoji, and Alira were almost dead last I saw," said Malya. "They were taken to some private rooms in the Temple to heal and rest."

"Almost dead?" said Carmaz, looking at Malya in confusion. "How did they get that way?"

"They were almost killed by a golem that broke into the Stadium," said Malya. "On the bright side, Raya won the Hollech Bracket Challenge, which means that she is going to become the next Goddess of Deception, Thieves, and Horses."

Carmaz groaned internally. *If Raya becomes a goddess, then that means I will* never *get away from her, at least not until I die. How wonderful.*

"Anyway, Carmaz, what are you doing back here?" said Tashir. "Why did the Loner God bring you back to World's End? I thought you were kicked out of the Tournament for breaking the rules."

Carmaz folded his arms over his chest. He found it hard to look at the others now, especially Braim, who he could feel glaring at him with nothing less than pure hatred. He tried his best to ignore Braim, however.

"I don't know," said Carmaz. "The Loner God thinks I could

help somehow, even though I don't have any magical powers or anything like that that I could use to help us defeat the Void."

"I have never understood how those southern gods think," said Tashir, shaking his head. "They are completely alien and incomprehensible."

"Eh, not really," said Braim. "I think that the Loner God probably just wants a tasty snack on hand. And since he can't really eat any of us because we're in the Tournament, he picked Carmaz instead."

"Braim, that's very rude," said Malya, looking at him in shock. "And that you would say that to Carmaz, of all people, is reprehensible."

"Am I the only one who remembers that Carmaz teamed up with the Ghostly God to turn me into a glorified magical experiment?" said Braim, the bitterness in his voice cutting Carmaz as deeply as any sword. "Or are we just going to conveniently forget that because there's a bigger problem at the moment?"

Both Malya and Tashir looked ready to argue in Carmaz's defense, but Carmaz raised his hand and said, "You two don't need to argue. It's fine. Braim has a point."

Braim looked at Carmaz like he couldn't believe what he had just heard. "What did you just say?"

Carmaz scratched the back of his head, but said, in a somewhat reluctant voice, "I said, you have every right to be angry at me for what I did. It was wrong of me and I have no excuse for doing it."

"You mean you *aren't* going to come up with a bunch of excuses to rationalize your betrayal?" said Braim. "Really?"

"Really," said Carmaz. He looked Braim straight in the eyes again. "I could come up with a bunch of excuses to deflect responsibility for my own actions, but I won't. I know that what I did was wrong. I've known that ever since I was kicked off the Tournament. And I'm not going to ask you to forgive me because I know that I have no right to expect that from you, not after what I did to you."

"I—" said Braim, but Carmaz wanted to continue speaking.

"I mean, not only did I put your life in danger, but I also caused you to lose your magical powers," Carmaz continued. "I've had a lot of time to think about this ever since I was sent home and realized that I was wrong, even if my reasons for doing it were understandable. If you want to keep hating me forever, then that is your right and there is nothing I can do to change that."

Braim looked like he was at a loss for words now. He rubbed his chin and looked at Tashir and Malya, who both shrugged their shoulders like they did not know how to respond to Carmaz's confession, either. It occurred to Carmaz that none of them had expected him to outright admit that he had messed up, which made him wonder whether that was because they had not believed it was a part of his character to do that or if it was simply because Carmaz had been kicked of the Tournament and thus unlikely to see Braim ever again.

In any case, Carmaz didn't care either way what their reactions were. In his view, he had already done the unforgivable. He didn't expect Braim to forgive him or even forget about what he'd done, but he felt better having confessed it all anyway.

Then Braim scratched the back of his neck and said, "Well …

Carmaz, I forgive you."

Carmaz was not sure he had heard Braim correctly. "What? Why? I caused you great harm. I caused you to lose your powers. Why are you forgiving me? Do you even remember what we're talking about?"

"I do," said Braim. "And I *did* plan on holding this grudge against you for as long as I lived, but when you outright admitted your mistakes like that ... well, I didn't think it would be very kind of me to do that."

"Wow," said Carmaz. "I didn't expect you to say that, Braim. I didn't expect you say that at all."

"I don't *want* to," said Braim. But then his shoulders slumped. "But I think that I *have* to, regardless of how I feel. We have a much greater enemy in the Void and you seem to be genuinely remorseful of what you did, so it's not fair of me to withhold forgiveness from you just because I am still angry at you for what you did to me."

"Well, thanks, Braim, for that,"said Carmaz. "I really do appreciate it."

Braim nodded, but he still looked troubled despite that. He looked around, then looked at Carmaz, Tashir, and Malya and said, "I have something I need to share with you guys, but you can't share it with anyone else. Okay?"

"We're listening," said Tashir. "What is it?"

Braim leaned in closer, probably so that the other godlings would not eavesdrop easily, and whispered, "I am dying."

Malya gasped, while Tashir and Carmaz exchanged surprised looks. None of the other godlings seemed to notice, although considering how loudly they talked among themselves, it wasn't very surprising that they hadn't heard it.

"Dying?" Malya repeated. She gulped. "What do you mean? Did the Void poison you? Why haven't you had Atikos look at whatever is ailing you?"

"The Void didn't do anything," said Braim, shaking his head. He put a hand on his chest. "I did it to myself. Remember when Yoji and I were trying to restore my magical powers earlier today?"

"No," said Carmaz.

"Well, you weren't here when that happened, but it happened nonetheless," said Braim. "Anyway, remember how the ritual seemed to fail?"

Both Tashir and Malya nodded, while Carmaz did nothing due to his lack of knowledge of this attempt to restore Braim's powers.

"Well, it didn't, at least not entirely," said Braim. "I mean, I didn't get my magical powers back, but I *did* get some powers: I got the divine energy of the gods flowing through my body."

"The energy of the gods?" said Malya. "Does that mean you are now a god yourself?"

"No," said Braim, shaking his head. "My friend, Darek, once told me about how he had been temporarily granted divine power by one of the gods in order to fight Uron. I think it's the same with me, only I got much more power than he did."

"Isn't that a good thing?" said Tashir. "The power of the gods is far greater than the power that even we mortal mages use. I don't see the issue."

"The problem is that my body is not designed to handle this kind of power for long," said Braim. "And it's not just a temporary power boost or whatever, either. The power has become a part of me and it is slowly killing me. Atikos herself told me that I will probably not live to see the next morning."

"How horrible," said Malya, putting her hands over her mouth in shock. "Is there a way to heal you?"

"Nope," said Braim, shaking his head. "Atikos couldn't remove it, and even if she could, then it wouldn't do me any good, because the process would still kill me. And I, frankly, don't want to die."

"Who does?" said Tashir.

"That's another thing I need to share with you," said Braim. He glanced at the other godlings, none of whom were paying any attention to their conversation, and then looked at Carmaz, Tashir, and Malya again with serious eyes. "I was told that when I die, my spirit won't simply go to the Spirit Lands, like most. When I die, my spirit will literally cease to exist."

"Cease to exist?" Malya repeated. "What does that mean?"

"It means it won't exist," said Braim. "I know that that's not an entirely satisfactory answer, but it's the best I can come up with. See, when someone dies, their spirit continues to exist even after their body decays into worm food. This applies to everyone, except for Uron, whose spirit was utterly destroyed after I got my body back from him."

"How do you know this is true?" said Tashir.

"The person who told me is someone who I trust," said Braim. "Of course, he did say that it was just a theory of his, but he seemed confident about it and I have no reason to doubt him, so I've been operating off the assumption that it's true for a while now."

"Oh," said Carmaz. "I see. The divine energy of the gods is slowly killing you from the inside out. And once you are dead, then you will literally cease to exist."

"Exactly," said Braim, nodding. "I did not tell anyone any of this because I didn't want to worry anyone, but I thought that you guys deserved to know, at least, because I trust you guys more than anyone else."

"Is there anything you can do to stop yourself from dying?" said Malya.

"I don't think so," said Braim. "I've been thinking about it for a while, but have been unable to come up with any plans that could save me. As far as I can tell, I am going to die and there is nothing that even the gods can do to stop that."

Malya and Tashir exchanged troubled looks, but it was clear that they were just as powerless as Braim was in this situation. Carmaz put his hands into his pockets, but he didn't know what to say, either. He knew very little about magic and understood even less about how to fix magical problems like this. He now wished that there was a way he could help Braim, especially after Braim had just forgiven him for his betrayal.

"I don't expect any of you to have a solution to my problems," said Braim, shaking his head. "I just wanted to tell you guys this because I wanted you to at least know the reason why I am going to die. That way, it won't come off as a nasty surprise when it happens."

"I wish there was some way we could help," said Malya. She rubbed her hands together anxiously. "What are you going to do, then?"

"Not sure," Braim said. "I originally intended to win the

Skimif Bracket Challenge and become the God of Martir, which I hoped would give me the immortality I need to survive, but with the Tournament delayed due to the Void's attack on the city, I am not sure I will be able to do anything except wait until the divine energy completely destroys me from the inside out."

Malya opened her mouth again, like she was going to say something, but before she could, the gods began to appear in the thrones in the lists. The gods appeared dozens at a time, until soon, in less than five minutes, nearly every god and goddess in Martir was present in the Temple. The only throne left empty was the massive throne at the other end of the room where the God of Martir was supposed to sit, although Grinf's throne was also empty and so were four others that must have belonged to the gods whose souls Tamra had taken earlier.

As soon as all of the gods were present, the Loner God reappeared in the throne reserved for the God of Martir, except he was too small to sit in it. As soon as he appeared there, three other gods appeared behind him. Two Carmaz recognized easily: Tinkar and the Ghostly God, but the third god was unfamiliar to him. She looked like a humanoid horse and wore a red tunic that looked like the tunics worn by all of the godlings, but Carmaz wasn't sure who she was. The goddess actually looked at him for a moment before hastily averting her gaze, which made Carmaz wonder why she did that.

But he stopped thinking about it when the Loner God stepped forward and said, "Welcome, my brothers and sisters! I am glad that you all answered Atikos's summons. Thought you might ignore them because of me, but I guess you guys still like me after all."

"Get on with it, brother," Ranama, the God of Language, shouted from his throne on the left side of the chamber. "Our city is under attack and we cannot waste any time listening to you babble on about anything. What did you call this meeting for?"

"Very well," said the Loner God. "I always prefer getting straight to the point myself, anyway. So let's do that: I called this meeting because I have good news and bad news to share."

"What's the good news?" said Atikos, who sat on a throne just to the right of the massive throne reserved for the God of Martir.

"The good news is that I killed the golems' leaders," said the Loner God. He folded his arms over his chest, looking quite pleased with himself. "They weren't that hard to kill. Oh, and that Tamra mortal is also dead, slain by our very own Braim Kotogs if I am not mistaken."

"What's the bad news?" said Ranama.

"The bad news is that the Void now controls the golems and has made them much harder to kill," said the Loner God. "And they're rampaging through the city destroying and killing everything they can get their rocky little hands on."

"We know that already," said Ranama in annoyance. He readjusted his glasses and then glared at the Loner God from across the vast chamber. "Do you know anything that we *don't*?"

"Not really," said the Loner God, shaking his head. "I just wanted to tell everyone about what I did, because unlike you guys, I actually tried to do something to stop the golems, just like I said I would."

The gods collectively groaned and more than a few looked like they wanted to leave and go deal with the golem army in the city rather than listen to the Loner God continue to speak, but then Tinkar stepped forward and said, "My siblings, there is actually more good news than our brother here suggests. There is a new Goddess of Deception, Thieves, and Horses, at long last."

While the gods gasped and muttered among each other at this pronouncement, Carmaz looked at the humanoid horse-like being standing behind Tinkar. Although he at first did not realize who he was looking at, he suddenly recognized the figure's mane—which appeared to be the same color and texture as the hair of a certain woman he once new—and her general figure. He hoped he was wrong, but when he looked at Braim, Malya, and Tashir and saw looks of recognition dawning on their faces, he realized that he probably wasn't.

"My brothers and sisters, please meet the newest addition to our ranks," said Tinkar, stepping aside to show the new goddess to the entire room, "Raya, Goddess of Deception, Thieves, and Horses and successor to our deceased brother Hollech."

"Raya?" Malya muttered. She looked at Carmaz. "*Our* Raya?"

"Is there any other?" Tashir muttered in response.

Carmaz suddenly started looking around, hoping to find a way to sneak out of here before Raya could come over to him, but then Tinkar continued speaking.

With one hand on Raya's shoulder, Tinkar said, "While one new goddess does not exactly restore the balance to the gods that we so desperately need, increasing our numbers is always a good thing no matter how you look at it. With Raya's power on our side, we should have a better chance at defeating the Void and saving World's End than we otherwise would."

"What about Xocion, Mica, Kos, and Hamin?" said Ranama. "The Loner God said that Tamra is dead. Have their spirits returned to their bodies?"

It was the Ghostly God who answered that, saying, "No. I checked on the bodies of our siblings, but they are as still and lifeless as ever. I suspect that the Void is keeping them from returning to their bodies after she took over Tamra's body, although I don't know for sure. That means that we will need to destroy the Void if we're going to rescue the lost souls of our brothers and sisters."

More worried murmurs swept through the gods, while the godlings also exchanged worried and confused looks.

"Then what are we waiting for?" said Ranama. "If we are all here, then we should go and fight the Void. We should destroy the golems that she leads. By combining our power, I think we can do it."

Many of the gods were nodding in agreement with Ranama, while others looked a little worried as if they doubted Ranama's words.

"Can we?" said the Loner God, putting his hands on his hips. "I think under ordinary circumstances, we could, but all reports suggest that the Void is getting stronger. At this point, I am not sure that we could beat her even if we combined all of our powers and completely annihilated World's End from existence."

"Then what do you suggest we do, brother?" said Ranama. "Do you think we should run and hide? Or maybe contact the Powers or the Mysterious One?"

"Nope," said the Loner God, shaking his head. "The Powers are too far away for us to contact them, and even if we sent someone to find them, Martir would be completely consumed by the Void by the time they got back, if they chose to help us at all.

And the Mysterious One is too busy with the Spirit Lands to help us here. Nah, I got a better idea, although I'm not sure if it will work or not."

"Say it, then," said Fojak, who sat in a throne next to Ranama. "We're all listening."

"All right," said the Loner God. "But first …"

The Loner God held out his hand and several long vines shot from his palm. They flew through the air, heading straight for the godlings, and then wrapped around Braim's waist. Before anyone could react, the vines jerked Braim off his feet and through the air until he landed on the massive throne next to the Loner God. The Loner God then pulled the vines back into his hand, while Braim stood there looking quite confused by this turn of events, as did everyone else in the Throne Room.

"Here he is," said the Loner God, patting Braim on the back. "The mortal who will save us."

"Braim Kotogs?" said Fojak, while the other gods exchanged uncertain looks with each other and many others—who were probably southern gods based on their monstrous appearances— were staring at the Loner God like he had lost his mind. "What do you mean that he is the mortal who will save us?"

"Exactly what I said, brother," said the Loner God. "As much as I hate to admit it, Braim Kotogs is our best bet for defeating the Void and saving all of Martir from her darkness."

"I am?" said Braim.

"He *is*?" said Raya, who sounded offended. "What about me?"

The Loner God apparently didn't hear anything Raya said, because he continued explaining his plan as if she had not spoken a word. "Now, I don't know if you all know, but Braim Kotogs is the only thing in Martir that the Void fears."

"*Used* to fear," Braim corrected. "When she attacked me earlier, she said she'd gotten over her fear."

"Yeah, but she could have been lying," said the Loner God. "In any case, the fact is that Braim Kotogs is the walking embodiment of everything the Void hates and fears. This give us a psychological advantage against her, because if she fears Braim, then she will probably not behave rationally if we sent him against her."

"Assuming that your psychoanalysis of the Void carries any weight, Braim is still a mortal, and not even a magical one at that," said Fojak. "Explain, then, how he is supposed to defeat her."

"But he's not a normal mortal," said the Loner God. "Thanks to a botched ritual, he now has divine power flowing through his veins. Even better, he's used this power to escape the Void just earlier today, when the Void attacked. Right?"

Braim nodded. "Yeah. I did."

"So here's what I think we should do with him," said the Loner God. "We need to send Braim to fight the Void. He can use his powers to drive her back, maybe even destroy her, or at least wound her so badly that she has to retreat beyond the edge of Martir, where she's supposed to be."

"I am not sure that that is such a great plan at all," said Fojak, shaking his head. "Even if Braim has as much power as us, he is still a mortal. I would rather not trust the fate of our world to a mortal, even to one like Braim."

"Do you have a better idea about how to defeat the Void,

then?" said the Loner God. He looked around at the other gods. "Does *anyone* have a better idea? Because I certainly am not hearing any other suggestions from the rest of you, that's for sure."

"I think our brother has a point," said Ranama, steepling his fingers together. "Braim may very well be our best chance at defeating the Void and saving Martir. I'm just shocked that the Loner God was the one to come up with this plan, seeing as he is a southern god."

"Hey, I said I hate to admit it," said the Loner God. "But unlike some of my siblings, I *am* willing to work with beings I might ordinarily eat for dinner if it means saving the world. The only other alternative is trying to stop the Void on our own and I think that our chances of doing that and surviving are even less than using Braim to defeat her."

"But how can one mortal—even with divine energy flowing through him—stop the Void, if we gods cannot?" said Fojak. "It makes no sense."

"We'll act as back up," said the Loner God. "Should Braim fail, we gods will still be here and will be able to fight the Void if he loses. Besides, I'd like to point out that Braim has already had a lot of experience fighting the Void, so he should at least be able to weaken her long enough for us gods to figure out how to drive her back if nothing else."

Carmaz looked around at the other godlings. None of them seemed to object to the idea, although Malya looked worried, as did Tashir. They were probably worried for Braim's safety, which was reasonable, especially after what Braim had just told them about what would happen to him if he died. As for Raya up on the

259

throne, she looked rather annoyed that Braim had taken the spotlight off of her, which made sense, considering how much Raya loved being the center of attention.

"So let's put it to a vote," said the Loner God. "All in favor of sending Braim to defeat the Void?"

Hundreds of hands—from among both the northern and southern gods—rose into the air, among them Tinkar and the Ghostly God, but with so many gods, Carmaz could not be sure whether that was more than half that were voting in favor of the plan or not.

"All right," said the Loner God. "And against?"

More hands rose into the air, but they were a definite minority in comparison to the amount of hands that had gone up in favor of the plan. One of them was Raya's, but considering how annoyed she seemed to be toward Braim at the moment, that was hardly surprising.

"Okay, then," said the Loner God. "Looks like the voice of the gods has spoken and it is in favor of sending Braim to defeat the Void."

Most of the gods nodded in agreement, although a handful— probably the ones who had voted against it—looked bothered at having lost. Still, even they kept quiet, probably because they did not want to speak out against the only plan that the gods had.

"But we aren't going to send Braim in alone," said the Loner God, shaking his head. "I think that we should send at least one god and another mortal with Braim. They will help him get past whatever the Void throws at him. So who wants to—"

"Me!" said Raya, her voice ringing throughout the Throne Room, holding up one of her hands. "I want to escort Braim to the

Stadium. I can do it."

The Loner God looked at Raya with a mixture of annoyance and amusement on his face. "Girl, you just became a goddess not half an hour ago. Don't you think that you need to get some more training in before you go up against the Void?"

"No," said Raya, shaking her head. "I can do it. I've fought the Void before and survived. I know exactly what I'm going up against."

The Loner Good still looked deeply skeptical about Raya's involvement in the mission, but then he shrugged and said, "Oh well. Becoming a god is the sort of job that requires hands-on training anyway. Now who will volunteer for the position of backup mortal?"

Carmaz didn't even stop to think. He just raised his hand and shouted, as loudly as he could so that everyone could hear him, "I volunteer."

The Loner God looked at Carmaz, but rather than the annoyance he had worn while looking at Raya, he looked rather pleased at Carmaz's volunteering. "Great. I expected you to volunteer, but no matter. Let's get the three of you out of here as quickly as possible, because the Void is certainly not going to wait for us to come up with a neat plan of action to defeat her."

"Wait!"

That single voice came from the thrones, causing Carmaz and everyone else to look up to see who had shouted. Carmaz immediately spotted an old-looking man sitting in the thrones, who looked more like a reanimated corpse than anything. Although Carmaz wasn't sure which god this was, a look of recognition had arisen on Braim's features and he looked like he wanted to run.

"What is it, Diog?" said the Loner God, who sounded annoyed. "Are you going to ask if you can kill Braim? Because if so—"

Diog—who Carmaz recalled had tried to kill Braim at the start of the Tournament—shook his head. "No, brother. Even though I would like to kill that unnatural abomination whose mere presence has brought us great misfortune, even I realize that the Void is the greater threat at the moment. I would merely like to help."

"Help?" the Loner God repeated. "Help how?"

"By providing Ragao to help him," said Diog. "Ragao is a half-god and therefore knows how to survive in the Void. By sending Ragao with Braim and the other two, they have a better chance of getting inside her and stopping her."

"That sounds like a good idea to me," said the Loner God. "Only question is, how can we be sure that Ragao won't try to kill Braim?"

"I will tell her not to," said Diog. "She isn't a very independent thinker, so she will go along with almost anything I ask her to do. Besides, I am well aware of what all of you would do to me if I ordered Ragao kill Braim now. I am not an idiot."

"All right," said the Loner God. "Your reasoning makes sense. The more advantages the better, I say, considering what we're up against."

Braim didn't look like he agreed with Ragao's inclusion in the team at all, but he didn't voice any objections to it. He did, however, eye Diog carefully, like he was trying to figure out what Diog's real reason for helping was.

"Anyway, if no one else has any other suggestions, let's get Braim and everyone out of here right away," said the Loner God, snapping his fingers. "We've got even less time to waste now than we did a few minutes ago, so let's do this."

Chapter Nineteen

BRAIM, CARMAZ, AND Raya stood in the alleyway between two buildings near the Stadium, where they were hidden from the view of the golems patrolling the outside of the Stadium. Raya had teleported them here with her new-found divine powers, which apparently included instant teleportation to almost anywhere in Martir. They had teleported here in order to get as close to the Stadium as possible without the Void seeing them, although Braim had the strongest feeling that the Void knew where they were regardless of where they hid.

Braim peered out from around the corner of the building. The Stadium was completely covered in the Void's shadows from bottom to top. It was the only building in the area to be covered, but other nearby buildings were constricted by the massive tendrils that emerged from the top of the Stadium. Several golems were walking around the Stadium on patrol, although unlike normal golems, these ones were clearly controlled by the Void, for her shadows could be seen in their joints and eyes and they walked in lockstep like they were controlled by one mind. There were no entrances into or out of the Stadium, which would make getting inside difficult, although not impossible if the plan worked.

Braim pulled his head back into the alley and turned to face Carmaz and Raya. Carmaz carried a crystalline sword in his hands given to him by the Soldiers of the Gods, who said that it would help him hurt the golems, while Raya was unarmed, although as a goddess she didn't need any weapons to be able to fight well. As for Braim himself, he still carried Devourer, which he had grown rather attached to ever since Fojak gave it to him earlier that day.

"All right," said Braim. "Do you two remember the plan?"

Raya nodded. "Of course. Carmaz and I are supposed to distract the golems, while Ragao creates an opening in the Void that you can use to enter the Stadium unharmed. Then you are supposed to explore the Stadium until you find the Void's center and then defeat it."

Braim nodded as well, but he found it hard to think of the powerful, horse-faced humanoid before him as Raya, even though her basic personality and clothes were exactly the same as they had been when she had been a mortal. He supposed it was just one of those things he'd have to get used to. "Right. It's a good plan."

"The only problem I have is that I am not sure how you're supposed to 'defeat' it," said Carmaz. "The Void doesn't necessarily have a 'core,' does it?"

"No," said Braim, shaking his head. "But the Void usually does have a being whose form it takes. Last I saw, she had taken control of Tamra's body, so I am going to look for Tamra when I get in there and take her out."

Carmaz nodded, but then looked around and frowned. "Where

is Ragao? I thought that Diog said she was going to help us."

Braim shuddered at the thought, but then he said, "Remember, Ragao was locked away beneath World's End, so they're probably going to free her. So I doubt we'll see her for another few minutes at—"

Braim was interrupted by the sounds of movement in the shadows in the alleyway in which they stood. His first thought was that it was the Void about to attack them, which must have been the first thoughts in the heads of Carmaz and Raya as well, because Carmaz whirled around holding his sword in defense, while Raya's hands glowed with a deadly-looking energy that Braim doubted would be fun to get hit by.

But then a massive, four-armed being stepped out of the shadows. It was Ragao, the Half-Goddess of Darkness, still wearing that tusked baba raga mask on her face while carrying her four slim swords. She towered over even Raya, her body cloaked in shadow.

"Oh," said Braim, though he didn't quite relax around her just yet. "There she is."

Ragao looked down on them all in silence. And then, suddenly, she said, in a very halting voice, "Ready?"

Braim, surprised that Ragao could talk at all, nonetheless managed to say, "For the attack?"

Ragao nodded.

"Well ..." Braim looked at Carmaz and Raya. "You guys ready?"

"Whenever you are," said Carmaz.

Raya brushed back her mane. "Of course. I am always ready to save the world."

266

Braim nodded. "All right. Then let's do this."

-

Braim and Ragao stood in the shadows of the alley, watching as Carmaz and Raya waited for the golem patrol to pass by so they could distract them. Braim felt uncomfortable standing next to Ragao, even though the half-god was not acting very hostile toward him at the moment, but he still didn't trust her one bit. Still, he supposed that you couldn't always choose your allies and that sometimes you had to make alliances with people you normally would have nothing to do with if that was what you needed to do in order to succeed.

She's a better ally than the Void, I suppose, Braim thought, *though that's not saying much, now that I think about it.*

Just then, Carmaz looked over his shoulder and said, "The golem patrol is on their way. We're heading out to distract them now. Get ready to run after us."

Braim and Ragao nodded. Braim checked Devourer again, just to make sure that it was not damaged in any way, and then looked up in time to see Carmaz and Raya run out into the streets.

Braim and Ragao followed, but then they stopped at the edge of the alley and Braim peered around the corner to see Carmaz and Raya running toward the golems. The Void-possessed golems, however, did not notice Carmaz or Raya running toward them until Raya fired two blasts of dark energy at their backs, striking them dead-on, but her attacks hardly scratched the golems' thick backs. Still, it got their attention, causing the golems to turn to face them, clearly not happy about Raya's attack.

"Hey, stupid rocks!" Raya shouted as she and Carmaz stopped

267

several feet away from the golems. "Come and catch us if you can!"

With that, Raya and Carmaz ran into another alley. The golems, thankfully, took the bait, and ran after them, disappearing into the alley after them with every step of their massive feet.

As soon as the golems were gone, Braim nodded an Ragao and the two dashed across the open street to the column of shadow that had once been the Stadium. Braim fully expected the Void to attack them from a distance well before they got there, but much to his surprise, they made it across the street without any problems and arrived in front of the solid black darkness quickly.

Then Ragao raised one of her hands over him and he and the half-god were covered in a sheet of darkness, yet Braim could still somehow see through it regardless. He supposed it was probably the half-gods' strange magic at work, but he didn't question it, as he knew that Ragao's magic would protect him from the worst of the Void's corrosive effects and that was what mattered to him at the moment.

Steeling himself for the worst, Braim stepped through the Void's solid darkness with Ragao by his side. As soon as he did, he instantly felt the Void's alien and cold presence sweep over him like an ocean wave, but Ragao's power seemed to work, because he did not feel like he was being eaten alive by the Void like he had earlier.

As soon as they stepped inside, Braim shouted, "Void! It's me, Braim Kotogs. The only being you've ever feared. And I am here to kick your ass. Show yourself."

At first, Braim's words seemed to fall on deaf ears, because he did not get a response.

Then the familiar but deadly voice of the Void echoed from the shadows. **Come in deeper, Braim Kotogs. I'm waiting for you not far ahead. Then you can see me.**

Braim didn't like hearing that, but he walked forward anyway. Ragao followed, keeping her shadow cloak over them both as they stepped over the debris on the floor from the shattered entrance. Due to the severity of the darkness, it felt like it was forever before Braim saw several figures standing just outside of the field of his vision, figures which became more and more visible the closer he drew to them.

There were four beings now standing in the ruins of what was once the Stadium lobby. One of them Braim recognized right away as Saia, or really Saia's body under the Void's control. It looked just as sadistic and monstrous as ever, even though last Braim had heard, it had been Grinf who had destroyed Saia's body. Perhaps the Void had recreated it.

The second was Tamra, although she was hardly recognizable as such now. Her skin was almost completely black now, while her eyes glowed a deep, dark blood-red that made Braim nervous. Braim saw none of the blood on her form from where he had stabbed her, but that was the least of his worries at the moment.

The other two beings Braim did not recognize. They were golems, based on their rocky skin, but they were the size of humans. One of them, which had a feminine body, had wings sprouting from her back, while the other, which was probably male, had a scorpion tail rising from his behind. Although Braim was certain he had never seen those two before, he could not help but feel like he had, although where and when, he could not recall right away. Maybe they were figures from his first life, although peka_

at didn't seem likely to him.

In any case, Braim could tell that all four were no longer living. Instead, they were puppets of the Void, reanimated corpses that had no wills of their own. It disgusted Braim just to look at them, especially at Saia's.

Then the Void's voice came from Saia's mouth, saying, **You asked me to show myself, Braim Kotogs, but I forgot to ask: Which self should I show you? Should it be Saia, the mortal who was once Carmaz Korva's best friend? Or Tamra's? Maybe you would like to see the bodies of the golem leaders, Lady Dia and Stalac, who died not long ago at the hands of the Loner God.**

Braim scowled. "You know exactly what I mean, Void. I'm here to put an end to you. One way or another, this will be the end of your attack on Martir. For good."

The Void's chuckled emanated from Tamra's mouth. **And what makes you think that you can defeat me? This will not end like the last time we fought, Braim. This time, I will not leave simply because you told me to. This time, I am going to tear you apart piece by piece and then consume them. I am done with putting up with your foolishness.**

"Then why didn't you kill me the second Ragao and I stepped in here?" said Braim. "Face it, Void. I still scare you, despite your protests. I'm the embodiment of everything you fear. You know you won't be able to stop me, even if you are more powerful than you were the first time we fought. Because guess what? I'm also a lot stronger than I was back then."

But are you strong enough to stop me? said the Void. **You still don't understand my true nature. I am a force of nature,**

like the wind and the ocean. You cannot stop me, any more than you can stop a raging hurricane or an erupting volcano. Give into despair and sleep.

Braim shook his head. "Sorry, but that doesn't work on me. I came here to save Martir, not let you talk me into doing something stupid. So why don't we skip the talking and go straight to the fighting?"

The Void did not respond at first, which made Braim think that maybe she agreed with him and that she was going to start attacking him.

But then, the Void chuckled again, this time coming from the mouth of the female golem who Braim assumed was called Lady Dia. It was a small chuckle at first, but then the other bodies started to chuckle along with her, and soon all four were laughing together in unison, each one sounding exactly like the other. It was the most chilling and surreal thing that Braim had ever heard and seen in his entire life, but he didn't run. He stood his ground, holding Devourer before him, ready to use it.

Then the Void's puppets suddenly stopped laughing, which made Braim think that she was finally going to attack, but then the Void's voice came from the body of Stalac.

I am not going to fight you, Braim Kotogs, said the Void. **I have no need to, because you will end yourself for me.**

Braim raised an eyebrow. "Why would I do that? I'm not suicidal. And even if I was, I wouldn't kill myself just because you told me to."

Let me show you, then, why you will kill yourself, said the Void.

Braim didn't know what the Void was going to do until an

ethereal portal popped open between him and the Void. As soon as it opened, two large golems stepped out of the portal, but they did not come by themselves. They carried in their hands two people Braim had not expected to see here. In fact, he was almost certain that they were not there, even though as far as he could tell, they were indeed the real thing.

Still, Braim said, "No ... Darek and Jenur?"

The two mages raised their heads when they heard their names, but as soon as Braim saw them, he winced. Darek's face was bashed in, looking more like bloody paste than a human face, while Jenur's forehead was crumpled and she seemed to barely be breathing.

"Braim ..." said Jenur, her voice sounding weak and close to death. "Help ..."

The golem holding Jenur squeezed her in its hand, causing her to scream in pain. Darek shouted, "Mother!" before the golem holding him poked him in the back of the head with one of its fingers. It must have been a more powerful blow than it looked, because Darek's face slammed forward into the hand of the golem holding him and he did not move again.

"Darek? Jenur?" said Braim. He blinked, unable to believe his eyes. "No way. They can't be here. They're back in the Great Berg, Jenur at North Academy and Darek at the Temple of Xocion. They can't be here."

But they are, said the Void. **This is no illusion. My power reaches across the vastness of Martir, to the point where I can grab anyone I want and take them wherever I want. I kidnapped them because I knew that you care about them, but also because I remember Darek Takren and how he stood**

ASCENSION OF THE CHOSEN

against me in the past. Killing him would satisfy me just as well as killing you.

"Let them go," said Braim, his voice harsh. "Now."

Of course, said the Void. **But only on one condition: That you take that sword of yours and drive it straight through your heart, which will kill you instantly.**

Braim looked down at Devourer. Its tip certainly did look sharp enough to pierce his chest, but he looked up at the Void again and said, "No way. I'm not going to kill myself. You'll just kill Darek and Jenur anyway."

True, said the Void. **Like all that live on Martir, it is their destiny to be consumed by me. But you don't have much of a choice, really. There isn't much you can do against my power. And I know how much you humans value your friends and family, how much you will do anything—even murder—for them. Do you really want to sacrifice them just to get a chance to kill me? Do you really value their lives that little?**

As much as Braim didn't want to admit it, he had to admit that the Void's question was a good one. He hadn't expected her to put the lives of the two people he was closest to in danger. He hadn't even thought that the Void was clever enough to try something like that.

The right answer, he knew, was to go and attack the Void, even if that meant sacrificing Darek and Jenur. But he wasn't sure if he could take the right answer, because Darek and Jenur were still his friends and he did not want to sacrifice them for anything.

I will give you five more minutes in which to make your choice, Braim Kotogs, said the Void. **Once those five minutes are up, I will kill them, unless you agree to my demands**

before then. The five minutes are starting … now.

Chapter Twenty

RAYA DUCKED AS a shadow bolt flew over her head and struck the wall of a building before her. She glanced over her shoulder and frowned when she saw that the patrol golems were still chasing after Carmaz and her. They had not yet caught up, but they were now shooting shadow bolts at her and Carmaz, and she knew that the golems just needed one shot to slow them down long enough for them to catch up.

But Raya wasn't going to slow down anytime soon because she was now a goddess, and she felt far more powerful now than she ever had in her life. Her legs, which had become more powerful since her ascension, allowed her to run across the streets of World's End with little effort. Indeed, her feet barely touched the streets, almost fooling her into thinking that she was actually flying across the streets, although that of course was a silly thought.

It was Carmaz who she was worried about. Carmaz was still an ordinary mortal and, although he somehow managed to keep up with her at the moment, Raya could tell that he was getting tired. Sweat ran down his face, his strides were becoming shorter and shorter, and he seemed to be getting out of breath.

The golems might not catch me, but they will catch Carmaz unless I can get him to safety somehow, Raya thought. *He really shouldn't be here at all, but I guess he wants to help save the world. That's what I've always loved about him, how brave and heroic he is even in the face of danger like this.*

Nonetheless, even Raya understood that bravery and heroism could not always make up for a mortal's weakness for long.

So as they ran, she shouted at Carmaz, "Carmaz! We need to split up. Look, there's a wall coming up ahead. You can go to the right and I'll go to the left."

"What if the golems come after me?" said Carmaz, who sounded almost out of breath as he ran beside her.

"They won't," said Raya, ducking again to avoid another incoming shadow bolt. "The Void always attacks what she considers to be the largest threat in the area, so they will come after me because I'm a goddess, which automatically makes me a bigger threat than you."

"All right," said Carmaz. "Let's try to lose them and meet back up at Anwan's Tailoring. I think it's somewhere near here and we should be able to find it easily."

Raya was about to say that she didn't want to meet up at that awful place, but then she realized that arguing with Carmaz over where they could meet up again was a waste of time. So she just nodded as they came upon the building before them and then split, Raya to the left and Carmaz to the right.

As Raya ran, she looked over her shoulder and was pleased to see both golems running after her. They seemed to have forgotten all about Carmaz, which was exactly what she wanted.

But Raya still didn't slow down. She kept running, turning

another corner, intending now to lose the golems in the maze of streets and alleyways that made up World's End. Then she would meet up with Carmaz at Anwan's Tailoring and the two of them could figure out what to do from there. Maybe they could go back to the Stadium and help Braim defeat the Void, although she hoped that by then Braim would have defeated the Void himself.

Just as Raya rounded another corner, an ethereal portal exploded open in her path ahead of her. Raya skid to a halt, readying her energy blasts to take out whoever was going to step out from the ethereal portal, but she was not prepared for the being who stepped out.

The figure was huge, at least as tall as Raya in her current goddess form, but much bulkier and armored. It had metallic skin, with joints creaking with every movement, and it had a skull-like face that Raya had never thought she'd see again.

Stepping back in surprise, Raya said, "Keeper?"

As the ethereal portal closed behind Keeper, Raya's old automaton bodyguard looked at her with harsh eyes. **No, but I certainly look like him, don't I, Raya Mana?**

Raya's fists shook. "The Void. I should have known it. You took over Keeper's body, didn't you?"

Yes, I did, said the Void. She raised Keeper's hands and turned them over, as if fascinated by them. **While this automaton's body is nowhere near as graceful or nimble as what I am used to, I know exactly what kind of psychological effect it should have on you, seeing me use the body of the bodyguard you once trusted so much.**

Raya would not admit it, but the Void had a point. Seeing Keeper again, especially after watching the Void cut him up into

277

pieces the last time she had seen him, hit Raya in a way that she had not expected. Still, she knew the Void well enough at this point not to show any weakness that the Void could exploit.

So Raya said, "I thought you were fighting Braim. What are you doing here?"

My consciousness can be in multiple places at once, said the Void, tapping the side of her head. **It is a part of my nature, that I can be in many places simultaneously. A useful ability, to be sure.**

Raya was about to say that she didn't care whether it was useful or not before she heard the sound of stone feet slamming into the street behind her. She looked over her shoulder and saw the two golems from before had finally caught up with her. They stood at the other end of the alley, standing side by side, making it impossible for anyone to walk in-between them. And with the Void in Keeper's body in front of her, Raya was effectively trapped.

Of course, I am not going to fight you with Keeper alone, said the Void. She pointed at the golems behind Raya. **I am also going to fight you with those two golems. I believe in strength in numbers, although in your case I don't need many numbers to destroy you.**

Raya smiled confidently, even though she certainly did not feel confident at the moment. "Well, I'd rather have you coming after me than Carmaz. At least I can deal with you on a somewhat equal level."

The Void shook Keeper's head. **You didn't think I forgot about Carmaz, did you? Oh, no. My followers are going to deal with him even as I speak. I imagine the poor mortal**

won't last even five minutes against them, which is also the time I estimate our own fight to take.

"You're lying," said Raya.

Why would I lie? said the Void. **To make you worry about your friend and be too distracted to fight effectively? I guess that is one benefit to lying, but in this case I am telling the truth, and nothing but the truth.**

"Then I don't have time to deal with you," said Raya. She raised her hand. "I am going to find Carmaz and save him from your followers. Bye."

Before Raya could teleport away, the Void raised her right hand and unleashed a shadow tendril that shot through the air toward Raya. The tendril wrapped around Raya's waist and raised her off the street before slamming her against the side of a nearby building. The blow was enough to stun Raya, but she recovered quickly and slashed at the tendril, cutting through it with her hand, which made her fall to the streets.

Just as she landed, however, Raya heard two explosions behind her and looked over her shoulder in time to see two fists from the golems flying at her. Raya jumped out of the way just in time to avoid getting hit, allowing the flying fists to go past her straight toward the Void.

The Void, however, opened an ethereal portal before her, allowing the fists to pass safely through. Closing the portal, the Void raised Keeper's hand and unleashed a volley of bullets at Raya.

Horrified, Raya was unable to dodge them, so she raised her arms instinctively and was surprised when the bullets bounced off her arms. Then she remembered that she was a goddess and therefore unable to be hurt by normal mortal weapons like bullets, although she still found it hard to relax.

But the thought did give her a little courage, enough to make Raya dash toward the Void. The Void unleashed another volley of bullets at her, but Raya saw them coming this time, so she managed to dodge them easily. She leaped into the air and kicked the Void in the face.

Her hoofed foot left a deep dent in the side of the Void's face, causing the Void to stagger from the impact. Then Raya followed it up with another kick, but this time the Void caught Raya's leg and threw her through the air. Raya flew uncontrollably through the air before she landed on the street, but she was back on her feet almost instantly, because she discovered that gods could recover more quickly from those types of blows than mortals.

But then Raya heard movement behind her and looked over her shoulder in time to see the two golems standing behind her, raising their hammers above their heads like they were going to bring them down on her head.

So Raya, moving faster than the golems, lashed out with her feet, kicking them in their knees and causing them both to fall to the street. Just as she did that, however, the Void ran toward Raya as fast as she could move in Keeper's body, every step of her massive feet sending tremors through the ground.

Raya, however, was not going to run from Keeper. She ran toward the Void and the two met halfway, slamming their fists together and getting stuck in a back-and-forth struggle for dominance. Although Raya had the strength of a goddess, she found it hard to stand against the Void, whose strength seemed to equal hers if the fact that she was not giving up was a clue.

You know you can't win, said the Void as she and Raya struggled against each other. **None of you can. My power grows with every hour. Soon, no one will be able to stand against me, not even you gods.**

Raya gritted her teeth. "After I just became a goddess? Unacceptable. I am going to live long enough to enjoy my powers, thank you very much."

With that, Raya slammed her knee into the Void's gut. Her knee struck hard and fast enough that the Void's force against her weakened ever-so-slightly, but it was enough for Raya to catch the Void and raise her above her head. The Void waved her arms and legs about uselessly, while Raya lifted the Void as high as she could.

"Now," said Raya through her gritted teeth, "let Keeper's body go!"

Raya turned and slammed Keeper's body down on the fallen golems as hard as she could. The golems' bodies were crushed into pieces under the impact, while Keeper's body shattered into pieces under the impact.

Standing upright, Raya stepped back from the pile of metal and rock and looked at it sternly. She expected the Void to get up and continue the fight, but to her surprise, neither Keeper nor the golems moved an inch from their spot. That was probably because their bodies were almost completely destroyed, meaning that movement was essentially impossible for them, but Raya was still puzzled by the complete lack of hints of the Void's existence there.

She must have run away, Raya thought with a smirk. *Probably realized that she couldn't beat me. Now, I should go see if Carmaz*

281

is all—

At that moment, a dozen black tendrils exploded from the pile of metal and rock that had once been Keeper and the golems. They burst out so suddenly that Raya was taken by surprise and unable to stop them from slamming into her with the force of a brick wall and knocking her over. And before she could get up again, the tendrils slammed down on her arms and legs, effectively pinning her to the street.

Then a dark face appeared in the tendrils, one with two eyes and a simple line mouth. It smiled horrifically, revealing deadly sharp gray teeth that made Raya feel sick.

You didn't honestly think that that would be enough to kill *me*, did you? said the Void. **Even as a goddess, you are as foolish as ever, Raya. Too bad that will be the last mistake you will ever make, for I am done playing with you. Time to die.**

With that, one of the Void's tendrils turned into a needle and struck Raya in the neck. Raya gasped in pain, the first pain she had felt since becoming a goddess, and screamed when she felt an ice cold liquid burning through her veins.

I am filling your body with my own essence, Raya, said the Void, malicious gleefulness in her voice. **And I would tell you to pray to your god, but then I realized that you are a goddess, so you have no one to pray to but yourself. And I doubt you will be able to hear your own prayers over the pain that will rip you apart from the inside.**

Chapter Twenty-One

CARMAZ RAN THROUGH the alleys of World's End, ran as fast as he could, even though he was well aware at this point that the golems had decided to chase after Raya rather than him. Still, Carmaz didn't want to waste any time going to Anwan's Tailoring, where he had told Raya to meet him, so he ran as fast as he could.

Even so, however, Carmaz was starting to think he was reaching his limits, because his movements felt far more sluggish now, until eventually he was forced to come to a stop and catch his breath. Sweat ran down his face, his legs were weak, and his lungs felt like they were about to burst.

Panting, Carmaz sat down on the stoop of a nearby building, brushing some of his sweaty hair off of his forehead. He looked to the left and to the right, but did not see anyone else nearby. He did, however, hear the sounds of battle in the distance, but he could not tell who was fighting who, though he guessed that it was probably Raya fighting the golems.

Guess that means she won't get to Anwan's Tailoring just yet, Carmaz thought, wiping sweat off his forehead. *That means I can afford to take a few minutes to sit here and rest. But not for long.*

What Carmaz wanted more than anything was a nice glass of cold water. His throat was dry and parched, because he had not had anything to drink in a while. Yet he saw no immediate source of water anywhere he looked, so he would have to keep going until he could find some.

Even though Carmaz was still tired, he rose from the stoop and resumed walking down the alleyway, but he only walked, and slowly at that. He did not have the strength to run, even though he wanted to. Besides, he didn't think that anyone was chasing him, so he didn't have any real need to run. As long as he kept moving, he knew he was going to be all right.

But Carmaz only made it a few steps away from the stoop before five ethereal portals popped open around him. Then half a dozen beings wearing ratty gray cloaks stepped out of the portals, each one carrying a sword as black as the Void's darkness, which they lifted up to their chests as the portals closed shut behind them with a collective *pop*. Carmaz recognized these beings as being members of the Empty, that katabans cult dedicated to worshiping the Void, and so he knew exactly why they were here.

Carmaz raised his crystalline sword immediately, even though he doubted he could fight off all six of these Empty followers at once. They completely cut off all possible escape routes, meaning that running away was not an option.

The lead Empty follower, who was taller than the others, stepped forward, a fanatical grin of crooked white teeth visible from underneath his black hood. "Carmaz Korva. We meet again."

Panting, Carmaz tilted his head to the side. "Meet again? When did we meet before?"

"Don't you remember?" said the Empty follower. "Anwan's Tailoring. You and I fought in Brother Anwan's storage room. You beat me and I had to flee."

Carmaz suddenly remembered what the Empty follower was talking about. "Oh, right. I almost forgot, because I didn't know your name."

"My name is Timik," the Empty follower snapped. "And the Void, blessed be her all-consuming presence, has given me the task of leading the others to slay you where you stand."

Carmaz looked at the other Empty followers. All of them were silent, but he could tell that they were all eager to hack him apart with their swords. And unfortunately, he wasn't sure he could stop them from doing that once they started.

Looking back at Timik, Carmaz said, "So the Void still trusts you even *after* you have failed her time and again?"

"Shut up," Timik said. He put a hand on his chest. "You don't know anything about the Void. She is far more gracious than she appears, but even if she wasn't, I deserve every punishment I receive from her, for she is just and I am not."

Carmaz could think of no word less appropriate to describe the Void with than 'just,' but he supposed that that wasn't a point worth arguing.

Instead, he said, "What makes you think that you can defeat me? After all, as you yourself said, you lost to me last time."

"I have my fellow followers to back me up," said Timik, gesturing at his silent friends. "But more than that, I have given myself wholly to the Void. She has granted me strength unlike any that I have known before. Look."

Timik raised one of his hands. A black tendril rose from it, flailing about momentarily before returning to his hand. He then clenched his fist and looked at Carmaz with a smirk on his face.

"So the Void granted you some of her power," said Carmaz. "So what?"

"You don't understand," said Timik. "She didn't just grant me and the others *some* of her power. We *gave* her our bodies."

"Gave her your bodies?" said Carmaz. "What does that mean?"

Timik chuckled, a mad chuckle that made Carmaz want to run and hide. "Have you not wondered why my fellow followers are so silent? They do not have souls anymore. They have willingly given the Void control over their bodies in the same way that she controls the bodies of the golems and the corpses of her deceased enemies."

Alarmed, Carmaz looked around at the Empty followers again. Now that he looked more closely, he noticed that they stood too erect and too perfectly for real people. They more closely resembled puppets under the control of a puppeteer. In fact, they didn't even seem to be breathing.

"Why?" said Carmaz, looking at Timik again. "Why would anyone ever willingly give their selves up to the Void?"

"Because the Void will consume us all one day," said Timik with a satisfied sigh. "It is her destiny, you know, to consume Martir. It is our job as her followers to aid her in that regard, and this is one way we have chosen to do it. By giving her our souls and our bodies, we are helping her achieve her goals in the most concrete way possible."

"That's horrifying," said Carmaz, shaking his head. "Didn't you even stop to think what would happen if you did that? Don't your friends realize that they can never come back? That they will never get their souls back?"

"That, my enemy, is the *point*," said Timik. He shuddered and looked down at his own body in disgust. "We do not want to live. We want to sacrifice our bodies, our lives, our very souls, at the foot of the Void. She has given us purpose where we had none, turned our desire to end our suffering into a force for a greater purpose, and this is how we repay her. It is a feeling you will never understand."

"It sounds to me like you are completely and utterly insane," said Carmaz. "And the worst part is that I am not sure if that is because the Void has corrupted your mind or if you have always been this way."

"It doesn't matter," said Timik. "What matters is that the Void has spoken and declared that you must be destroyed. And we will happily obey, because we are to never question her commandments no matter what."

"Why aren't you a puppet like the others?" said Carmaz. "You still seem to be yourself. Are you not as devoted to the Void as your friends were?"

Timik snarled. "Don't you dare accuse I, Timik, a Priest of the Void, as lacking devotion to her greatness. I have simply asked to retain my individuality long enough to get my revenge on you, because I still remember how you soundly defeated me not long ago and I will not die until I can satisfy my revenge."

Carmaz looked at the puppets again, but none of them looked likely to move. That was when an idea came to mind that might help him survive, but he would have to put it into action quickly so that he could ensure its success.

"If you want your revenge against me so badly, Timik, then why don't you fight me by yourself?" said Carmaz. He gestured at the puppets standing around them. "Or are you so weak and cowardly that you need five other people to back you up?"

"The Void ordered us to kill you," said Timik. "But if necessary, I could kill you on my own."

"Then why don't you?" said Carmaz. "After all, even if I do beat you, I will still have to deal with your friends, who will probably be able to beat me because I will be so tired from fighting you. And if you win, then you will both please the Void and satisfy your own desire for revenge. There's no way you can lose here."

Timik looked like he was seriously considering Carmaz's offer, his eyes shifting to the right and then to the left, like he was now lost in thought. Carmaz hoped that Timik would take up his offer. He knew his chances of beating all six of the Void's puppets was as low as the chances of the southern gods collectively renouncing mortal hunting as a sport, but his chances of beating Timik in a one-on-one fight were high even in his tired state. He just had to bet that Timik valued getting revenge over obeying his mistress's orders.

Finally, Timik nodded and said, "Very well then, Carmaz Korva. I will accept your offer to fight one-on-one, to the death, of course."

"Of course," said Carmaz. "I expect nothing less."

Timik gestured at the puppets, which walked backwards until they had created a much wider area for Carmaz and Timik to fight in. Timik stepped forward, holding his black blade with one hand, while Carmaz carefully watched the katabans's body language in order to guess what Timik's first move was going to be.

Then Timik ran toward Carmaz faster than Carmaz expected. Carmaz raised his sword in time to block Timik's blade, which hit him with surprising force. Carmaz was almost knocked off his feet, but he retained his balance and forced Timik back.

The two struggled against each other like this briefly before Carmaz tried kicking Timik. But the katabans jumped backwards, avoiding Carmaz's kick, and then thrust his sword forward again. Yet Carmaz blocked it and slashed at Timik, which the katabans dodged as gracefully as a dancer.

But Carmaz slashed at Timik again, his sword catching Timik's robe and cutting through it. Unfortunately, his sword did not cut through Timik's skin, although he had little time to dwell on that misfortune because Timik stabbed at him. Carmaz jumped backwards and brought his sword down on Timik again, but the katabans blocked the blow with his own sword and pushed Carmaz back.

Taken by surprise, Carmaz staggered backwards, leaving his chest wide open. He registered that mistake right away, but before he could defend himself, Timik slashed at his exposed chest.

Blood exploded from Carmaz's chest as Timik's sword cut through his flesh. Pain shot through Carmaz's body as he stumbled and fell on his back. And before he could get up, Timik was upon him, pointing the tip of his black blade underneath Carmaz's chin.

"This is the end for you, Carmaz Korva," said Timik, his voice full of mad glee. "Your days of opposing the Void are finished. By the end of this day, the Void will be unstoppable and there will be nothing in Martir that can stop her. Too bad you will

289

not live long enough to see it."

Chapter Twenty-Two

TWO MINUTES LEFT, said the Void, her voice coming from the collective mouths of Saia, Tamra, Lady Dia, and Stalac. **Make your choice quickly, Braim Kotogs, because time is running out.**

Braim looked between the unconscious Darek and Jenur in the golems' hands and his own sword. There was no way in hell that he would ever kill himself just to satisfy the deranged demands of the Void, but neither was he willing to sacrifice Darek and Jenur, either. Yet he did not see any way out of this situation that would end well for either him or Darek and Jenur. Even if he tried a ranged attack—which he didn't think he could, even with the divine power flowing through him—there was no way he could hit the Void fast enough to save his friends.

Time is ticking, Braim thought. *And I can't bet on the Void deciding to give me even just a few extra seconds to think. I have to come to a conclusion now.*

Braim looked at Darek and Jenur again. The two were now so still that he almost suspected that they actually were dead. But of course, if they were, then the Void wouldn't have any leverage over Braim and her threats would be pointless.

Timothy L. Cerepaka

But then Braim thought about it. It didn't make any sense to him that the Void would have both Darek and Jenur. While the Void's reach was probably extensive, he found it odd that he had not heard about their kidnapping until just now. Maybe Darek and Jenur's kidnapping had happened just a few hours ago, but Braim had a feeling that if they had indeed been kidnapped, he would have heard about it at some point from one of the gods, even if they had been kidnapped only recently. After all, Darek and Jenur were not involved in the Tournament. It would seem like a lot of work on the Void's part to kidnap Darek and Jenur and bring them all the way here, especially because there was no way the Void could have guessed that Braim would have the power to fight her, which was the whole reason she had kidnapped Darek and Jenur in the first place.

One minute, Braim, said the Void, snapping him out of his thoughts. **I am surprised that you have not immediately obliged. I thought that you valued your friends enough to die for them. I guess you humans really do only look out for yourselves after all.**

Braim gritted his teeth, but didn't respond. He tried to think of a way out of this and focused on the fact that this situation did not make any sense.

Then it hit him like lightning, and he smiled.

Why are you smiling? said the Void. She sounded as authoritative and strong as ever, but also slightly confused and even scared. **Does seeing your friends' lives threatened amuse you?**

"Nah," said Braim, shaking his head, "because those aren't my real friends."

The Void, in all four of the bodies that she controlled, looked stunned. **They aren't your friends? What are you talking about? Of course they are your friends. Why have you chosen to reject them?**

"My feelings toward my real friends hasn't changed a bit," said Braim. "What has changed is that I know exactly what you are doing: You faked my friends."

Faked? the Void repeated. **What do you mean?**

"Those two people in your servants' hands?" said Braim, gesturing at the two unconscious beings. "Those aren't the *real* Darek and Jenur. They're illusions created by your shadows. The *real* Darek and Jenur are still safely in the Northern Isles, well away from your grasp."

The Void's four hosts did not move. Neither did the golems. That made it hard for Braim to tell whether he was correct in his accusation. He was confident that his theory was correct, but he still had no way of knowing that for sure until the Void confirmed it herself.

Finally, the golems squeezed Darek and Jenur ever more tightly. Darek and Jenur screamed in pain, realistic screams that made Braim almost doubt his own theory. The pain in their eyes, the thrashing of their heads … it was all too real.

But just when their screams reached their zenith, Darek and Jenur exploded into shadows. The golems then lowered their hands to their sides, leaving absolutely no sign that either Darek or Jenur had even been there in the first place.

You are smarter than you appear, Braim Kotogs, said the Void. **Yes, those were illusions I crafted in order to crush you without having to lift a finger. I clearly underestimated your**

intelligence and understanding, however.

"Obviously," said Braim. He raised Devourer. "Now that I don't have to worry about you harming any of my friends, I'm going to go all out against you. Get ready to go down for good."

Why should I? said the Void. **After all, it is you who are about to 'go down for good,' as you put it.**

Braim raised an eyebrow. "By what? Your golems? Your hosts?"

One of my hosts, said the Void.

"Which one?" said Braim. "No, hold on. Let me guess. It's Tamra, isn't it?"

It will be none of these hosts, said the Void, gesturing at all of the assembled hosts. **But if you want to know who it is, I suggest looking behind you.**

Frowning, Braim looked over his shoulder in time to see a large and heavy-looking hammer falling down toward him. Braim and Ragao jumped forward to avoid the hammer, which slammed into the floor with enough strength to shake the building and cause portions of the ceiling to fall.

"Another golem?" said Braim, trying to get a good look at whoever had just attacked them, though it was difficult due to the darkness of the Void.

It was Ragao, squinting her eyes, who answered the question in a trembling voice: "Not a golem. But a god."

Ragao's answer was followed by a brilliant burst of fire that illuminated the being that had tried to attack them. The fire was in the hand of the person, floating above their palm, but Braim's attention was drawn not to the fire but to the face of the being holding the fire.

It was the face of Grinf, with his strong jaw and light-colored hair visible in the glow of the fire. The God of Justice, Fire, and Metal was as large and imposing as ever, the fire in his eyes burning as brightly as a furnace.

"Grinf?" said Braim. "I thought that the Void had consumed you."

That was when Braim noticed streaks of darkness on Grinf's body. They looked almost like the strings of puppets, which immediately told Braim what the Void was doing to Grinf.

Before Braim could say that aloud, however, the Void behind him said, **Grinf is under my control now. I haven't consumed his soul just yet, because godly souls are harder to consume than mortal souls, but he is wholly and fully under my control and there is nothing he can do to fight against me and free himself from my control.**

"Am I going to have to fight him, then?" said Braim, though he did not look over his shoulder at the Void when he said that.

Of course, said the Void. **But I doubt you will win. Grinf still has his divine power and energy. He is so far above you that it won't take him much time to eliminate you, especially with my own power augmenting his.**

Braim gulped. He knew that the Void had a point. While Braim did indeed have the divine power of the gods flowing through him, he was quite aware that he was not much of a match for an actual god, especially if that god was being controlled by the Void. The best he could hope for was maybe somehow surviving for a few minutes, but even that struck him as too optimistic.

But it wasn't like Braim could run away anywhere. With the

Void's other hosts behind him and Grinf before him, he was effectively trapped. That meant that Braim had no choice but to fight to the best of his ability, even though he was quite sure at this point that his best was nowhere near enough to beat Grinf.

So Braim raised Devourer, but just as he did that, Grinf raised and hurled the fireball in his hand at Braim. The fireball grew rapidly the further it traveled through the air until it was soon large enough to consume Braim entirely if it hit him.

But at the last moment, Ragao stepped in between the fireball and Braim. She raised her swords just as the fireball collided with her form, causing it to explode and send flames everywhere and forcing Braim to duck to avoid getting his hair burned off his scalp. Nonetheless, he looked up at Ragao, who had not even moved an inch when the blast hit her, although there was now smoke rising from her body where she had been hit.

"Ragao?" said Braim. "Why did you—"

Ragao looked over her shoulder at Braim and said, "Distraction."

Then Ragao dashed toward Grinf, swinging her swords through the air at him. Grinf raised his gavel and ran toward her and soon the god and the half-god were dueling, Ragao slashing and stabbing at Grinf with her four swords, Grinf blocking each blow with his gavel.

That was when Braim realized what Ragao meant. She was going to distract Grinf in order to give Braim time to fight the Void. It was a brilliant move, one he wished he had thought of, but it didn't matter because he now had an opportunity that he could not afford to waste.

Turning around, Braim was about to run toward the Void, but

stopped when he saw a strange sight. The four hosts of the Void were now standing in a square formation, with the golems separating Braim from them, but that wasn't the oddest part. The oddest part was the shadowy tendrils that were attached to the heads of each of the Void's hosts, which were in turn all connected to a swirling ball of darkness in the center of their formation.

As Braim watched, Saia, Tamra, Lady Dia, and Stalac were drawn into the swirling black ball like they were being sucked into a whirlpool, which had now grown as large as Braim himself. The sound of lightning striking and electricity sparking came from the sphere, growing louder and louder, until Braim was certain that the sphere was about to explode.

But then the sphere stretched until it resembled a thin black bar rather than a sphere. Then the shadow fell away from its body, revealing a new being that Braim had never seen before.

The being resembled a horrific combination of human and golem. Half of its face was human, the other half golem. Its body and arms and feet were golem in appearance, while its hands were organic human hands that were extremely large. The figure's face had dual-colored eyes, one green and the other yellow, and a mouth that had both human and golem teeth in it. The abomination had the wings and tail of Lady Dia and Stalac rising from its back, too, which made it look even larger than it already did.

"What the hell?" said Braim. "What did you do?"

I combined my hosts, of course, said the Void, her voice issuing forth from the monstrosity's misshapen and unnatural mouth. **I decided that I would be stronger in one body than in**

297

four. How do you like it?

"I don't," said Braim.

I didn't expect you to, said the Void. **Now, why don't we make this battle our last? Even if Grinf will not be able to defeat you, I can still do it myself.**

Braim nodded and, without saying another word, ran toward the Void with Devourer before him. The two golems standing between him and the Void moved to meet him, but Braim charged Devourer with some of the divine energy flowing through him and slashed at the two golems, sending an energy slash toward them. The golems were too slow to dodge and the energy slash cut them both in half, sending their remains falling to the floor as Braim dashed past them toward the Void.

The Void pointed at Braim and several dozen shadowy tendrils lanced forth from her arm toward him. Braim, however, jumped over the tendrils as they came toward him and landed on the tendrils themselves before cutting through them with his sword. The tendrils immediately dissipated, causing Braim to fall back to the floor, but he hit the floor running and soon was right in front of the Void.

With a yell, Braim slashed the Void with Devourer. But the Void blocked the blow with the thick, stone forearm of her right arm and then tried to punch him with her other fist, which Braim dodged by jumping backwards out of her reach. He slashed at her again, sending an energy blast that hit the Void dead on, but unfortunately it did not cut her in half like it did to the golems.

Still, the Void visibly cringed when the slash hit her, which told Braim that he could indeed harm her. He moved in to get closer, but had to jump backwards again to avoid her fist. Just as he landed, however, the Void pointed her tail at him and an ice blast shot out from it.

Braim jumped to the side, allowing the ice blast to smash into the ground where he had been standing mere moments before. He then leaped at her with his sword held high, but the Void held up both of her arms to block the blow. Then she tried to shoot him with ice again, but Braim dropped to the ground before the ice could hit him and, taking advantage of the opening the Void provided, stabbed her in the stomach with his sword as hard as he could.

Despite the Void's rock solid skin, Braim's sword sank into her stomach as easily as if it was made of butter. Then he channeled his divine energy through the sword and into her body, causing the Void to let out a roar of pain that sounded unnatural and eerie, but Braim kept digging his sword in deeper while pouring more and more divine energy into her body.

But then Braim heard her tail above her gathering energy and, yanking his sword out of her body, jumped backwards, again avoiding her ice beam just in the nick of time. He walked backwards several feet, watching as the Void fell to her hands and knees as a strange reddish-black liquid that might have been blood poured from the wound Braim had created. She looked close to death now, but Braim didn't let down his guard just yet.

"Ready to give up and go back where you belong, Void?" said Braim. "It's pretty clear by now that your body is clumsy and useless. If you give up now, I'll let you go back to whatever rock you crawled out from with your dignity in tact."

The Void looked up at Braim with pure hatred in her eyes. **Getting a body was a mistake. I don't need a body to kill you.**

Without warning, the Void's body hit the floor with a *thump*. A second later, the Void's shadows burst from the monstrosity's back like a geyser, causing Braim to hold Devourer defensively in order to defend against any frontal attacks.

But then several tendrils lanced out from the darkness and wrapped around Braim's arms and legs. They jerked his arms backward, causing him to drop Devourer, which fell to the floor with a clatter. Braim struggled against the tendrils, but they were stronger than they had been even just a couple of hours ago, and now they barely budged under his strength and effort.

I am finally *done* playing with you, Braim Kotogs, said the Void, which sounded like it was speaking from everywhere at once. **It is time for you to die like the worm you are.**

A dozen shadow tendrils appeared in front of Braim. He only had enough time to register that, because the tendrils then started slashing at his chest, body, and face. Every slash was like getting cut by the sharpest sword in the world, sending blood flying everywhere and making Braim scream, only for each scream to be cut off by another slash that tore through his skin like the claws of a swamp tiger. He couldn't defend himself, couldn't do anything except feel the wrath of the Void come down upon him.

Die, die, die, said the Void, whose voice now sounded beyond madness. **Die!**

Every slash of the Void's tendrils sent fresh waves of pain into his brain that he was simply unable to ignore. He couldn't even struggle against the tendrils holding limbs back anymore. All he could do was stand there and let the Void rip him apart piece by piece.

This is it, was the only rational thought that Braim could think

300

amidst the terrible pain ripping through him. *I'm finished.*

Yet as those thoughts passed through his head, Braim felt a fiery, burning energy in him that he had not noticed before. It was like the divine energy from before, only this time it was rising within him as rapidly as lava rose from an erupting volcano. The Void, in her mania to kill him, didn't seem to notice, but Braim did because this rising, burning energy was now starting to eclipse the pain he felt in his body. He was starting to think clearly and rationally again, like the pain from each of the Void's blows meant nothing at all.

With a roar of anger, Braim ripped his arms and legs out of the tendrils holding them back. The other tendrils, the ones slashing him, paused and Braim could feel the Void watching him in shock, as if she had not expected him to start fighting back.

Impossible, said the Void. **How did you do that?**

"I don't know," said Braim. He breathed heavily, feeling the wet blood on his clothes, but he ignored it for the moment. "What I do know is that you are going down for good, just like I said before."

No, I won't, said the Void. **If you won't let me kill you that way, then let's try another!**

The shadow tendrils in front of Braim retreated back into the darkness. Braim held Devourer to defend himself again, but then he noticed that all of the shadow and darkness in the Stadium lobby was slowly being sucked away. Light returned where the darkness left, allowing Braim to see the lobby a little easier than before, but his attention was not on the light returning. Instead, he focused on the massive darkness building up before him, which was grower larger and larger every second, until soon a massive pillar of shadow rose before him. It was far larger than even the golems and its tip was pointed and sharp.

Then, without warning, the Void's spear turned and rammed down on him. Braim lifted up Devourer and blocked the spear, even though it was five times bigger than he was. In fact, he blocked it easily, without being pushed back at all.

Impossible! the Void said again, her voice full of rage and confusion. **You shouldn't be able to hold back against my full wrath. No mortal can.**

Braim smiled. "Then maybe I'm not your ordinary mortal."

With that, Braim sent all of the divine energy in his body into the sword. And with a yell, he pushed back against the Void as hard as he could, sending all of his energy through his blade into the Void herself.

The effect was instantaneous. A massive, brilliant burst of light exploded from the point where Braim's sword met the Void's spear. The light was brighter and greater than anything Braim had seen in his life, even greater than the light of the sun. It reached into every corner of the Stadium, and even went beyond it, though Braim was not quite sure how he knew that. Perhaps it was because the light was an extension of his own will and body, which allowed him to feel the light reach for every inch of the Void's shadow, driving it back or eliminating it entirely wherever it touched.

And all the while, the Void roared in sheer agony, sounding like she was being torn apart. But Braim did not care, did not let up, and poured as much of his own energy into the light as he could.

Then, just as suddenly, the light faded and Braim blinked

several times before his vision adjusted and he saw the results of the explosion.

The Void was almost completely gone now. There was a slight afterglow everywhere he looked, even on his body, which had actually been healed now, apparently by the light of the explosion itself. The coldness of the Void was gone as well, replaced instead by a pleasant warmth, like a blazing fire on a cold winter's night. Braim heard a grunt behind him and looked over his shoulder to see both Grinf and Ragao lying on the ground unconscious, wisps of shadow floating from Grinf's body like smoke.

Then Braim heard a groan of pain and looked back in front of him to see a shadowy sphere floating in the air before him. He immediately knew what it was: The Void, or what remained of her, anyway.

Well ... played, Braim Kotogs, said the Void, her voice no longer strong and boasting, but weak and pathetic. **You destroyed me where the gods ... where your gods failed. But the Void will always exist. You can never destroy me forever. I will return, and when I do, you will be the first to die.**

Braim didn't respond. He simply raised Devourer—which still glowed with divine energy—and slashed the Void's remains. In one stroke, the Void's spherical form dissipated like smoke in a strong breeze.

As soon as the Void's remains vanished, four bright balls of energy—one brown like dirt, one white like snow, one blue like water, and another a dreamlike purple—shot out of its shadows and flew away through the ceiling. But before they left, the spheres stopped briefly and seemed to look at Braim for a moment.

Then Braim heard four voices in his head say, *Thank you.*

And then the spheres were gone, and after they left, Braim realized that those had been the spirits of the four gods that Tamra had taken. They were now returning to their bodies, which meant that the Void really was gone.

Lowering his weapon, Braim turned and walked over to Grinf and Ragao. Both were heavily wounded from their fight with each other, but they both appeared to be alive. Braim bent over Grinf and said, "Hey, Grinf, are you awake?"

Grinf's eyes opened. They were still on fire, but they no longer had the darkness of the Void clouding them. He did, however, look confused. "Braim Kotogs? What … what happened? Is the Void—"

"She's gone," Braim said. "And she won't be coming back anytime—"

Braim stopped speaking abruptly. A horrible, burning pain surged through his body. He dropped Devourer, which fell to the ground with a clatter, and then keeled over backwards himself even as Grinf shouted, "Braim!"

But Braim didn't pay attention to anything Grinf said. The divine energy in his body—or what was left of it, anyway—was now tearing him apart on the inside. And he could tell that his time was up, that the energy was finally going to end his life, just as Atikos had warned.

That was the final thought that passed through Braim's head before he drifted off into unconsciousness.

Chapter Twenty-Three

THE ICE COLD poison that flowed through Raya's veins was almost too much for her. And she couldn't force it out no matter how hard she tried. The Void was pouring more and more of herself into Raya's mouth, the darkness paralyzing Raya and making it impossible for her to get rid of it. It felt like the Void was killing her, and there was nothing Raya could do to save herself.

Someone ... Raya thought, although even her thoughts were becoming less and less effective. *Save me* ...

Then, without warning, everything was suddenly consumed by a bright light. The light washed over Raya and the Void and the golems in the alleyway, blinding Raya, but not leaving her deaf. She could hear the screams of the Void, which sounded like they were coming from within and without her brain. It was the loudest and most painful sound Raya had ever heard in her life, but also the most satisfying, because she understood that she was listening to the final screams of the Void as she was driven away from World's End.

But more than that, Raya felt a familiar presence in the light, Braim's presence, which reassured her that this was a friendly force and that she would not be harmed. She felt the poisonous darkness in her veins evaporating, until soon the pain and cold was gone and Raya felt normal once again.

As quickly as it came, however, the light vanished. Raya blinked several times, but her eyes did not need to take much time to adjust to the light. She saw a pleasant afterglow on everything, but more importantly, the Void was nowhere to be seen.

Raya sat up, her limbs now free from the Void's control, and looked at her body. There were no clues whatsoever that the Void had even touched her. It was like the light had healed her of any injuries or imperfections that she had suffered from.

That was Braim's light, Raya thought. *And he defeated the Void.*

But then Raya suddenly remembered that Carmaz was still in trouble. She stood up and used her divine powers to search the city for Carmaz's presence, which she immediately found not far from her current location. She then teleported across the next few streets and alleys until she found herself in the same alley as Carmaz, where she spotted a disturbing sight.

Carmaz was lying on the street, apparently alive, but all around him lay dead katabans in gray cloaks, which identified them as Empty followers. It looked like they had simply collapsed, as if someone had taken their souls from their bodies.

Only one of them stood: A tall katabans who was staring down at his hands for some reason. His face was hidden by his hood, but even Raya could tell that this katabans was shocked by something that had just happened to him.

"The Void ..." said the katabans. He started patting his body and feeling his face. "Where is she? Why can't I feel her anymore? Where is her loving embrace, her familiar coldness? Did she abandon me? But why would she do that?"

"Hey!" Raya shouted, causing the katabans to look up at her suddenly. "Leave Carmaz alone, you monster!"

The Empty follower, a panicked look on his face when he recognized Raya, held out his hand, probably to open an ethereal portal from which to escape. Raya moved to stop him, but then Carmaz rose to his feet behind the Empty follower, crystalline sword in hand, and drove the sword straight through the Empty follower's back.

The Empty follower gasped as the tip of Carmaz's sword tore through his chest, blood pouring out from the wound. Then Carmaz pulled his sword out and the Empty follower collapsed among his fellows in a rapidly-expanding pool of his own blood. He did not so much as stir as the blood stained his gray cloak.

"That ..." Carmaz panted, but he managed to finish his sentence. "... was for Saia, you bastard."

Raya, temporarily stunned by Carmaz's action, shook her head and then ran over to Carmaz, reaching him in a few seconds. She then scooped him up into her arms and hugged him as tightly as she could, saying, "Oh, Carmaz, I'm so glad you're alive! I thought for sure that you were going to die!"

"Raya?" said Carmaz, whose voice sounded tight. "I might still die if you don't let go of me right away."

"Oh, right, sorry," said Raya as she put Carmaz back down on the street and let go of him. "I am just so happy to see you. Did you see that light from before?"

Carmaz, who was now rubbing his ribs rather gingerly, nodded. "The one that destroyed the Void. It was Braim's doing."

"I know," said Raya. She clapped her hands together, which created a clopping sound due to the hooves on her fingers. "We should go and see if Braim is all right and make sure that the Void really is gone."

"Good idea," said Carmaz. "Let's go to the Stadium."

Raya nodded, grabbed Carmaz's hand, and then teleported them both back to the Stadium's destroyed entrance. The two of them then dashed inside, but stopped as soon as they saw the scene before them.

Braim was lying on the floor without any wounds or injuries visible on his body (although his clothes were cut up for some reason). His sword, Devourer, lay by his side, while Grinf knelt over him with a surprisingly concerned expression on his divine features. Ragao was there, too, but she stood to the side, like she was not sure what to do.

"Lord Grinf?" said Raya as she and Carmaz approached. "What happened to Braim? Is he all right?"

Grinf looked up at Raya and Carmaz suddenly, instinctively reaching for his gavel before he recognized them. Then his hand returned to his side. "Oh. You must be the new goddess that I sensed."

"Yes, I became a goddess," said Raya, nodding. Then she looked at Braim's unconscious form. "But what about Braim? He looks dead."

Grinf frowned and looked down at Braim's prone body. "He is in the last stages of his life. I don't know how much longer he has left, but I doubt it is much. We are seeing the last stages of his life."

"But why?" said Raya. "I don't understand."

"Braim is being killed by the divine energy inside him, even after he left out most of it in that last attack against the Void earlier," said Grinf. "And there is nothing that I or any of the other gods can do to save him. Not even you could save him, Raya."

"But if he dies ..." Carmaz trailed off like he was remembering something important. "Then his soul will be completely extinguished. That's what he told us."

"Even if that is true, that does not change the fact that we gods are powerless to save him," said Grinf, shaking his head. "If we had given him his divine energy ourselves, then we could have saved him, but because he gained his powers via that ritual, it is impossible for us to save him on our own."

"Then what are we supposed to do?" said Carmaz. "Just let him die?"

"Unless your knowledge of rescuing the dying is better than the collective knowledge of the gods, then yes, that is exactly what we must do," said Grinf. "I don't like it any better than you do, but even I have to acknowledge when there is nothing that we gods can do to help people like him."

Raya fell down by Braim's side and looked him over. Although he was still breathing, Raya could feel the divine energy in him burning away at his life. She, too, did not know how much longer Braim had, but that just made it all the more urgent to save him right away.

But what am I supposed to do? Raya thought. *I'm a new goddess. I don't have as much power or experience as Grinf or any other god or goddess. And if Grinf says it's impossible, then it probably is impossible to save him.*

309

Even though Raya understood that thought, a part of her rebelled against it anyway. Just because the gods said it was impossible didn't mean that it was. After all, Braim himself was an impossibility, a mortal who came back from the dead. Why shouldn't it also be possible to save him from dying again?

"I have an idea about how we can save Braim," said Raya. She gestured at herself and Grinf. "Because we two gods are here, I think we can save Braim by ascending him to godhood."

Grinf bit his lower lip and glanced down at Braim again. "But that can only be done in the Ascension Ceremony and with a southern and northern god."

"Are you sure?" said Raya.

"Yes," said Grinf, nodding. "We're both northern gods, so the Ceremony could not be done even if we were both willing to do it."

Raya looked down at Braim again before saying, "Then I will be a southern god. Or a southern goddess. Is that how it works?"

She looked up at Grinf again, who appeared taken aback by her sudden willingness to become a southern god. "Is it?"

"For new gods, yes, they can choose which Pantheon they want to join," said Grinf. "But why would you want to do that? You do realize that southern gods hate mortals, don't you?"

"I do, but if this will help me save Braim, then I must do it," said Raya. "All right?"

Grinf looked deeply skeptical about this, but then he nodded once more and said, "Very well. But be warned that when you choose an affiliation, you cannot change it back. And if you become a southern god, then your interaction with mortals will be limited by its very nature."

"I will do whatever it takes to help Braim," said Raya. "Now, are you going to help me ascend Braim or not? We can use Braim's own divine energy to ascend him, since we don't have access to the well of divine energy underneath World's End at the moment."

Again, Grinf looked skeptical, but he placed his hands on Braim's chest, as did Raya. Carmaz took a couple of steps back, even though Raya wasn't sure that that was necessary on Carmaz's part.

But Raya soon forgot all about that as she focused on accessing the divine energy in Braim's body. She could still feel it burning away at his body, mind, and soul, even smell his flesh starting to burn, but eventually she gained access to it, as did Grinf.

Because Raya was not sure what to do next, she followed Grinf's lead as he refocused the energy in Braim's body. She felt Grinf begin to distribute the energy all throughout Braim's body in an even way, and she helped, although she could not help nearly as much as she wanted to due to her own inexperience as a goddess.

Even with Grinf's help, it was hard to do, because the divine energy in Braim's body did not want to be contained. It felt wild and destructive, almost like the Void, except without her intelligence and cruelty. Raya even felt it biting at her own soul, but as a goddess, she was immune to the pain it was trying to inflict upon her and so she did not react.

But eventually, the divine energy's burning power grew less and less, while Braim's body grew warmer, although it was a comforting warmth rather than a lethal one. Braim's breathing—

which had grown weaker since he fell unconscious—was getting stronger with each passing second. His skin no longer burned, nor did his hair or clothes. Raya could now tell that Braim was no longer in danger of dying and in fact was perhaps better now than he had ever been at any point in his life.

Raya and Grinf removed their hands from Braim's chest. As soon as they did, Braim's eyes shot open and he gasped. He sat up, feeling his forehead and gasping for air. He looked around wildly, like he wasn't sure where he was or what happened.

"Am I dead?" said Braim. "Or was I dreaming?"

Grinf, who looked too astonished to speak, nonetheless said, "No, Braim, you are alive. You were dying, but now you are not."

Braim looked at Grinf in confusion. "The last thing I remember was falling unconscious from my own power trying to kill me. Are you telling me that I'm not going to die after all?"

"Yes," said Grinf. "Raya and I saved you by ascending you to godhood. Your body is now strong enough to handle the divine energy in you, which means that you will not—and cannot—die."

Braim looked at Raya in surprise. "Wait a minute. *You* helped me?"

"Of course," said Raya with a smile. "After all, I am a gracious and loving goddess who always rewards those who help her. Especially friends like you, who deserve to be helped no matter what."

Braim started feeling his body. "I *do* feel a lot more powerful than I did before, but what is my domain? What, exactly, am I the God *of*?"

Grinf tapped his chin in puzzlement for a moment before realization dawned in his eyes. "Oh."

"Oh?" said Braim, looking up at Grinf again suddenly. "Oh what?"

"I just realized that you are now the God of Martir," said Grinf. "That is how the ascension process works. We gods who ascend mortals have no say in what areas they become gods. It is based purely on their destiny, so that means that you are the God of Martir."

"I am?" said Braim. He sounded both delighted and confused. "Really? But I didn't win the Tournament."

"I know," said Grinf. "But there's no changing it now. When a mortal becomes a god, they *stay* a god until they are destroyed. Therefore, Braim Kotogs, you are now the God of Martir, whether you won the Tournament or not."

"So does that make me your leader?" said Braim.

"Yes," said Grinf, though he sounded rather reluctant when he said that. "But you are still inexperienced, seeing as you have not been a god for even fifteen minutes yet."

"I know," said Braim. "But still … I can't believe it. I'm the God of Martir. That's amazing."

Although Raya was happy for Braim, she did feel a little bit jealous. That meant that he was now in charge of her, but more than that, it meant that she would never have a chance at the spot of Goddess of Martir ever again. That almost made her depressed, but then she told herself not to feel so bad about Braim's success and that what mattered was that he wasn't going to die.

"What should we do now?" said Braim, looking around at everyone.

"Go back to the Temple and inform the others of what happened," Grinf said. "No doubt everyone has noticed the

313

banishment of the Void, but they also need to know the exact details, as well as your ascension."

"All right," said Braim. He stood up and now Raya noticed that Braim suddenly looked a lot handsomer and stronger than before. "And let's throw a citywide party while we're at it."

Grinf frowned when he heard that. "A party?"

"To celebrate the fact that we defeated the Void," said Braim, grinning as he patted Grinf on the shoulder. "Let's get all of the best musicians in the city to play at it and all of the best dancers to dance at it and all of the best chefs to cater to it. We could even mark today as a holiday, though not sure what to call it."

"First things first," said Grinf as he and Raya rose as well. "We must go to the Temple and inform everyone of what happened. After that, we can discuss things like parties and the like."

Braim nodded. "Sounds good to me. What are we waiting for? Let's go."

Chapter Twenty-Four

WHEN CARMAZ AND the others returned to the Temple of the Gods, they were immediately greeted with cheers from both the gods and godlings, who, as Grinf suspected, had felt the Void's banishment. The gods even allowed Braim to sit on the throne reserved for the God of Martir, although due to his small size he still had to stand on it rather than sit on it. Braim then explained to the assembled gods and godlings all about how he defeated the Void, although it was Raya and Grinf who had to explain how and why they ascended him to godhood.

It was the other godlings' reaction to this explanation that interested Carmaz the most. Most of the godlings seemed happy for Braim's ascension, but a few did not, which Carmaz assumed were other participants in the Skimif Bracket who had not been given a chance to win the title of God of Martir for themselves. Carmaz said nothing to them, however, because he could not think of anything to say to comfort them.

Not to mention that a handful of the gods appeared dissatisfied by Braim's ascension as well. Diog and the Ghostly God both failed to cheer Braim when he told the gods about his ascension, which made Carmaz wonder if Braim was going to punish those two for what they did to him in the past now that he was stronger than him. Considering Braim was not a very vengeful person, Carmaz doubted that that would happen, but he doubted that Diog or the Ghostly God would enjoy Braim's rule very much nonetheless.

In any case, the gods did agree to throw a citywide party in World's End to celebrate this success, with many of the gods and goddesses already leaving the Temple to start to gather resources and plan out the celebration, although there was talk of rebuilding any destroyed or damaged buildings first. Many of the godlings started chatting excitedly about whether they would be allowed to stay in the city for the celebration, which sounded like it was going to be the grandest celebration of all time based on the way Braim described it.

While Carmaz was just as happy as anyone else about the Void's defeat and Braim's ascension, he nonetheless sneaked out of the Throne Room and into the lobby to be alone, where the voices of the chattering gods and godlings were muted. Closing the doors behind him, Carmaz's shoulders slumped and he sighed before walking over to a nearby support beam and leaning against it. He was so exhausted from the excitement and challenges of the day that he could barely stand, which was one of the reasons he had removed himself from the others. He needed time alone to think.

Raya and Braim are now gods, Carmaz thought. *The Void is defeated. Martir is safe. And no doubt the next three godlings to ascend to godhood will be chosen in short order. This is all great news, yet my home ...*

"Long time, no see, Carmaz Korva," a familiar authoritative and feminine voice said, causing Carmaz to snap out of his thoughts and look up.

Judge Alira was walking toward him, although it was more like limping. She was limping with wooden crutches, like she was recovering from a serious injury, which actually was the case, as Carmaz recalled hearing that Alira had been badly injured trying to save Raya and Yoji from a golem. He had not, however, expected to see her again so soon.

"Alira," said Carmaz. His voice sounded exhausted, which he made no attempt to hide, because he did not feel any need to. "You look awful."

"You don't look much better yourself," said Alira, stopping a few feet away from him. She glanced at the closed doors to the Throne Room, where the sounds of cheering and chattering gods and godlings could still be heard. "I felt the Void's defeat and Braim's ascension."

"Yes," said Carmaz. "Looks like Martir is going to survive after all, doesn't it?"

"It does," said Alira, nodding. "And the Tournament will still go on as well, seeing as there are still a few godly positions left that have not been filled. I have no doubt that we will fill them soon enough, however, because there is now nothing to stop us from completing the Tournament in a timely manner."

Carmaz looked at Alira in surprise. "You mean you still want to judge the Tournament anyway? Even after all that's happened?"

Alira looked down at her feet. She pushed her glasses up the bridge of her nose. "I don't *want* to, but it is my job. It is the whole purpose of my existence. And Martir still needs its gods."

317

Carmaz nodded, but then said, "Have you thought about what you will do *after* the Tournament is over, though? I remember you didn't answer that question when I asked you about it back on Ruwa."

Alira looked up at Carmaz again, but before she could speak, Raya suddenly appeared next to Carmaz and said, "Carmaz! I was wondering where you went. Why aren't you in the Throne Room with everyone else celebrating the—"

Raya cut herself off abruptly when she saw Alira. Alira, meanwhile, had closed her mouth and stared at Raya as well. The two stared at each other in a rather awkward way, which made Carmaz wonder what had happened between the two since he had last seen them. Alira looked like she wanted to run away, which was an odd trait to associate with her, as Carmaz had never thought of Alira as being particularly timid or afraid of anything.

Then Raya said, in an awkward voice, "Oh, so you are doing all right, Alira. I was wondering if you would recover from the attack or not."

"That I did," said Alira, although she was just as awkward as Raya. "That I did. Even better, the Void's darkness is gone from within me, eliminated, I think, by Braim's light explosion from earlier, so I am no longer dying like I was previously."

"That's good to hear," said Raya, although she was deliberately avoiding looking at Alira now. "Very good to hear."

"Um," said Carmaz, catching both of their attention. "Am I missing something or—?"

"It's nothing," said Alira, shaking her head. "Raya and I … it's nothing. I should return to bed now. I still need rest."

With that, Alira turned and walked away, using her crutches

318

for support, while Carmaz and Raya watched her go, Carmaz with confusion, Raya with relief. Once Alira was gone, Carmaz looked at Raya.

"What was that all about?" said Carmaz.

"Nothing," said Raya, too quickly for Carmaz's tastes. "I mean, it's none of your business. So don't worry about it, all right?"

Carmaz was still intensely curious about what had happened between Raya and Alira to leave things so awkward between them like that, but he had always believed in respecting the privacy of others.

So Carmaz nodded and said, "All right. I won't ask you any more questions about it, then."

Raya sighed in relief. "Good. Anyway, why aren't you back in the Throne Room with everyone else?"

Carmaz shrugged. "I need my privacy. So much has happened that I just couldn't take all of the cheering and screaming. I needed some silence, some space to think about everything."

"Oh," said Raya. "Okay. But are you going to stay for the party, at least? Braim says there's going to be enough wine to fill the entire Crystal Sea. I'm not much of a drunkard, of course, but —"

"No," said Carmaz. "I want to go home to Ruwa and make sure that everyone there is all right. Then we will rebuild ... or rebuild what little we can, anyway."

Raya frowned. "Can I help?"

Carmaz scowled and looked Raya straight in the eyes. Even though he was just an ordinary mortal and Raya was a goddess, she still stepped back when he looked at her with anger in his

319

eyes.

"Would you just cut that out already?" said Carmaz. He no longer hid the anger in his voice. "We are *never* getting together. I don't care whether you're a goddess, a princess, or whatever. I have *zero* interest in marrying a woman like yourself. I am loyal to Ruwa first and foremost, and any woman who cannot see that cannot stand with me. Do you understand that or must I use simpler language to cut through that thick skull of yours?"

Raya looked offended, even hurt, by Carmaz's words, but he didn't care. While he didn't hate Raya, he certainly did not want her to entertain any illusions about the two of them ever getting together or marrying. If that meant being harsher than usual, then so be it.

Then Raya said, in a hurt voice, "I was only offering to help because we're friends and I wanted to change the fact that the gods have ignored your homeland. But if that's how you *really* feel about me, then maybe I shouldn't have offered to do that at all. Bye."

Too late did Carmaz realize his mistake, and by the time he thought of something a bit kinder to say, Raya was gone, having teleported away, probably back into the Throne Room, where Carmaz did not want to go.

And standing alone in the lobby of the Temple of the Gods, listening to the cheers of the gods and godlings in the next room, Carmaz cursed himself for being such an idiot, turned, and walked away. He had no particular destination in mind. He only wanted to leave World's End and never return.

Chapter Twenty-Five

OVER THE NEXT month, so many things happened that even Braim, with his new godly brain, had a hard time keeping up with it all.

The Tournament of the Gods was restarted the very next day, with Tashir winning his bracket and becoming the God of Spiders and Sleet, Malya winning her bracket and becoming the Goddess of Birds, and Samvan winning his bracket and becoming the new God of Humans. Braim was present to watch every victory, but he also congratulated the losers for doing a good job and made sure that all of them were safely returned to whatever lands they came from.

In addition, the four gods that had lost their souls to Tamra—Xocion, Mica, Kos, and Henim—personally thanked Braim for his saving them in front of the other gods shortly after the Tournament ended. Their thankfulness was sincere and emotional and also seemed to make the rest of the gods respect Braim more, because in the days and weeks afterward he noticed that the other gods, even the southern gods like the Loner God, started to treat him with more respect than they did before the four gods thanked him.

Not only that, but Darek and Jenur (along with Archmage Yorak and her pupil Auratus) arrived in World's End a few days after the end of the Tournament to congratulate Braim on his ascension. They also brought with them one of the Divine Carvers, who carved a statue of Braim for Jenur, as the Magical Superior of North Academy, to use in order to contact Braim whenever she needed. It was kind of funny standing there and posing for the statue, but Braim thought that the finished statue looked great and so he didn't complain about having to do that.

As for Alira, after the Tournament, she requested to leave World's End, much to Braim's surprise. When Braim asked her where she wanted to go, Alira replied that she did not know but that she would find out. It seemed like an odd thing for someone like Alira—who was always so certain about the rules and always strove to abide by them to the letter—but Braim granted her that request and so Alira left the island a week after the Tournament's end. Braim didn't know where she was now or what she was doing, but he figured that she was probably going to be all right no matter what she did or where she went.

Even King Malock and Queen Hana arrived in the city via the ethereal to congratulate Braim. They brought with them a strange automaton that Braim had never seen before, but which they called 'Divine-Keeper,' who was apparently supposed to be Raya's bodyguard, even though Raya was a goddess and did not need a bodyguard. Nonetheless, Raya had seemed overjoyed to see the new version of Keeper, so Braim didn't worry about it.

As for Carmaz, he did not stay on the island for long. He said that he had to return to Ruwa to help his people. Braim offered to help Carmaz rebuild Ruwa, which to his surprise Carmaz accepted. Braim said that he would start helping to rebuild Ruwa after the citywide celebration was over, which Carmaz also agreed to. Despite that, there was a melancholy about Carmaz that Braim did not understand, although he chose not to question it because Carmaz gave off the attitude that he was in no mood to answer personal questions right now.

And then there was the citywide celebration exactly one month after the end of the Tournament and after the damage to World's End was repaired. Every single god and goddess in both Pantheons was on World's End on that day, as well as every katabans in the world. The streets were packed with katabans musicians singing and playing their instruments, with party-goers and dancers, and the entire thing lasted a week. It was indeed the grandest party in the world, just as Braim said it would be, and Braim was right in the midst of it, even though he was the God of Martir and therefore probably should have kept his distance. But he didn't care too much about that right now because all he wanted to do was celebrate, not just the fact that Martir was going to continue, but his own life and the fact that he was not going to cease to exist.

It was on the day after the end of the festival, when the gods scattered across Martir to return to ruling their domains and their katabans servants followed them back and the katabans remaining in the city started the long but important process of cleaning up after the party-goers, that Braim stood on Last Beach, his hands in his pockets, as he looked at the Void. It was still a black wall of shadow, but after becoming the God of Martir, Braim had made sure to restore and strengthen its original boundaries and keep it from being able to escape and cause any harm on Martir ever again. It was now as it had been since the day the Powers laid the foundations of Martir, and it would always be thus as long as Braim ruled Martir.

Braim was the only person on the beach and so he was the only person to feel the cool ocean wind and feel the warm rays of the sun overhead. He was glad that he could still feel all of these sensations even as a god, because they reminded him that he was still alive and not dead.

Then Braim heard someone walking across the sand behind him and looked over his shoulder to see who it was. It was the Mysterious One, who walked up to his side, his bony joints clicking as he moved.

"Mysterious One," said Braim in surprise. "When did *you* get here?"

"As soon as I heard that you became the God of Martir," said the Mysterious One. He put one hand on Braim's shoulder. "I wanted to let you know that I am proud of you and think you will make a great ruler of Martir."

Braim scratched the back of his neck sheepishly and looked back over the ocean at the Void. Although the Void was unable to cross over into Martir, he could feel her hatred and anger toward him for preventing her from consuming everything. But he didn't let it worry him one bit, because he knew that she could not even touch him without his permission.

"Thanks," said Braim, "but I'm still learning. I'm just happy that I'm alive and won't die anytime soon, if ever."

"That is good," said the Mysterious One. He glanced at the Void. "Still worried about her?"

Braim shook his head. "Nah. The Void's boundaries are pretty firm, firmer than before, actually, because I wanted to make sure that she couldn't get over here or even influence the actions of anyone else to help. I think that Martir is going to be safe from her shadows for a long time, maybe forever if we get lucky."

The Mysterious One nodded. "Good. I have grown rather fond of this little world and its inhabitants and I would rather not see it consumed by the Void's darkness. That would be depressing."

Braim chuckled. "Same here. Anyway, is that all you came to do? Just congratulate me? Not that I am complaining, but—"

"No," said the Mysterious One. "I also came to speak with you about something else."

Braim looked at the Mysterious One with a frown. "Please don't tell me that the Dark Lady is up to something and we have to stop her."

"My sister is still fuming about Uron's death and isn't in much of a position to harm anyone at the moment," said the Mysterious One. "Even if she was, I am perfectly capable of handling whatever she has up her sleeves. No, I came to discuss a different issue."

"And what is that?" said Braim.

"Your resurrection," said the Mysterious One.

Braim sighed. "That? I thought we already talked about that to death."

"I know," said the Mysterious One. "But I wanted to tell you that I've learned much about your resurrection since you returned to life so many months ago now. I've learned—"

Braim held up a hand, silencing the Mysterious One instantly. "Don't tell me. I don't want to know."

"But why not?" said the Mysterious One, who sounded

annoyed at being interrupted. "Wouldn't you want to know the truth about your resurrection so your knowledge can be complete? The darkness in the back of your mind—"

"Is gone," Braim finished for him. He smiled. "Gone since I became a god. I've put that behind me. Right now, I am looking toward the future—my future and the future of Martir—and not my past, however mysterious it may be."

Even without skin, the Mysterious One was quite skilled at making himself appear annoyed that he was not allowed to share what knowledge he had learned about Braim with him.

But then the Mysterious One nodded once more and said, "Very well. I don't think I'll ever quite understand the way you mortals and gods think, but I accept your decision to not know. But if you ever do wish to know, you know where to find me."

With that, the Mysterious One vanished, and Braim—deciding that he was ready to return to the city—turned and walked back up the beach to World's End, to his city, to help his people. And he smiled while doing it.

THE END OF TOURNAMENT OF THE GODS.

Glossary:

Aorja Kitano. A former student at North Academy who specialized in musical magic. Though she is good at pretending to be kind and intelligent, in truth she is insane and violent and is currently on the run from the authorities for her crimes against Martir. She has a 'pet' half-god called Zeeree who she managed to tame. She is also a mage known as a 'Limitless,' which means that she has access to unlimited magical energy (although that does not make her invincible).

Aquarians. A species of fish-like humanoids that live in the Undersea, which is the name for the part of Martir underneath the Crystal Sea. Like humans, aquarians worship the northern gods and can use magic, although they have different names for the gods and also do magic differently from their human counterparts. They have a variety of different appearances and races, much like humans, although their differences tend to be even more dramatic than the ones between humans.

Automatons. Mechanical beings created by the Mechanical Goddess to carry out her will, although the Carnagian Royal Family has been experimenting with making automatons of their own in recent years.

Darek Takren. The adopted son of Jenur Takren and a graduate of North Academy. He specializes in pagomancy, or ice magic, and is currently the leader of the Xocionian Monks. He was the protagonist in the Mages of Martir novels and is a good friend of Braim Kotogs.

Diog. The God of the Grave. Aquarian name: Hamafa.

Godling. Name for human beings who are destined to become gods.

Half-gods. The prototypes of the gods that the Powers abandoned in the Void after finishing Martir. Half-gods, while stronger than mortals, are not quite as strong as gods, although they can give the gods a good fight. They also tend to be more animalistic and lack some of the higher reasoning functions of the gods themselves due to their incompleteness, which makes it possible for beings who are weaker than them to control or manipulate them. The most well-known half-god is Zeeree, the Half-God of Poison, who serves Aorja Kitano.

Harnum. The world that existed before Martir. It was destroyed by Uron, one of its inhabitants, and everyone who lived there was killed off. The Powers arrived many years later and used Harnum's remains as the foundation for Martir, although some Harnumian buildings and objects can still be found deep beneath Martir's surface.

Jenur Takren. A native of Ruwa and current Magical Superior of North Academy and adoptive mother of Darek Takren. Like Malock, she was a major character in the Prince Malock World novels. In her youth, she was a member of the Dark Tigers Guild, an assassin's guild based in Ruwa, but eventually left it when she became disgusted with the Guild's mission. She adopted Darek Takren when he was only five years old after his birth mother was murdered by an enemy of hers.

Katabans. A species of intelligent beings who exist to serve the gods. 'Katabans' means 'minor spirit,' as katabans are spirits who often take on physical forms in order to follow the gods' commands. Their appearances range from human to beast, depending on their preferences, personality, and what they need to complete whatever mission given to them by the gods.

King Tojas Malock. The son of Queen Markinia and King Halock of Carnag. Current King of Carnag. He was the protagonist of the Prince Malock World novels and is married to Queen Hanarova. He is a fair and just ruler, although he spoils his daughter too much.

-Mancy. A suffix usually attached to Latin prefixes that denotes the name of a magical discipline. For example, hydromancy means 'water magic,' pyromancy means 'fire magic,' panamancy means 'healing magic,' and so on.

North Academy. The most prestigious and most difficult to get into magical school in the world. It is located in the northernmost reaches of the Great Berg and can only be reached with great difficulty. It is run by Jenur Takren, who is the current Magical Superior of the school.

Northern Isles. A region of the world located on the northern half of the Dividing Line that consists of thousands of island nations of various sizes. It is where almost all of Martir's human population is located, as well as many aquarians.

Northern Pantheon. The gods who rule the northern half of Martir. In contrast to their southern siblings, the northern gods are kinder and more respectful to mortals. They also tend to take mortal names (for example, Grinf), rather than titles translated from Godly Divina (for example, the Loner God).

Ooka. The God of Knives and Shadow. Aquarian name: Ooka.

Queen Hanarova. The katabans wife of King Malock and mother of Princess Raya Mana. Like Malock, she was a major character in the Prince Malock World novels. While not a bad person, she has a fierce rivalry with Jenur Takren that started in their youth and continues to this day.

Rock Isle. The most secure prison in the Northern Isles. Home to many of the most dangerous criminals in the Northern Isles.

Silver spoon. A slang term, common in the Northern Isles, usually applied to princesses, especially spoiled or bratty ones. The male equivalent is gold blood and the terms come from the folk song *Princess Silver Spoon and Prince Gold Blood.*

Skimif. The previous God of Martir. He was once an aquarian farmer who was chosen by the Powers to announce their return to Martir back in the Prince Malock World series. The Powers eventually made him into the God of Martir, but he was killed by Uron thirty years after his ascension.

Southern Pantheon. The gods who rule the southern half of Martir. In contrast to their northern siblings, they hate mortals and see them as no different than any other kind of animal. They tend to be more vicious and animalistic and don't understand humans as well as their northern siblings do.

The Almighty Ones. A group of four beings who live in the Spirit Lands and are responsible for judging and guiding the spirits of the dead. Originally consisted of the Dark Lady, the Arbiter, the Great Snake, and the Mysterious One before the Arbiter and the Great Snake were killed. They are far more powerful than the gods, but typically do not directly interfere with the physical realm, preferring to focus instead on the Spirit Lands where they rule.

The Dividing Line. The exact line that divides the northern and southern sides of Martir. This line can be crossed by any god or mortal, but if a southern god crosses it, then this god cannot kill any mortals on the northern side.

The gods of Martir. Super-powerful and immortal beings who each control a particular domain of Martir, such as the elements or even abstract concepts. The gods used to be one united force, but after the Godly War, they were separated into the Northern Pantheon and the Southern Pantheon and have remained that way ever since.

The Godly War. An ancient conflict that took place shortly after the creation of Martir eons ago. The War started over a disagreement between the gods over how to treat mortals. Half of them wished to use mortals for sport and food, while the other half wanted to have them as worshipers and followers. The two sides waged a war that killed many gods and countless mortals before the Powers stepped in, ended the conflict, and wrote up the Treaty to govern relations between the two sides.

The Ghostly God. The God of Ghosts and Mist. A southern god. Highly intelligent, but cruel and antisocial. Has an intense fascination with studying the dead and where ghosts go after their bodies die.

The Mechanical Goddess. The Goddess of Machines. A southern goddess. She is the creator of the automatons. Queen Hanarova served her in her youth.

The Mysterious One. One of the Almighty Ones. Originally pretended to be the mythical God of Mystery and Magic before revealing his true identity at the end of the Mages of Martir series. Strange and enigmatic, he nonetheless cares about Martir and does what he can to help protect it.

The Powers. A group of six powerful and ancient entities who created Martir, the gods, humanity, and everything else within

Martir. Their exact nature is a mystery, but it is known that they are currently creating other worlds beyond the Void. They have only visited Martir once since creating the world but otherwise are not actively involved in the world's day-to-day functions, which are instead regulated by the gods themselves.

The Spirit Lands. A land where all spirits go when they die and where they are judged by the Mysterious One for their deeds in life. Those who are judged as righteous go beyond the Gates to rest eternally, while the ones judged wicked are banished to the Unknown to be tortured forever.

The Thief's Way. A magical discipline generally practiced by followers of the late Hollech, the former God of Deception, Thieves, and Horses. Practitioners of the Thief's Way can travel through shadow and also detach body parts and have them emerge from the shadows to attack someone or steal from them. Most practitioners of the Thief's Way are scorned by their fellow mages and generally treated as criminals even if they do not actually commit any crimes.

The Treaty. A document that governs relations between the Northern and Southern Pantheons, written by the Powers themselves.

The Void. A powerful and evil force that exists beyond the edge of Martir. Its sole purpose is to destroy and devour everything that exists. While the Void does not technically have a gender, it is usually referred to with female pronouns.

Tinkar. The God of Fate and Time. One of the oldest gods and a northern god. Aquarian name: Seyar.

Uron. A powerful being who existed in the world before Martir, where he was a bitter scientist who was hated by everyone. He allowed the Almighty One known as the Great Snake to possess him so he could get back at his people, but due to a series of unforeseen events, Uron and the Great Snake ended up banished to the physical realm without a body for centuries. After Uron got a body, he then attempted to destroy Martir, but was ultimately destroyed by Braim Kotogs and now no longer exists as a spiritual or physical being.

World's End. Also known as the Throne of the Gods. The final island in the southern seas and home to most of the katabans on Martir.

About the Author

Timothy L. Cerepaka writes fantasy as an indie author. He is the author of the Prince Malock World fantasy novels, the Mages of Martir fantasy novels, and the Two Worlds science-fantasy series. He lives in Texas.

Find out more at his website: www.timothylcerepaka.com.

Other books by Timothy L. Cerepaka

Prince Malock World:

The Mad Voyage of Prince Malock

The Return of Prince Malock

The New Era of Prince Malock

The Coronation of Prince Malock

Mages of Martir:

The Mage's Grave

The Mage's Limits

The Mage's Sea

The Mage's Ghost

Two Worlds:

Reunification

Alliance

Allegiance

Retaliation

Desinence

Tournament of the Gods:

Gathering of the Chosen

Betrayal of the Chosen

Invasion of the Chosen

Ascension of the Chosen

The War-Torn Kingdom:

Kingdom of Magicians

Kingdom of Heirs

Kingdom of Dragons

Kingdom of Gods

Standalones:

The Last Legend: Glitch Apocalypse

www.ingramcontent.com/pod-product-compliance
Lightning Source LLC
Chambersburg PA
CBHW05054726026
47157CB00002B/471